PIETRO DI DONATO was born on April 5, 1911, in West Hoboken, New Jersey, the son of an immigrant, whose death, like that of the Geremio of his famous novel *Christ in Concrete*, sent Pietro to work at age twelve as a bricklayer. In 1937 he published an autobiographical short story in *Esquire* magazine which was named "Best Short Story of 1938" and became the basis of his bestselling and critically acclaimed novel, *Christ in Concrete* (1939). Di Donato's seminal novel influenced a generation of Italian American writers, including Gay Talese. His other works include a sequel, *Three Circles of Light* (1960), as well as *This Woman* (1958), *Immigrant Saint: The Life of Mother Cabrini* (1960), and *The Penitent* (1962). *Naked Author* (1970) is an anthology of his short stories and excerpts from his longer works. Di Donato died of bone cancer at his home in Setauket, Long Island, on January 19, 1992.

CHRIST IN CONCRETE

A NOVEL BY

PIETRO DI DONATO

Preface by Studs Terkel
Introduction by Fred L. Gardaphé

A SIGNET CLASSIC

SIGNET CLASSIC
Published by New American Library, a division of
Penguin Putnam Inc., 375 Hudson Street,
New York, New York 10014, U.S.A.
Penguin Books Ltd, 80 Strand,
London WC2R 0RL, England
Penguin Books Australia Ltd, Ringwood,
Victoria, Australia
Penguin Books Canada Ltd, 10 Alcorn Avenue,
Toronto, Ontario, Canada M4V 3B2
Penguin Books (N.Z.) Ltd, 182–190 Wairau Road,
Auckland 10, New Zealand

Penguin Books Ltd, Registered Offices:
Harmondsworth, Middlesex, England

Published by Signet Classic, an imprint of New American Library,
a division of Penguin Putnam Inc.

First Signet Classic Printing, July 1993
10 9 8 7 6 5

 REGISTERED TRADEMARK—MARCA REGISTRADA

Library of Congress Catalog Card Number: 92-39372

Printed in the United States of America

To
ANNUNZIATA AND GEREMIO

CONTENTS

PREFACE

1939 was the year for me. Two of the most powerful American novels of our time were published in 1939. One was *The Grapes of Wrath* by John Steinbeck, the other was *Christ in Concrete* by a young bricklayer named Pietro di Donato. While they dealt with different cultures, they shared a similar theme: in one case the journey of the Okies to California in search of a better life; in the other case, an Italian immigrant in New York in search of a better life. Both novels portrayed the travails of working people faced with obstacles, battling overwhelming odds in their attempts to survive troubled times. In both cases the heroism of the non-celebrated was celebrated.

Pietro di Donato's story is the story of so many immigrant peoples whose dreams and realities were in conflict. It is the story of fathers and sons and the hard-bought legacy. In the case of di Donato the son, as with Tom Joad, the sanitized American Dream is challenged, and both face up to the hard truth. When the young man, myself, first read *Christ in Concrete* in 1939, the impact was indelible.

Today, more than fifty years later, with a new Depression, euphemistically called a recession, *Christ in Concrete* more than holds up. It is a powerful contemporary novel. And while for too long novels of working class life have been out of fashion, the hard reality of our day makes them as pertinent and timely as ever.

INTRODUCTION

1939, the year that Pietro di Donato's *Christ in Concrete* appeared as a novel, was monumental in American history. In the cultural arena James Joyce published *Finnegan's Wake*, John Steinbeck's *The Grapes of Wrath* topped best-seller lists around the country, and Judy Garland made her debut in *The Wizard of Oz*. In politics, the Hitler-Stalin pact shocked the American left, Germany and the U.S.S.R. invaded Poland, and while America remained neutral, Britain and France declared war on Germany. Technological breakthroughs included Edwin H. Armstrong's invention of FM radio and David Sarnoff's unveiling of the first television at the World's Fair in New York.

While critics disagreed as to the novel's formal merits, they unanimously concurred that a major voice had broken into the American literary scene. After a brief period of national attention, *Christ in Concrete* was relegated to the margins of mainstream American culture where it lay dormant as a minor classic. Overlooked by literary historians, the novel rarely appeared in American literature courses. The author, while a favorite guest speaker in the rare course on Italian/American culture, survived primarily as a bricklayer, the trade he had mastered in his teens.

Reprinted only once, in 1976, the novel's fiftieth anniversary in 1989 passed without celebration. In fact, until recently, all of Pietro di Donato's books, *Christ in*

Concrete, This Woman, Immigrant Saint: The Life of Mother Cabrini, Three Circles of Light, and *The Penitent,* remained out of print. In 1990, *Immigrant Saint* was re-issued and generated some renewed interest in di Donato's writing and life.

Born in West Hoboken, New Jersey, in 1911, of Abruzzese parents, di Donato became a bricklayer, like his father, shortly after his father's tragic death on Good Friday, 1923. "Christ in Concrete," his first short story, recounted his father's death, and was published in the March, 1937, issue of *Esquire*; the story was reprinted in Edward O'Brien's *Best Short Stories of 1938* and was expanded into a best-selling novel that was chosen over John Steinbeck's *The Grapes of Wrath* as a main selection of the 1939 Book-of-the-Month Club. Di Donato never dreamed of becoming a writer, but *Christ in Concrete*'s success placed him in a national spotlight that many critics believe blinded his artistic vision for life.

In an early review, E. B. Garside called him "a shining figure to add to the proletarian gallery of artists." Garside then dismissed the young author with a prediction that di Donato "would never create a prose [sic] equal of Leopardi's *A Silvia*, nor will the latter-day rebellion rise to the supple power of *Pensieri*." Garside's nativist chauvinism becomes obvious when he attempts to provide insight into the Italian soul: "But it must be understood that the Italian soul is essentially 'thin.' The Italian peasant and work man live themselves out fully as part of a family, or of an aggregate of some sort all committed to the same style."[1]

Louis Adamic, an immigrant himself and editor of *Common Ground* and thus perhaps more sensitive to di Donato's characters, saw that *Christ in Concrete* was unlike the staple fare of the laboring class that he characterized as "reflections of the economic treadmill on the tenuous cheesecloth fabric of an ideology." Yet, in spite of this sensitivity, Adamic's review betrayed a stereotypical notion of the Italian in America when he characterized the writing as "robust and full-blooded and passionate, now and then almost to the point of craziness; . . . he has imagination and a healthy sense of the source of poetry in the Italian. . . . Sometimes one feels as though bricks and stones and trowelfuls of mortar have been thrown on the pages and from them have risen words."[2]

The only book-length study of the literature of the 1930s which mentions di Donato is Warren French's *The Social Novel at the End of an Era* (1966). And while French acknowledges the "fresh and vigorous viewpoint" that di Donato "brought to the American social scene," he portrays di Donato as an example of "the very irresponsibility that destroyed the age." French includes di Donato, along with Richard Wright, in an epilogue subtitled "Beginner's Luck."

Only recently have critics begun to realize the value of di Donato's contribution to American letters. In a resurrection of di Donato's speech presented at the Third American Writers' Congress in 1939, Arthur Casciato helps us to understand why writers like di Donato have been ignored by the literary establishment of the period. As Casciato points out, di Donato refused to adopt "the prescribed literary posture of the day in which the writer would efface his or her own class or ethnic identity in order to speak in the sonorous voice of 'the people.' "[3]

In spite of his absence in historical and critical studies of American writers, di Donato is perhaps the most well known of the early Italian-American writers because of the impact *Christ in Concrete* had and continues to have on its readers. Through this novel we gain an unprecedented insight into the mysteries of Italian immigrant life. Whether he is describing a work site or a bedroom, di Donato's imagery vibrates with the earthy sensuality that early Italian immigrants brought to their American lives.

For many critics, di Donato's first novel has become the prototypical "ethnic" American novel, in spite of the fact that a number were published long before his. One of the reasons for this stems from the fact that the peculiar aspects of Italian immigrant culture are represented in this novel as in no other writing yet produced by an Italian American.

Di Donato's *italianita* becomes most obvious through the novel's diction. As mediator between the Italian culture of his parents and the American culture he was born into, di Donato masterfully effects our understanding of both through his unique linguistic representations of both. His word choice and word order recreate the rhythms and sonority of the Italian language. He does this through two methods: recording the broken English which results when the immigrant tries to speak English, as evidenced by the speech of Mike the Barrel-mouth, "I don't know myself, but somebodys whose gotta bigga buncha keeds and he alla times talka from somebodys elsa!"; and by translating the immigrants' Italian literally into English, as in the speech of Uncle Luigi as he lies in a hospital with a leg crushed from a work accident, "Nurse-nurse, I sense badly . . . nurse-doctors, I sense ill." Di Donato renders the Italian reflexive verb *sentirsi*, "to feel," into the English "sense." In this way, di Donato captures, as no writer before him, Italian-American English, a language that is neither Italian nor English, but an amalgam of the two.

Christ in Concrete transcends the self-congratulatory autobiographical portrayals produced by many immigrant writers of the period. While other Italian-American writers were portraying characters who struggled to fit into American life, di Donato was rejecting the American dream by documenting a crisis situation that threatens an Italian-American family. In the process he spoke for a whole population involved with building industrial America. Using the *Esquire* short story as a foundation, di Donato built a novel through episodes which present the Italian-American experience through literary snapshots. In this way, *Christ in Concrete* differs greatly from the retrospective novels produced during and after World War II by writers like Mari Tomasi (*Deep Grow the Roots*, 1940), Carl Marzani (*The Survivor*, 1958) and Mario Puzo (*The Fortunate Pilgrim*, 1964). Unlike these novels, which have more traditional plot structure, *Christ in Concrete* strings together episodes as though the writer had no idea of the future that awaited these characters. The end result is that heavy emphasis on the existential nature of the immigrant experience.

What separates di Donato from other American writers of his generation is his representation of a Catholicism that has its roots in pre-Christian, matriarchal worship. As di Donato himself admitted, "I'm a sensualist, and I respond to the sensuality of the Holy Roman Catholic Church, its art, its music, its fragrances, its colors, its architecture, and so forth—which is truly Italian. We Italians are really essentially pagans and realists."[4] This sensuality becomes evident through his visceral descriptions and complements his recreation of a troubled Catholicism.

Annunziata, the mother in *Christ in Concrete*, becomes the key figure in di Donato's revision of the Christian myth. She controls her son's reaction to the work-site "murders" of his father and grandfather by calling on him to put his trust in Jesus, the son of Mary. This is a trust that has led immigrants to accept poverty as their fate and passivity as their means of survival in a world bent on turning them into disposable tools of the rich. This trust is a myth that di Donato, through his protagonist, Paul, refuses to accept.

Christ in Concrete is one of the most mythical texts of American literature. As a myth it presents an heroic figure, Paul, who searches for God, in the form of Christ, whom he believes, as he was trained, can save his family from the terrible injustices brought upon them through a heartless society. The novel is divided into five parts: "Geremio," "Job," "Tenement," "Fiesta," and "Annunziata," each focusing on the key figures in the myth, each representing stages in the development of Paul's life.

In "Geremio" and "Job," di Donato presents Job as a god-like antagonist which controls the Italian workers led by his father Geremio, through the human forces of Mr. Murdin, the heartless foreman, the State Bureaucracy that sides with the construction company during a hearing into Geremio's death, and the Catholic Church through an Irish priest who refused to do more than offer the family a few table scraps from his rich dinner.

"Job," which appears without definite articles such as "the" or "a," is depicted as a living thing that "loomed up damp, shivery gray. Its giant members waiting." Job serves as the means by which "America beautiful will eat you and spit your bones into the earth's hole," as one worker predicts. In "Tenement," young Paul comes to learn about the forces of good and evil in the world and realizes that good comes only from the workers' community, which is portrayed in "Fiesta."

Paul's mother, Annunziata, pregnant at the opening of the novel, serves as the figure of the Madonna representing the immigrants' faith in God, whom she invokes through prayers such as, "God of my fathers, God of my girlhood, God of my mating, God of my innocent children, upon your bosom I lay my voice: To this widow alone black-enshrouded, lend of your strength that she may live only to raise her children." In "Annunziata," the chapter devoted to her "widowhood," Annunziata attempts to raise her children according to the Christian myth, but in the process her son Paul loses the faith she hopes to pass on to him through her recollections of her husband's show of faith.

An heroic struggle occurs between man and God through Geremio and Job. Through Job, Geremio believes he can gain the means to live and to eventually achieve the American Dream of a haven from Job, where "no boss in the world can then rob me of the joy of my home." But the money saved for the house must be used to bury Geremio, who along with the workers become sacrificial victims to Job through the greed and insensitivity of the construction company. Paul is forced to take up the struggle where his father left off. He learns to see through the masked mechanism of this myth and realizes that the only way to beat Job is not to become part of the system that supports it; instead he must fight against it. This realization is vividly depicted by di Donato through one of Paul's dreams.

Toward the end of the novel Paul has a dream in which he is about to die as his father did. His godfather attempts to save him and is tossed off a scaffold by the foreman who was threatening Paul. Paul fails to save his godfather but remembers who can save him: "[I]t is our Lord Christ who will do it; he made us, he loves us and will not deny us; he is our friend and will help us in need! Bear, oh godfather bear until I find Him." Paul then takes off in search of Christ and runs into his father who is on his way to work. The work site becomes a shrine for the workers who have now become saints; Mr. Murdin, the foreman, appears as a magician who "each time he revolves and shouts at Geremio and Paul he has on a suit and mask of a general, a mayor, a principal, a policeman." Job falls apart and Paul is the only one who tries to save himself. Paul sees himself in his father's crucified form. He is then carried off to "the Cripple," the hag who earlier in the story had conducted a seance for Paul and his mother. Paul sees his father hovering over "the Cripple," and as they embrace Geremio sighs, "Ahhh, not even the Death can free us, for we are . . . Christ in concrete." Paul's dream quest ends here with the failure of Christ to save him and his family. Paul realizes that only he can save himself. This realization is dramatized in the last scene of the novel.

By the end of the novel, Paul's faith is nearly destroyed as evidenced by his crushing of a crucifix offered to him by his mother. However, the final image of the novel suggests that the matriarchal powers still reign. The image we are left with is an inversion of the *Pieta* in which son is holding a mother who is crooning a deathsong/lullaby which hails her son as a new Christ, one that her children should follow. But this haunting image also suggests that it is the mother who has become the new Christ, who in witnessing what America has done to her son, dies and through her death frees her son from the burden of his Catholic past. This death is quite different from the death of his father which leads Paul in search of Christ. His rejection of Christ as the means to survive in this world contributes to his mother's collapse. She then becomes the basis for a new faith, a faith in himself, a faith that his mother urges her children toward as she tells them to "love . . .

love ... love ... love ever our Paul." For di Donato, this figure of the dying *Mater Dolorosa* replaces Christ as the figure through which man can redeem himself. There can be no redemption through the father, for if Paul stays in the system, if he continues to interact with Job, he will share the same destiny as his father, Geremio. For di Donato the immigrant laborer may become a hero through martyrdom, but his life becomes not a model to emulate, rather, something to avoid. Through the father, America remains the dream of an immigrant anchored in God and the belief that God will provide the means by which the immigrant will prevail. Geremio's hope that all his children will be boys is tied into his perception of the American dream: "... I tell you all my kids must be boys so that they someday will be big American builders. And then I'll help them to put the gold away in the basements!" And so, what is a dream for the immigrant becomes a nightmare for the child Paul, who as a witness to the tragedies that have befallen his immigrant family must become not a new Christ, but more a St. John the Baptist figure who wanders through life preparing humanity for the revolution, seeking redemption through the women he encounters.

By directing his characters' rage at the employers who exploit immigrant laborers, Pietro di Donato argues for solidarity among American workers and requires that they look to each other to solve their problems. Just as it is the Italian community, through the extended family, that keeps Geremio's family together, it is the extended family of the workers that must help each other. Di Donato's revision of Christ points to the failure of American Catholicism as a force that controls and subdues the immigrants' reactions to the injustices of the capitalist system that exploits as it maims and kills the Italian immigrant. His deconstruction and remaking of the Christian myth forces us to re-read his masterpiece as more revolutionary than it has been portrayed by past critics.

Di Donato's rewriting of the myth of Christ leads him back to the pre-Christian roots of Italian culture. This return, while implicit in *Christ in Concrete*, becomes explicit in nearly all his subsequent work. Di Donato's ability to see through the repression created by a Christianity which aligns itself with a capitalist power structure leads him toward a socialistic vision of the world. For Di Donato, the solution to the problems created by capitalism would come not in the form of an organized church, but rather through a spiritual quest for truth that would lead him back to pagan sensualism that he would record in his second novel.

This Woman, di Donato's long-awaited sequel to *Christ in Concrete*, appeared in 1958 and was greeted with a plethora of negative reviews. As a work of art, the novel does not achieve the status of his first. However, for readers of di Donato, it is an incredibly important work. In the novel, di Donato describes the path taken by the young Paolo after his rejection of both the American dream and the traditional myth of Christ. Significantly, the protagonist, Paolo, has been given the surname di Alba (Paul of Dawn or Paul reborn) and becomes, "The boy who later felt the terrible exultation of pagan freedom when his mother died in his arms." This freedom from the strictures of Italian and American traditions enables the protagonist to re-create himself through a new moral order built on a triad of masonry, sex and soul: "The three-act drama of his mental theatre would revert first to the factual solidity of building construction, evolve to the mercury of sex, and then culminate with the spiritual judgement."

Much of di Donato's later work continues to portray this conflict of the sacred and the profane. In *The Penitent* (1962), he recounts the story of Alessandro Serenelli, the man who killed the virgin Maria Goretti—later sainted by the Catholic Church. Di Donato attempts to understand the murder as a crime of nature-driven passion committed by a man who as a fisherman lived the pagan life of the sea.

In *Three Circles of Light* (1960) di Donato returns to the material of his first novel and recounts the years prior to his father's death. In episodic fashion, this novel depicts Paolo's coming-of-age in the West Hoboken setting and suggests that his father's infidelity might have been the cause of his early death. After destroying the traditional myth of a Christianity by showing how it has been corrupted by temporal powers, di Donato builds a new myth for his readers, that of man as surviving best within the naturally spiritual institution of family which is constantly being threatened by a world corrupted by the artificial institutions created through a material-hungry capitalism.

Even into the eighties, di Donato continued his criticism of American society in a daring project called "The American Gospels." A mixture of Dantesque *terza rima*, Joycean stream of consciousness, and biblical prose, the entire work is a testament to di Donato's life. Yet unpublished, "The Gospels" demonstrates the continuation of di Donato's lifelong commitment to social criticism through story. Through this novel, which should be read as his primal scream out of the world just as *Christ in Concrete* was his cry into the world, di Donato takes his "revenge on society" by revealing "all the nonsense of authority and of Church" through what he calls a "conscious evaluation of myself."[5] To di Donato, salvation for the world lies in man's ability to become his own god, to take responsibility and control of the world he's created and to act for the good of all.

Fred L. Gardaphé
Columbia College, Chicago

NOTES

1. E. B. Garside, *Atlantic Monthly*, August 1939.
2. Louis Adamic, *Saturday Review of Literature*, August 26, 1939.
3. Arthur D. Casciato, "The Bricklayer as Bricoleur: Pietro di Donato and the cultural politics of the popular front," *Voices in Italian Americana* (Fall 1991), pp. 67–76.
4. Von Huene-Greenberg, "A *Melus* Interview: Pietro di Donato," *Melus* XIV (1987), pp. 33–52.
5. Ibid., pp. 33–34.

I
GEREMIO

1

March whistled stinging snow against the brick walls and up the gaunt girders. Geremio, the foreman, swung his arms about, and gaffed the men on.

Old Nick, the "Lean," stood up from over a dust-flying brick pile, tapped the side of his nose and sent an oyster directly to the ground. "Master Geremio, the Devil himself could not break his tail any harder than we here."

Burly Julio of the walrus mustache and known as the "Snoutnose" let fall the chute door of the concrete hopper and sang over in the Lean's direction: "Mari-Annina's belly and the burning night will make of me once more a milk-mouthed stripling lad . . ."

The Lean loaded his wheelbarrow and spat furiously. "Sons of two-legged dogs . . . despised of even the Devil himself! Work! Sure! For America beautiful will eat you and spit your bones into the earth's hole! Work!" And with that his wiry frame pitched the barrow violently over the rough floor.

Snoutnose waved his head to and fro and with mock pathos wailed, "Sing on, O guitar of mine . . ."

Short, cheery-faced Tomas, the scaffoldman, paused with hatchet in hand and tenpenny spike sticking out from small dicelike teeth to tell the Lean as he went by, in a voice that all could hear, "Ah, father of countless chicks, the old age is a carrion!"

Geremio chuckled and called to him. "Hey, little

Tomas, who are you to talk? You and big-titted Cola can't even hatch an egg, whereas the Lean has just to turn the doorknob of his bedroom and old Philomena becomes a balloon!"

Coarse throats tickled and mouths opened wide in laughter.

The Lean pushed his barrow on, his face cruelly furrowed with time and struggle. Sirupy sweat seeped from beneath his cap, down his bony nose and turned icy at its end. He muttered to himself. "Saints up, down, sideways and inside out! How many more stones must I carry before I'm overstuffed with the light of day! I don't understand . . . blood of the Virgin, I don't understand!"

Mike the "Barrel-mouth" pretended he was talking to himself and yelled out in his best English . . . he was always speaking English while the rest carried on in their native Italian. "I don't know myself, but somebodys whose gotta bigga buncha keeds and he alla times talka from somebodys elsa!"

Geremio knew it was meant for him and he laughed. "On the tomb of Saint Pimple-legs, this little boy my wife is giving me next week shall be the last! Eight hungry little Christians to feed is enough for any man."

Tomas nodded to the rest. "Sure, Master Geremio had a telephone call from the next bambino. Yes, it told him it had a little bell between instead of a rose bush. . . . It even told him its name!"

"Laugh, laugh all of you," returned Geremio, "but I tell you that all my kids must be boys so that they someday will be big American builders. And then I'll help them to put the gold away in the basements!"

A great din of riveting shattered the talk among the fast-moving men. Geremio added a handful of Honest tobacco to his corncob, puffed strongly, and cupped his hands around the bowl for a bit of warmth. The chill day caused him to shiver, and he thought to himself: Yes, the day is cold, cold . . . but who am I to complain when the good Christ Himself was crucified?

Pushing the job is all right (when has it been otherwise in my life?), but this job frightens me. I feel the building wants to tell me something; just as one Christian to another. Or perhaps the Easter week is making of me a spirit-seeing pregnant woman. I don't like this. Mr. Murdin tells me, Push it up! That's all he knows. I keep telling him that the underpinning should be doubled and the old material removed from the floors, but he keeps the inspector drunk and ... "Hey, Ashes-ass! Get away from under that pilaster! Don't pull the old work. Push it away from you or you'll have a nice present for Easter if the wall falls on you!" ... Well, with the help of God I'll see this job through. It's not my first, nor the ... "Hey, Patsy number two! Put more cement in that concrete; we're putting up a building, not an Easter cake!"

Patsy hurled his shovel to the floor and gesticulated madly. "The padrone Murdin-sa tells me, 'Too much, too much! Lil' bit is plenty!' And you tell me I'm stingy! The rotten building can fall after I leave!"

Six floors below, the contractor called. "Hey, Geremio! Is your gang of dagos dead?"

Geremio cautioned the men. "On your toes, boys. If he writes out slips, someone won't have big eels on the Easter table."

The Lean cursed that the padrone could take the job and all the Saints for that matter and shove it ...!

Curly-headed Lazarene, the roguish, pigeon-toed scaffoldman, spat a cloud of tobacco juice and hummed to his own music ... "Yes, certainly yes to your face, master padrone ... and behind, This to you and all your kind!"

The day, like all days, came to an end. Calloused and bruised bodies sighed, and numb legs shuffled toward shabby railroad flats ...

"Ah, bella casa mio. Where my little freshets of blood and my good woman await me. Home where my broken back will not ache so. Home where midst the monkey chatter of my piccolinos I will float off to blessed slumber with my feet on the chair and the head on the wife's soft full breast."

These great child-hearted ones leave one another without words or ceremony, and as they ride and walk home, a great pride swells the breast . . .

"Blessings to Thee, O Jesus. I have fought winds and cold. Hand to hand I have locked dumb stones in place and the great building rises. I have earned a bit of bread for me and mine."

The mad day's brutal conflict is forgiven, and strained limbs prostrate themselves so that swollen veins can send the yearning blood coursing and pulsating deliciously as though the body mountained leaping streams.

The job alone remained behind . . . and yet, they also, having left the bigger part of their lives with it. The cold ghastly beast, the Job, stood stark, the eerie March wind wrapping it in sharp shadows of falling dusk.

That night was a crowning point in the life of Geremio. He bought a house! Twenty years he had helped to mold the New World. And now he was to have a house of his own! What mattered that it was no more than a wooden shack? It was his own!

He had proudly signed his name and helped Annunziata to make her X on the wonderful contract that proved them owners. And she was happy to think that her next child, soon to come, would be born under their own rooftree. She heard the church chimes, and cried to the children, "Children, to bed! It is near midnight. And remember, shut-mouth to the paesanos! Or they will send the evil eye to our new home even before we put foot."

The children scampered off to the icy yellow bedroom where three slept in one bed and three in the other. Coltishly and friskily they kicked about under the covers; their black iron-cotton stockings not removed . . . what! and freeze the peanut-little toes?

Said Annunziata, "The children are so happy,

Geremio; let them be, for even I would dance a Tarantella." And with that she turned blushing. He wanted to take her on her word. She patted his hands, kissed them, and whispered. "Our children will dance for us . . . in the American style someday."

Geremio cleared his throat and wanted to sing. "Yes, with joy I could sing in a richer feeling than the great Caruso." He babbled little old-country couplets and circled the room until the tenant below tapped the ceiling.

Annunziata whispered, "Geremio, to bed and rest. Tomorrow is a day for great things . . . and the day on which our Lord died for us."

The children were now hard asleep. Heads under the cover, over . . . snotty noses whistling, and little damp legs entwined.

In bed Geremio and Annunziata clung closely to each other. They mumbled figures and dates until fatigue stilled their thoughts. And with chubby Johnny clutching fast his bottle and warmed between them . . . life breathed heavily, and dreams entertained in far, far worlds, the nationbuilder's brood.

But Geremio and Annunziata remained for a long while staring into the darkness . . . silently.

At last Annunziata spoke. "Geremio?"

"Yes?"

"This job you are now working . . ."

"So?"

"You used always to tell me about what happened on the jobs . . . who was jealous, and who praised . . ."

"You should know by now that all work is the same . . ."

"Geremio. The month you have been on this job, you have not spoken a word about the work . . . And I have felt that I am walking into a dream. Is the work dangerous? Why don't you answer . . . ?"

2

Job loomed up damp, shivery gray. Its giant members waiting.

Builders donned their coarse robes, and waited.

Geremio's whistle rolled back into his pocket and the symphony of struggle began.

Trowel rang through brick and slashed mortar rivets were machine-gunned fast with angry grind Patsy number one check Patsy number two check the Lean three check Julio four steel bellowed back at hammer donkey engines coughed purple Ashes-ass Pietro fifteen chisel point intoned stone thin steel whirred and wailed through wood liquid stone flowed with dull rasp through iron veins and hoist screamed through space Rosario the Fat twenty-four and Giacomo Sangini check . . . The multitudinous voices of a civilization rose from the surroundings and melted with the efforts of the Job.

The Lean as he fought his burden on looked forward to only one goal, the end. The barrow he pushed, he did not love. The stones that brutalized his palms, he did not love. The great God Job, he did not love. He felt a searing bitterness and a fathomless consternation at the queer consciousness that inflicted the ever mounting weight of structures that he *had to! had to!* raise above his shoulders! When, when and where would the last stone be? Never . . . did he bear his toil with the rhythm of song! Never . . . did his gasping heart knead the heavy mortar with lilting melody! A voice within him spoke in wordless language.

The language of worn oppression and the despair of realizing that his life had been left on brick piles. And always, there had been hunger and her bastard, the fear of hunger.

Murdin bore down upon Geremio from behind and shouted:

"Goddammit, Geremio, if you're givin' the men two hours off today with pay, why the hell are they draggin' their tails? And why don't you turn that skinny old Nick loose, and put a young wop in his place?"

"Now listen-a to me, Mister Murdin—"

"Don't give me that! And bear in mind that there are plenty of good barefoot men in the streets who'll jump for a day's pay!"

"Padrone—padrone, the underpinning gotta be make safe and . . ."

"Lissenyawopbastard! if you don't like it, you know what you can do!" And with that he swung swaggering away.

The men had heard, and those who hadn't knew instinctively.

The new home, the coming baby, and his whole background, kept the fire from Geremio's mouth and bowed his head. "Annunziata speaks of scouring the ashcans for the children's bread in case I didn't want to work on a job where. . . . But am I not a man, to feed my own with these hands? Ah, but day will end and no boss in the world can then rob me the joy of my home!"

Murdin paused for a moment before descending the ladder.

Geremio caught his meaning and jumped to, nervously directing the rush of work. . . . No longer Geremio, but a machinelike entity.

The men were transformed into single, silent beasts. Snoutnose steamed through ragged mustache whip-lashing sand into mixer Ashes-ass dragged under four-by-twelve beam Lean clawed wall knots jumping in jaws masonry crumbled dust billowed thundered choked . . .

At noon, dripping noses were blown, old coats thrown over shoulders, and foot-long sandwiches were toasted at the end of wire over the flames. Shadows were once again personalities. Laughter added warmth.

Geremio drank his wine from an old-fashioned mag-

nesia bottle and munched a great pepper sandwich . . .
no meat on Good Friday.

Said one, "Are some of us to be laid off? Easter is
upon us and communion dresses are needed and . . ."

That, while Geremio was dreaming of the new house
and the joys he could almost taste. Said he, "Worry not.
You should know Geremio." It then all came out. He
regaled them with his wonderful joy of the new house.
He praised his wife and children one by one. They listened respectfully and returned him well wishes and
blessings. He went on and on. . . . "Paul made a radio—
all by himself, mind you! One can hear *Barney Google*
and many American songs!"

"A radio!"

"An electric machine like magic—yes."

"With music and Christian voices?"

"That is nothing to what he shall someday accom-
plish!"

"Who knows," suggested Giacomo amazed, "but that
Dio has deigned to gift you with a Marconi . . ."

"I tell you, son of Geremio shall never never lay
bricks! Paulie mine will study from books—he will be
the great builder! This very moment I can see him . . .
How proud he!"

Said they in turn: "Master Geremio, in my province
it is told that for good luck in a new home, one is to
sprinkle well with salt . . . especially the corners, and on
moving day sweep with a new broom to the center and
pick all up—but do not sweep it out over the threshold!"

"That may be, Pietro. But, Master Geremio, it would
be better in my mind that holy water should bless. And
also a holy picture of Saint Joseph guarding the door."

"The Americans use the shoe of a horse . . . there
must be something in that. One may try . . ."

Snoutnose knew a better way. "You know, you know."
He ogled his eyes and smacked his lips. Then, reaching
out his hands over the hot embers . . . "To embrace a
goose-fat breast and bless the house with the fresh milk.

And one that does not belong to the wife . . . that is the way!"

Acid-smelling di Nobilis were lit. Geremio preferred his corncob. And Lazarene "tobacco-eater" proudly chawed his quid . . . in the American style.

The ascent to labor was made, and as they trod the ladder, heads turned and eyes communed with the mute flames of the brazier whose warmth they were leaving, not with willing heart, and in that fleeting moment the breast wanted much to speak of hungers that never reached the tongue.

About an hour later, Geremio called over to Pietro, "Pietro, see if Mister Murdin is in the shanty and tell him I must see him! I will convince him that the work must not go on like this . . . just for the sake of a little more profit!"

Pietro came up soon. "The padrone is not coming up. He was drinking from a large bottle of whiskey and cursed in American words that if you did not carry out his orders—"

Geremio turned away disconcerted, stared dumbly at the structure and mechanically listed in his mind's eye the various violations of construction safety. An uneasy sensation hollowed him. The Lean brought down an old piece of wall and the structure palsied. Geremio's heart broke loose and out-thumped the floor's vibrations, a rapid wave of heat swept him and left a chill touch in its wake. He looked about to the men, a bit frightened. They seemed usual, life-size, and moved about with the methodical deftness that made the moment then appear no different than the task of toil had ever been.

Snoutnose's voice boomed into him. "Master Geremio, the concrete is re-ady!"

"Oh, yes, yes, Julio." And he walked gingerly toward the chute, but not without leaving behind some part of his strength, sending out his soul to wrestle with the limbs of Job, who threatened in stiff silence. He talked and joked with Snoutnose. Nothing said anything, nor seemed wrong. Yet a vague uneasiness was to him as certain as the foggy murk that floated about Job's stone and steel.

"Shall I let the concrete down now, Master Geremio?"

"Well, let me see—no, hold it a minute. Hey, Lazarene! Tighten the chute cables!"

Snoutnose straightened, looked about, and instinctively rubbed the sore small of his spine. "Ah," sighed he, "all the men feel as I—yes, I can tell. They are tired but happy that today is Good Friday and we quit at three o'clock—" And he swelled in human ecstasy at the anticipation of food, drink and the hairy flesh-tingling warmth of wife, and then, extravagant rest.

Geremio gazed about and was conscious of seeming to understand many things. He marveled at the strange feeling which permitted him to sense the familiarity of life. And yet—all appeared unreal, a dream pungent and nostalgic.

Life, dream, reality, unreality, spiraling ever about each other. "Ha," he chuckled, "how and from where do these thoughts come?"

Snoutnose had his hand on the hopper latch and was awaiting the word from Geremio. "Did you say something, Master Geremio?"

"Why yes, Julio, I was thinking—funny! A—yes, what is the time—yes, that it what I was thinking."

"My American can of tomatoes says ten minutes from two o'clock. It won't be long now, Master Geremio."

Geremio smiled. "No, about an hour . . . and then, home."

"Oh, but first we stop at Mulberry Street, to buy their biggest eels, and the other finger-licking stuffs."

Geremio was looking far off, and for a moment happiness came to his heart without words, a warm hand stealing over. Snoutnose's words sang to him pleasantly, and he nodded.

"And Master Geremio, we ought really to buy the

seafruits with the shells—you know, for the much
needed steam they put into the—"

He flushed despite himself and continued, "It is true,
I know it—especially the juicy clams ... uhmn, my
mouth waters like a pump."

Geremio drew on his unlit pipe and smiled acquies-
cence. The men around him were moving to their tasks
silently, feeling of their fatigue, but absorbed in con-
templations the very same as Snoutnose's. The noise of
labor seemed not to be noise, and as Geremio looked
about, life settled over him a gray concert—gray forms,
atmosphere and gray notes. . . . Yet his off-tone world
felt so near, and familiar.

"Five minutes from two," swished through
Snoutnose's mustache.

Geremio automatically took out his watch, rewound
and set it. Lazarene had done with the cables. The tone
and movement of the scene seemed to Geremio strange,
differently strange, and yet, a dream familiar from a
timeless date. His hand went up in motion to Julio. The
molten stone gurgled low, and then with heightening
rasp. His eyes followed the stone-cementy pudding, and
to his ears there was no other sound than its flow. From
over the roofs somewhere, the tinny voice of *Barney
Google* whined its way, hooked into his consciousness
and kept itself a revolving record beneath his skullplate.

"Ah, yes, *Barney Google*, my son's wonderful radio machine ... wonderful Paul." His train of thought quickly
took in his family, home and hopes. And with hope
came fear. Something within asked, "Is it not possible to
breathe God's air without fear dominating with the pall
of unemployment? And the terror of production for
Boss, Boss and Job? To rebel is to lose all of the very little. To be obedient is to choke. O dear Lord, guide my
path."

Just then, the floor lurched and swayed under his feet.
The slipping of the underpinning below rumbled up
through the undetermined floors.

Was he faint or dizzy? Was it part of the dreamy afternoon? He put his hands in front of him and stepped back, and looked up wildly. "No! No!"

The men poised stricken. Their throats wanted to cry out and scream but didn't dare. For a moment they were a petrified and straining pageant. Then the bottom of their world gave way. The building shuddered violently, her supports burst with the crackling slap of wooden gunfire. The floor vomited upward. Geremio clutched at the air and shrieked agonizingly. "Brothers, what have we done? Ahhh-h, children of ours!" With the speed of light, balance went sickeningly awry and frozen men went flying explosively. Job tore down upon them madly. Walls, floors, beams became whirling, solid, splintering waves crashing with detonations that ground man and material in bonds of death.

The strongly shaped body that slept with Annunziata nights and was perfect in all the limitless physical quantities thudded as a worthless sack amongst the giant débris that crushed fragile flesh and bone with centrifugal intensity.

Darkness blotted out his terror and the resistless form twisted, catapulted insanely in its directionless flight, and shot down neatly and deliberately between the empty wooden forms of a foundation wall pilaster in upright position, his blue swollen face pressed against the form and his arms outstretched, caught securely through the meat by the thin round bars of reinforcing steel.

The huge concrete hopper that was sustained by an independent structure of thick timber wavered a breath or so, its heavy concrete rolling uneasily until a great sixteen-inch wall caught it squarely with all the terrific verdict of its dead weight and impelled it downward through joists, beams and masonry until it stopped short, arrested by two girders, an arm's length above Geremio's head; the gray concrete gushing from the hopper mouth, and sealing up the mute figure.

Giacomo had been thrown clear of the building and

dropped six floors to the street gutter, where he lay writhing.

The Lean had evinced no emotion. When the walls descended, he did not move. He lowered his head. One minute later he was hanging in mid-air, his chin on his chest, his eyes tearing loose from their sockets, a green foam bubbling from his mouth and his body spasming, suspended by the shreds left of his mashed arms, pinned between a wall and a girder.

A two-by-four hooked little Tomas up under the back of his jumper and swung him around in a circle to meet a careening I-beam. In the flash that he lifted his frozen cherubic face, its shearing edge sliced through the top of his skull.

When Snoutnose cried beseechingly, "Saint Michael!" blackness enveloped him. He came to in a world of horror. A steady stream, warm, thick, and sickening as hot wine, bathed his face and clogged his nose, mouth, and eyes. The nauseous sirup that pumped over his face clotted his mustache red and drained into his mouth. He gulped for air, and swallowed blood. As he breathed, the pain shocked him to oppressive semiconsciousness. The air was wormingly alive with cries, screams, moans, and dust, and his crushed chest seared him with a thousand fires. He couldn't see, nor breathe enough to cry. His right hand moved to his face and wiped at the gelatinizing substance, but it kept coming on, and a heartbreaking moan wavered about him, not far. He wiped his eyes in subconscious despair. Where was he? What kind of a dream was he having? Perhaps he wouldn't wake up in time for work, and then what? But how queer; his stomach beating him, his chest on fire, he sees nothing but dull red, only one hand moving about, and a moaning in his face!

The sound and clamor of the rescue squads called to him from far off.

Ah, yes, he's dreaming in bed, and, far out in the streets, engines are going to a fire. Oh, poor devils! Suppose his house were on fire? With the children scattered about in the rooms he could not remember! He must do his utmost to break out of this dream! He's swimming under water, not able to raise his head and get to the air. He must get back to consciousness to save his children!

He swam frantically with his one hand, and then felt a face beneath its touch. A face! It's Angelina alongside of him! Thank God, he's awake! He tapped her face. It moved. It felt cold, bristly, and wet. "It moves so. What is this?" His fingers slithered about grisly sharp bones and in a gluey, stringy, hollow mass, yielding as wet macaroni. Gray light brought sight, and hysteria punctured his heart. A girder lay across his chest, his right hand clutched a grotesque human mask, and suspended almost on top of him was the twitching, faceless body of Tomas. Julio fainted with an inarticulate sigh. His fingers loosed and the bodiless headless face dropped and fitted to the side of his face while the dripping above came slower and slower.

The rescue men cleaved grimly with pick and ax.

Geremio came to with a start ... far from their efforts. His brain told him instantly what had happened and where he was. He shouted wildly. "Save me! Save me! I'm being buried alive!"

He paused exhausted. His genitals convulsed. The cold steel rod upon which they were impaled froze his spine. He shouted louder and louder. "Save me! I am hurt badly! I can be saved I can—save me before it's too late!" But the cries went no farther than his own ears. The icy wet concrete reached his chin. His heart appalled. "In a few seconds I will be entombed. If I can only breathe, they will reach me. Surely, they will!" His face was quickly covered, its flesh yielding to the solid sharp-cut stones. "Air! Air!" screamed his lungs as he was completely sealed. Savagely he bit into the wooden form pressed upon his mouth. An eighth of an inch of its surface splintered off. Oh, if he could only hold out long enough to bite even the smallest hole through to air! He must! There can be no other way! He must!

There can be no other way! He is responsible for his family! He cannot leave them like this! He didn't want to die! This could not be the answer to life! He had bitten halfway through when his teeth snapped off to the gums in the uneven conflict. The pressure of the concrete was such, and its effectiveness so thorough, that the wooden splinters, stumps of teeth, and blood never left the choking mouth.

Why couldn't he go any farther?

Air! Quick! He dug his lower jaw into the little hollowed space and gnashed in choking agonized fury. Why doesn't it go through! Mother of Christ, why doesn't it give? Can there be a notch, or two-by-four stud behind it? Sweet Jesu! No! No! Make it give ... Air! Air!

He pushed the bone-bare jaw maniacally; it splintered, cracked, and a jagged fleshless edge cut through the form, opening a small hole to air. With a desperate burst the lung-prisoned air blew an opening through the shredded mouth and whistled back greedily a gasp of fresh air. He tried to breathe, but it was impossible. The heavy concrete was settling immutably and its rich cement-laden grout ran into his pierced face. His lungs would not expand and were crushing in tighter and tighter under the settling concrete.

"Mother mine—mother of Jesu—Annunziata—children of mine—dear, dear, for mercy, Jesu-Giuseppe e' Mari," his blue foamed tongue called. It then distorted in a shuddering coil and mad blood vomited forth. Chills and fire played through him and his tortured tongue stuttered, "Mercy, blessed Father—salvation, most kind Father—Saviour—Saviour of His children, help me—adored Saviour—I kiss your feet eternally—you are my Lord—there is but one God—you are my God of infinite mercy—Hail Mary divine Virgin—our Father who art in heaven hallowed be thy—name—our Father—my Father," and the agony excruciated with never-ending mount, "our Father—Jesu, Jesu, soon Jesu, hurry dear Jesu Jesu! Je-sssu ... !"

His mangled voice trebled hideously, and hung in jerky whimperings. Blood vessels burst like mashed flower stems. He screamed. "Show yourself now, Jesu! Now is the time! Save me! Why don't you come! Are you there! I cannot stand it—ohhh, why do you let it happen— where are you? Hurry hurry hurry!"

His bones cracked mutely and his sanity went sailing distorted in the limbo of the subconscious. With the throbbing tones of an organ in the hollow background, the fighting brain disintegrated and the memories of a baffled lifetime sought outlet.

He moaned the simple songs of barefoot childhood, scenes flashed desperately on and off, and words and parts of words came pitifully high and low from his inaudible lips.

Paul's crystal-set earphones pressed the sides of his head tighter and tighter, the organ boomed the mad dance of the Tarantella, and the hysterical mind sang cringingly and breathlessly, "Jesu my Lord my God my all Jesu my Lord my God my all Jesu my Lord my God my all Jesu my Lord my God my all."

II

JOB

1

Paul, lugging a pail of coal through the hallway, halted frightened, then saw it was Di Angelo the stonecutter with an excited woman.

"Oh, I thought you were Master Geremio," she said. "You do not know if he has come home ... O Dio, Dio ..." Angelina could hardly speak, and she ran up the stairs. "Annunziata, where is Master Geremio ... when comes he ... ?"

"Angelia, Angelina, what happened? Why Geremio?"

"Oh, it is not Geremio," Angelina cried. "Julio—the police have come on a motorcycle—my Julio lies in hospital ... and badly!"

Annunziata clasped her hands. The women embraced, and the children gathered round.

"Angelina, courage-courage, sister mine ... it may not be anything ... nothing ..."

Swishing skirts and pointed shoes tripped up the stairs.

"Geremio!"

"Master Geremio!"

"Geremio ... for the love of God tell us—tell me about my Giacomo!"

"My Michael!"

"Why isn't Master Geremio home ... my Nick ... the hospital ... the police ..."

"Annunziata, help us, our world is ending—our men are away from us."

Di Angelo moved about woodenly, attempting to speak, and kept asking, "But what has happened—what *has* happened, may one know?"

"The police on motorcycle—"

"—Hospital—"

"My man!"

"The father of my children . . ."

Annunziata backed to the wall, her lips quivering. With a motion of the hands as though she were leading a distant symphony, she intoned: "It will all come out . . . the Lord will not permit . . . fathers are needed . . . wait, and my Geremio will come and assure you . . . wait . . . partake of my cake and wine . . ."

The children looked to the hot golden pastries hungrily. And Good Friday brought a trembling to the house.

Saint Prisca's bell-voice sang seven tolls.

More women came . . . more cries.

"Paul, away to the house of Tomas, and ask of your father."

The women munched cakes and cried.

"Has a scaffold broken . . . ?"

"What has happened . . . ?"

"No one knows anything."

"And when will Master Geremio come to relieve our hearts . . . ?"

Shortly after, Paul burst into the kitchen.

". . . Mama! Tomas is dead!"

O Jesus O Jesus!

"A block from Tomas' house I heard screams and near the building was a crowd of people . . . everybody said it was Cola going crazy—I was scared . . ."

A gray hand swept over faces, and lips mumbled swiftly, agonizingly.

Saint Prisca sang the hours away.

No Geremio.

The cakes had cooled, would never again know warmth. And not only they had lost their warmth.

Di Angelo sat dumbly and said things that meant nothing.

No policeman on motorcycle.

Paul and Maria asked Bessie Donovan to accompany them to the police station ...

And Annunziata became a human metronome, rocking ... communing with invisible worlds.

"Go on home, you kids, and tell your mother not to worry. Your old man Geremio is safe on tirra-foima ... yeah—yeah there's been a lotta trouble on the job an' there's a warrant out for him too."

... "So you see, mama, there's nothing to worry about ... the police wouldn't tell a lie."

The home of Geremio, builder, became cold ... and cried the children to sleep; as Annunziata rocked, and Paul watched her with wide questioning eyes ... while their lives floated in chill, ill-lit and strangling spheres.

"Sister mine."

"Sister of ours," said they.

"Praise Jesu that Geremio is alive in hiding. ..."

Said Annunziata to Di Angelo, "Bring out the food and drink. Give to the good paesans that which will not make them sad."

Wives whose husbands were safe at home carried life with full arrogance. And the home of Geremio was whither, whither?

Annunziata rocked on incessantly and murmured, "My beautiful Geremio, my round strong arms, my dark twinkle and pressing self, do you not know that I await with child ... our child soon to come ... who awaits your presence with me?"

Paul trembled with the vibrations of his changing world. He ran breathlessly about with Hail Marys and Our Fathers falling fast. The police station ... back ... the police station again. ... "Ha haha kid, your ole man's safe on ter-rer firma ... you're all right kid—he'll get outta it."

Then the trolley ride to the boardinghouse where uncle Luigi lived.

"Ci Luigi! Ci Luigi!"

But Luigi kept repeating, "Huh? Huh?" to Paul's attempt to convey his message, and he answered in his low-throated Italian: "The building ... ah yes, yes, it has been told me that Geremio has bought a home; may the Saints bless it ... and perhaps, with the will of the Lord, even I will have there a little room." "No no no, Ci Luigi ... No no no ... Look ... the newspaper here ... see ... papa's job—la jobe-a collapsed; the building—fell ... ca—caduta ...!"

Mountain-shouldered Luigi peered from under his shaggy brow and his twisted eye twitched as the picture dawned upon him. Luigi sighed a great, soft sound ... like the anguished cry of a mute ... and sank his iron teeth into his hands until the calluses showed deeply. He raised his eyes to the dirty ceiling, and cried in volcanic roars, "Dio ... Dio!" and then his slab-muscled frame shook violently with choking, inward sobs. It was strange to Paul and he whispered frightenedly, "Ci Luigi, Ci Luigi, papa is hiding ... the police and the papers—that's what they say, and they wouldn't tell a lie."

Luigi sat, and rolled his big tousled head on the bare table, crying. "Geremio, but why? But why, Geremio ...?"

Paul soothed the hands that broke stones, and led him out through the doorway.

Holy Saturday was unfriendly, in shabby mood, with sky spitting fickle rain, and clouds teasing the sickly sun. Di Angelo and Ci Luigi had gone to Job and watched the firemen and workers raise the girders and sprawled walls ... each member an oppressive weight on their hearts. "No! Fer Chris' sake, there ain't no more guys under them walls!" Life had stopped and changed for some, but the living could not help themselves, and went on living. Old man Donovan had swept his so-many streets with the so-many required strokes that week, and sat at the kitchen window smoking his pipe, resting, thinking nothing and watching old lady Loban squatting, her time-seared legs askew, on a rusty Socony can down in the littered back yard ... whisky-soused, belching and croaking: "Hey—hey Don-O-van—Yesh we have nooo bananashs—hawhaw hey Don-O-van—hey hahaha." Her string-bean husband foaming curses at her from the window above the Geremio flat ... she, screaming in return her obscene ecstasy, Donovan serenely puffing, thinking of nothing ... and at the next window sat Annunziata, rocking.

"Geremio, we wait ... we await thee ..."

Saint Prisca sang nine calls, and echoed away on the lashing tails of the March winds. Tomorrow would be bright Easter. The paesanos and relatives had slipped away; their husbands and children impatiently seeking the hands that would luscify the leaven dough and white pimpled fowl.

"All must be in order with much rejoicing, for tomorrow the Son of God will rise ..."

"We go now, sister. Courage and heart of steel." And with that they had disappeared.

At Easter dawn the street door closed and footfalls sounded up the stairs. Paul nodded shock-awake, and called frantically, "Papa!"

Annunziata flew to the door, and as she reached out her arms ... the policeman lowered his eyes and slowly removed his cap.

Easter morning bright. Slender dark-eyed Paul, holding little Annina's hand, entered the police station. He beat his thin fingers and stood nervously before the high desk.

"Whadya want, sonny?" asked the desk sergeant.

Paul shivered.

"Mama sent me because she couldn't come.... God's going to give her another baby—and she's sick—"

He hesitated and trembled. The sergeant waited.

"You kids get over to the radiator."

They looked at him, and timidly moved over to the warm radiator.

The sergeant rested his elbows, peered forward, and finally said, "Well, what is it, kiddo?"

Paul opened his mouth to speak, but instead, round wet tears came down his cheeks and through the wavery blur he saw the high brown desk, the policeman, and behind him a big red, white and blue flag. He closed his eyes and gasped:

"On Friday—Good Friday—the building that fell—my father was working—he didn't come home— his name is Geremio—we want him—"

The sergeant thought for a moment, and called to the next room: "Hey Alden, anything come in on a guy named—Geremio?"

A second later, a live voice from the next room loudly answered: "What?—oh yeah—the wop is under the wrappin' paper out in the courtyard!"

2

"Arrived!"

Trained hooves picked their way lightly over bald cobblestones. A black wagon moved properly to the curb, and high rubbered wheels with long-fingered spokes became gracefully inactive. Deft, white-gloved hands made absolutely correct arrangements, and somber faces accompanied. From the wagon's accomplished shell was tendered a fine and solid casket.

"Careful!"

"It is understood . . ."

On the entrance door-jamb was pinned a visiting sign of thin ribbons and white carnations. Hands clutched breasts, and mute respect cried, "Attend! By the love of God, attend! The man of the house has come home!"

He had left his house. He had dressed for the last time, and in the vestments of labor. He had passed the bedroom where the prolificacy of his blood dreamed innocently, and when he had gone out into the street world, the woman at his home's window sent her heart away with him. He went. He had to go. Job called him. And now Job called no more. Christians lined the banisters in the anemic shades of the hallway, and gazed on in blank silence. Carnations, roses, lilies, ghostly virgin, fugued in ritual melody and brought into a home the scented herald of the new Dead.

She, the woman of the house, sensed his entrance. The unearthy hothouse nostalgia shrank her nostrils, and her lips were bitten.

The children drew back from the visit and clasped her in fright.

Measured professional steps trod the stairs. A flowery drug rose through the hallway.

"Arrived!" they cried. "Home. Home has come the Dead!" But not to stay.

Four men in black fought the big box through the skinny parlor door. The living breathed with difficulty to think that the corpse was so oppressed in his protection.

Practiced fingers undid screws. A lid was raised. But none there to raise the Dead.

"Ahh-hh," came the swelling and falling wave. "It *is* Geremio. That is he." And hands signed the cross with automatic fervor.

How will she do now? It is expected she sorrows before us, for was he not her husband live, who lies there cold?

Annunziata did not move. From her bulk the newly-made widow stared.

Flowers, dainty and hypnotic. Flowers such as are seen in showcases, and grace the dinner tables and boudoirs of the rich as in books and the movies.

Candles. Costly waxy hands, sending up the prayered light. In such profusion! And she, a hostess, an impor-

tant figure in a large audience! Only ... above a re-
splendently cased dummy there read

Geremio——Born——Died——

on a shiny plate set in white and puffy silk.

The friend and lover, the patriarch of her children,
lay mute in cloistered refinery. Still, she remained. And
her breast called abandonedly: Light of my life! Flame
of my blood, how can it be? while within her swollen
entrails his blood of her blood kicked in the urge for
birth.

The cross was again signed throughout the room,
slowly.

"Poor Christian, it seems she will not know him."

"So he is dead, and what can she do?"

But she remained, belly full-bursting, and overworked
breasts sprawled, showing dumbly with her ungraceful
limbs. She turned and looked for her Jesu. May he not
be there? There were only faces, looking upon her in-
tently.

No message.

She caressed her moving stomach and her lips
formed, submissive, wistful ... "Do not the children of
their father come to kiss his hand? And he has come
home ..."

"She has reasoned justly!"

"Right! Right! Bring to the father his children!"

"Quick! The little ones must see ..."

"Yes, to them it must be recorded, so that they shall
grow up without delay!"

Paul cried: "Oh, no! I cannot go in—I cannot
look—O Jesus, no! No!"

The children shivered and bawled.

Annunziata looked to them.

"It is they that cry—and I am dry-eyed and tired. It
is too much. Overmuch. O travail, what have I done to
thee?"

Thin little Paul walked the rooms. He stumbled
along, his eyes a spring of weeping. The big people
made way. They watched him. He faltered and felt at

the walls as he went. The tears were his own and tasted
of salt; he sniffed and sucked them in. The grown
watched.

"Yes, boy-child. Loss. Grief . . ."

Faces used to the wrinkle and coarse stubble, and
women from above their round hips and bulge breasts,
watched wonderingly. Paul had crossed the rooms. The
threshold of the parlor charged him with a trembling
shock. From him flew the rising cry: "I can't, Jesus, I
can't!" And he clung shaking to the door.

Ci Luigi had been in the corner of the room, his
bowed head buried in the angle and the peak of his old
cap clutched in his teeth. He wiped his eyes on hearing
Paul's cry. His rough face softened and he whispered
across the room, "Little uncle. Little uncle mine. Not
like that. It must not be . . . as that . . ."

His great shoulders rolled over to Paul. Paul straightened.

"Ci Luigi—good Ci Luigi—I will go by myself—
forgive me."

Luigi ripped his cap. His mighty arms yearned to tear
apart a world and return to life his sister's man . . . as
she, Annunziata, remained columned in the center of
the room.

Night came again. Only . . . miserable. The children
slept, not the same as before. Geremio's mouth had not
kissed them to bed. Annunziata was eternity, rocking;
and Luigi, still in his work-soiled clothes, remained to
converse with the Dead. He touched tenderly the hair
and made-up features of his Geremio, he who had wed
his little sister.

"But can you not answer me, O friend? Why do you
not speak to me? Have you not a message for
Annunziata whose song has been stilled? Is there no
word for the children who bear your form and smell?
You are safe with me. Speak. I am your big Luigi, your
Gigi, who carried you on his shoulder in Abruzzi and
gave you sweet things to eat. Ah, Ger, Ger, will you not

tell me how it was? Did it not wound you terribly to become thus—and having left against your desires?"

His tears rained blessing, and far into the daylight of
burial morn he caressed and brothered the quiet form,
and never ceased questioning: "But why, Geremio—but
why?"

The day that followed was lived.

The Dead left, once more accompanied with the certain formality that numbed the senses. That of him
which answered to a name and number in the society of
laws was lowered into his first real estate.

"First must the children scatter earth upon the
father . . ."

They did. And the heavens wept as the released laborer embraced the fresh earth . . . while pointed spades
turned in upon him, his last home.

And earth to Paul became flesh of dirt, and burial
deep was cold rank to his heart. He carried his father's
life, and every granule of earth that planted his father
tighter beneath the footsteps of the living, he felt upon
himself . . . earth on his body—earth suffocating his
mouth and earth crushing his soul. Earth was a terrible
thing, a solid dead-live sea of clay and stems, a brown
foundation vastness hysterically firm. And now a still
man, dignified by death, was oppressed into its womb of
soil. The damp rose from the mud and up Paul's
straight thin limbs.

"Had he only broken a leg on the way to Job . . ."

"Or remained abed to enjoy the wife . . ."

"Or put behind bars in a dungeon—even for no
reason . . ."

"Thirty-six!"

"A strong tree broken . . . yes!"

". . . Ahhh, good Christian . . ."

They were an oblong ring. They were his comrades
of Job.

Postures of the wheelbarrow, scaffold and kitchen—
statures of stonecarriers and childbearers—splay-footed,

square-handed and poised of labor unpainted and unadorned—they were not pretty.

They were of the roots.

"My man was dark and strained because the good spirit Geremio could not place him on that job of sorrow ... but now, how I praise the Virgin and cling to Raffaele's legs ..."

Why could not mother Annunziata say that ... ? And Paul's lips were caught.

"It was yesterday in Abruzzi when he and his wife met at the feast of Saint Mary. It was I who first said they would marry. Yes, 'A matrimony, a matrimony,' said I."

"Yesterday? A yesterday of twenty years."

"At the joining, Pilone's great hound attacked Geremio (mercy on his spirit) and to save him Luigi received his twisted eye. Ah dear-dear, better said that it were a century ago, not yesterday."

"And to me, I, who am old, it is as a few breaths back."

"Time has given to time and made time. You speak of the old world. This is another world."

Tears dripped from Ci Luigi's broad mustache. Shaggy head rolled on right shoulder, mouth open, and, searching dumbly through his twisted eye, he gazed. Words-words-words, and a grave is filled! He held out his great hands questioningly to the mound and said with brother's sadness, "This ... could I ever believe?"

For a space the living were still; then, slowly gathering, they made to move.

Go? Go! And leave father drowning forever under the earth? Am I not he? ... His fire and hunger—Am I not my father's son!

The feet of the grown were leaving respectfully.

"Come, little Paul ..."

"He is ill."

Papa-papa-papapapapapa *rise*!

Ci Luigi caught Paul as he fell and lifted him to the carriage.

Back to the grave saluted the eyes of fellow workers. Before departing, once-familiar voices keened: "Good-by, Geremio. To God, Geremio."

3

"Bear—Annunziata—bear ..."
"... one door and opens another."
Dear mother, what can I do to awaken you softly—so rock, dear mother, rock.
"... Lord needed him."
"... sees all."
"And knows best ..."
Dear mother, what are they saying?
"... also died for us ..."
Dear mother, is not all this a wrong story?
"... prayer and giant's will!"
And gone were the mourners. Their breasts and knotted hands were called for in other home worlds.
Funeral was over and night floated down upon Tenement. They had to go. They could not stay forever.

Quiet, quiet.
Garish sickness of sweating yellow narrow kitchen walls in the slowly dying gaslight.
Quiet my heart, and a music sings that drifts my senses and drains my blood. My children, weep. Weep, for I know not how. Weep, for you have cause. Weep, for our light is cold.
Quiet.
Quiet and she rocks.
And the children sleep in tired lump.
Quiet ... and worlds rush past ...
His life holds me fast—
Quiet ... and he I cannot embrace
fast-fast-fasterfas*ter*
"*Geremio!*"

Paul jumped up.

"Mama—? Mama, sit down—"

Annunziata stood with hands pushing her breast as it came hard and short. Closer and closer circled her tension. She thrust her hands to her mouth and bit them in terrible brace.

With desperately resolute eyes she stalked to the window.

Her wounded hands opened the window, and from her came a voice: "Husband—husband . . ."

"Mama!" screamed Paul. *"No!!* Ohnonononono!"

He ran to her and chained her legs.

The children had been frightened awake, and their soft whimpering rose.

"Kids! *Kids!"* called Paul in lucid delirium, "come quick, come!"

They were sucked out of bed, and they bumped and rolled out into the kitchen clinging to one another. Paul rose, and led her back to the rocker.

"Mama—what will happen to the kids—"

Through my mysterious vale I see his and mine.

"Papa is in Paradise . . . watching . . ."

A new melody called to her. Faintly it came. She listened.

"God has taken him, and will send us another— Geremio . . ."

Slightly-slightly her lips parted. And clutching her hands Paul said: "Mama do not cry—mama, do not cry—I—I—shall be the father—"

A door was opening, a thin young door, and of his and hers . . . *I shall be the father.*

And dammed grief leaped and cascaded with wife-force.

For hours her love's violence flowed.

O Jesu in Heaven, and husband near, whither . . . and how? Pieced from the living are we now both. Bread— bread of Job and job of Bread has crushed your feet from the ground and taken your eyes from the sun, but

nowhere are we separate—never-never in this breathing
life shall I be away from you. Day and night will I kiss
your wounds, with my flesh shall I keep the rain from
you, these tears shall comfort you in heat, and with the
cold shall I breathe upon you my warmth . . . husband
great.

It is not of mine to ask—*Why?* But tonight must I
gather strength to carry yours and mine—to place their
feet safely upon this earth. Content for that am I to
suffer—to live—and then to join you. Join you.

And her hand caressed the bed haloed of his form.

4

Annunziata awoke to the beating of a life within her.

It pulled and gripped her back and thighs.

"Send for the dame Katarina, and prepare clean
sheets."

Luigi returned with the dame Katarina, and with
them came Tomas' widow big-titted Cola all in black,
the Regina Govanni, Theresa the Meatball, and the
peasant woman Grazia la Caffone. Dame Katarina was a
huge wizened creature, high priestess of ceremonials
from cradle to grave. Slinging her big sack from off her
pointed shoulders and dropping it at Annunziata's feet,
she said: "Eh? Annunziata—eh? Swollen like the dead
horse in July—eh?"

Then swinging around with her scything motions she
growled: "Well, unmount the pot, you public whores,
and prove yourselves Christians! Hot water! Clean
rags!" Under her breath she muttered, "Finger in
mouth—finger in mouth, the way they porch themselves you'd think they had never shot out babies . . ."

She rummaged in her sack among the herbs, evil-eye
amulets, love mixtures and dirty linen, and brought out
soap and a pocket knife. Swiftly she pared her nails and
washed her hands. Reaching into the folds of her end-

less many-colored garments, she brought forward an ancient pair of spectacles which she put on and tied in place with red string. She rolled up her sleeves, sprinkled talcum on her dried-up hairy arms, lifted the blanket from Annunziata, and went to work.

Annunziata moaned slightly.

"The signs are masculine!" said the dame. "And soon he will walk out by himself!"

Luigi arranged chairs for the women, gave weak coffee and stale bread to the children, and brought back into the bedroom a gallon of wine and two round loaves of bread. He broke the bread with his hands, and passed around, first to the dame and then to the other women, large glasses of the red wine.

The dame produced from her sack an earthen bowl and two long pointed hot peppers. She filled the bowl with wine, sandwiched the peppers between two rough chunks of bread, soaked all in wine, and swallowed ravenously.

As the dame was devouring her second bowlful, the Regina Govanni gave her breast a lift, motioned toward her and said, "Poor beast, how it loves the grape."

"It's the blood of our sweet Christ!" And with a circling movement the dame signed the cross.

"But it is not expected to swim in His blood."

"Better than in water, which decays great steamboats and drowns the Christians ... Now when I was a girl—"

"Nine years before the Lord was born."

"Water was not invented, and all women were great beauties—"

"Such as yourself who frightens even sin."

"And we bathed, and washed the streets, in wine—"

"So that is why you no longer bathe!"

"Quiet! And the elders taught us to drink it, for it painted real color in the cheek, put milk in the tit and fire in the stove.... Bah, you holes askew will yet become baloney-eating Americans!"

The Regina straightened her breasts, and asked coyly,

"Between us pigeons—is it true, Dame Katarina, that you once rubbed bellies with the Devil . . . ?"

"The pot calls the kettle black! You have not earned the name of the Regina Govanni who fornicated with a bull, for nothing!"

"Aie-aie-aie!" cried the dark-eyed Cola as she held her pumping breasts of laughter.

"You this" and "you that" . . . laugh sisters laugh, for even the twisted eye of Luigi lights up—laugh mouth laugh stomach laugh heart and soul laugh hahahahehe-he*hahahaha*!

Voices. And how do I lie here with pain of child? Voices—and the living carry life with full jest. Voices, and I would laugh with them. Voices and I am looking upward.

"I am bursting!"

All became sharply silent.

"Yes yes yes yes, little daughter," said the dame tenderly. She searched into Annunziata once more, and then with holy water she anointed her forehead and naked stomach hill.

"Now. Without comedy, sister. Behind the bed, Luigi my son, and hold strongly her arms. To the legs, Grazia, Cola."

The dame bent over Annunziata.

" 'Twas I, little daughter, who brought the very you to the light, and 'twas I who brought forth each of your little Christians. And now, attended by Jesu, the Saints, and the spirit of Geremio, we shall bring your last one to this world."

". . . His and mine."

"His and yours."

Annunziata whispered softly:

"Dame, we both prayed for a little woman. But now . . ."

"And now, a Geremio . . ." And the dame smoothed Annunziata's hair and kissed her forehead.

"Force, Annunziata."

"Force . . ."

"Yes, force."

Why do I live and give life when there is not Geremio to hold my hand . . . ?

"Tighter, her arms, Luigi. Wider her legs, Grazia, Cola!"

And the dame lay prone and squinted as one trying to look forward into a growing dusk.

"The head is seen. All shall be well! Force, my child, force!"

Annunziata breathed in long, hard movement . . . then felt a ripping within.

"Aie! Aie! A—ie!"

"It comes!"

"Aie, Jesu, aieeeeeeeee . . ."

And with dark torture slowly and sheerly was disgorged part of a soft hairy head.

. . . Repent ye . . . repent ye . . . for the Kingdom of God is on high.

As the pulpy head appeared, Annunziata bit her tongue and twisted. The dame coaxed its oozing passage with puckered mouth and intent care.

"Ah—*Je—su—ahhhhhhh*—Geremio—carrrro—"

The head retreated a bit and remained still. Cola made a fearful face and hastily cried, "Why doesn't it come? Something has happened?"

"No—God forbid—"

"Ah! Ah! *Ahh!*" sighed Annunziata, and she turned her head into the pillow.

"Katarina—Dio—she looks badly—Jesu-Giuseppe e' Mari—Jesu-Giuseppe e' Mari—" wailed the Regina.

"Stuck! Twisted! Instruments of iron will be needed yes yes . . . mal-fortuna!"

Katarina paid no heed, and worked Annunziata's stomach.

"O his and mine . . ." moaned Annunziata. "Poor they."

Luigi, frightened from the very first, lowered his head and sobbed.

"Sister mine—Dio—sister mine!"

When the women's fears joined in concert, Katarina clenched her jaws, raised her face to them and shouted, "Quiet!"

Silence echoed upon her cry and she said in even low voice, "Nature will follow its way."

"Sister-sister—" began Luigi.

"To Hell out of here, old woman!" ordered Katarina. And Luigi left, weeping. Katarina rubbed Annunziata's stomach and soothingly said, "Né' né' né', Annunziata, strain not overmuch. Pause. The little beggar is resting and in a minute will cannonade himself out; the little son of a bitch . . . the little angel."

Luigi corralled the children in the adjoining bed-room.

"Little uncles mine, pray-pray to father for mother." Paul ranged them at the bedside.

"Why mus' we?" asked Joie.

"Pray, kids," begged Paul. "Pray."

Katarina watched Annunziata's tired heaving stomach. "The sea is collecting force and will soon wave up high on shore our little visitor."

Annunziata's thighs tautened, and a power within pushed the child from her. Katarina gathered it as it came, and placed it safely on the bed. The Regina hastily wiped the child, and exclaimed:

"It's masculine—by the Madonna, it *is* a boy!"

The infant's mouth and nostrils dilated, and from it exploded sucking-bursting screams; shrilly it bellowed itself from pale blue-white to live pink.

"Benedictions on him, benedictions to him," exclaimed Grazia. "What a mouth of mouths!"

"All mouth!"

Luigi looked up on hearing the newborn's riot.

"Dame Katarina . . . how?" he called. "*How?*"

"What desires he?" questioned Katarina as she arranged the infant's navel.

"Pleasure me to answer . . . how, sisters, how?" called Luigi.

"A boy. And most beautiful! And all well, praise God," responded Cola.

Luigi's fears flew from him and he became childishly eager to re-enter the bedroom. He opened the door timidly and peeked in.

"Away-away!" admonished the Regina. "This is not territory for men!"

"Yes," affirmed Cola, "occupy yourself away from here. Have you no shame? Go purchase a paper bag of sweets for the children. . . . And for us too."

Luigi excused himself and did as he was told.

"What weathervanes that twist with each wind; what turn-banners—what gypsies!" hissed the dame.

"You are always giving names," said the Regina. "But is it nice that any man should be in the room of birth?"

Katarina rubbed Annunziata's stomach, looked in the direction of the Regina and muttered, "Madonna, what fools and hypocrites. You women should be lashed over the bare tail with a wet rope!"

Cola shouted with bursting laughter, "Or with maybe that other thing."

Suddenly she realized her widow-weed and broke into furious weeping. Grazia, Theresa the Meatball, and the Regina shook their heads sorrowfully, and tended to the infant.

Slowly and carefully, Katarina worked over Annunziata and examined her closely. She gathered all the waste into newspapers, washed Annunziata, and covered her. She aided Theresa in the cleansing and anointing of the infant with olive oil and talcum; then stood over the infant admiringly and said:

"Kick and swing your tiny jigger-limbs, load and fire your one-note opera . . . sing and live, live and sing—his mother's little man—her little rose . . ." and kissing him with tender frenzy of woman-love she sang, ". . . And the sweet little blessed cock of his own mother true!"

She sent for Luigi and the children. When they en-

tered she picked the infant up and held it by the feet,
naked and upside down, high above her head, and
sang, "Who will buy my fish? Who will buy my fish today . . . ?"

She brought the infant to the bed. "Gaze, little pi-
geon . . . upon the . . . new Geremio . . . ?"

From Annunziata's heavy eyes, a smile ushered two
clear tears. As those about her bowed their heads and
signed the cross, a great weight carried Annunziata off
into mouth-wide sleep.

When all was quiet, the infant swaddled, and placed
near to Annunziata, the dame Katarina put on her
shawl, slung her sack, and went close to Annunziata.
She wet her finger with spittle and did benediction
upon the brow of Annunziata.

"Repose, little daughter . . . and the great Christ with
you."

At the threshold, she said to the world of herself: "May it be understood . . . But what *does* one
know . . . ?"

Who are they who visit my bedside to gaze with
warming eye and word—who are these—not my other
selves? whose hands touch these my own . . .

"Mama," whispered Paul, "Missus Olsen, and Missus
Donovan and the other tenants are here."

". . . sorry."

". . . do you feel now?"

". . . he was a fine-looking man. Rest his soul."

". . . lovely child!"

". . . God's grace."

"Yes, He will help you . . ."

Let me go! Let me escape! This role I do not wish to
play!

"Mama, are you tired . . . that you do not speak?"

"Little son, what can I say . . . ?"

". . . we know, we know . . ."

"Time will heal."

Time . . . time-time-time will destroy time and will

never bring him back! The Dead depart but never have they returned. And could I ever accept this truth? Who grows upon me this ceremony and robs me of him who alone I desire? Who directs my heart? Who is there to answer its questions?—Jesu-Giuseppe e' Mari!

Then came stories. . . . Of how, and when, she, and he, and they, had met death. . . . At home, or far, or at birth, or in dismal hospital, or on Job, and what they said before they left, and why.

". . . and in these arms he breathed his last . . ."

". . . while washing clothes they brought me the news, and I—"

Who recounts me these tales, and why? Can words recourse this elegy that bears from me my senses?

"I tore my hair, I was goin' mad—"

With him am I buried, and the oceans shall bring tears for weeping to my soul. Why-why have I power for so great a love, and no one to set just this loss? Ah, forgive me Lord, and know that my faith is unfailing . . . my God my Lord my all.

"She is tired and the baby is hungry."

"We go."

The women had talked and now were leaving. Did Annunziata hear all they said . . . did it matter? Unlovely bodies in any sort of cheap clothes, greasy red hands, pinched faces, hungry eyes, and draggy turned-over heels. Ungraceful young and yet more ungraceful old had been there consoling Annunziata in the dark consumptious bedroom in the dark rank flat in the cancerous dark tenement in the dark close street in a dark world. The poor alone had visited the poor.

Yes, the friends and neighbors have come to pay witness to my position. And to my ears is brought my new name—the widow—the widow Annunziata. For from my home has been shorn its main wall and upon these my children shall rain every heat and cold; their only covering to be the indelible stigma . . . the fatherless. Already are we left alone and avoided—for we have nothing to give—except our need. And day and night have changed semblance and are as white and black towers that besiege us in turn. For the walls who destroyed the father of his own lie as the earth upon me and mine and must ever by us be borne.

Where first shall I turn? . . . to whom with my broken speech shall I say: "Stricken widow with hungry brood am I. Help me and mine and these weak arms shall pray Heaven's blessing ever upon thee"? Whom shall my children seek? Who will now put food into the open mouths of my little birds?—for they must live and blossom as tall-tall pillars in this land that swallowed their father—I must live so that they shall *live*!

And she pressed little Geremino tightly as he hungrily suckled her hot breast.

Quiet-quiet, and Geremino's nose-bud zzzzzzzed.

Quiet Luigi quiet Paul and in the streaming silence Annunziata contemplated the dirty yellow walls as from them perspired pimples of chill damp.

At the other end of the railroad flat Joie cried:

"I'll tell mammm-a . . . !"

"Quiet! . . ." came Annina's voice.

Zzzzzzz-zizzed Geremino.

And also in the room three other souls breathed each in their time and concentration.

Live quiet.

The toilet above flushed with watery roar, pish-thrash-gargled down the exposed pipe and trick-trickled away in its hollow metal throat.

The street door sounded below and a frigid draft blew through Tenement.

"Jack—hey Ja-ckie!"

Above, a door rattled open and from it re-echoed.

"Be right dow-un—"

And a mad downward stumble of young feet.

Heavy steps rushed to the door and Mr. Olsen's raw voice bombed the hall-shaft, *"Shut the goddamn door!"*

The door exploded shut and shocked quiet trembled

down the crooked stairway down the rope-woody dumbwaiters down the soil pipes down away . . .

Quiet balanced itself and moved with level time.

The dimming window said day was leaving, and soon the chill bedroom was dark. A saffron light splotched in from the high-set hall window streaking the wet yellow walls near the ceiling and telling with its gasps that the hallway gas-lamp was being lit.

Luigi rested his elbows on knees, cupped his face and thought.

Through the dark the gaslight's wavering glare reflected and palely illumined Annunziata's face.

Paul's gaze searched in awe her light brown eyes, heart-shaped face, slender nose, baby-pure skin, and long brown hair.

Annunziata raised a small fine hand to her face and brushed delicately from her forehead a wisp of hair, her little mouth forming softly O.

Mother, my life is now your shield. Nothing, nothing in the world can now harm you. These limbs shall hurl back the world and raise you to glory . . . beautiful Madonna mine!

And Paul clutched his fists.

Luigi lapped the quiet with a sigh and said respectfully, "Little sister . . ."

Annunziata lay in floating fatigue.

"Mama," whispered Paul.

Annunziata turned her head wearily.

". . . Yes, good brother . . . ?"

Luigi leaned forward and held his huge hands in front of him.

"Sister cruelly hurt, the thirtieth of March has brought woe to the home of Geremio—" he paused. "Malediction-malediction! . . . Ahhhh. . . . But now he is at rest, and with the Geremino at your breast, let us to make the count and measure the distance ahead."

Paul listened attentively.

"Thirty-five are you, and with eight Christians in

your arms. The Dead are in their world—and we in ours. We have problems."

"Geremino has not left me. 'Never shall I desert you,' said he."

"You are yet young."

"One man has God united me with—the dearest man in the universe. He was Christian clean and strong, whose beauty delighted my being."

"Blessings to his spirit."

"His love I have in the eight pillars for whom I must live."

"For them you must live."

"I give thanks to the good God for my Geremio. And I know he hovers above me aiding me to protect his and mine—and then to join him."

"Amen. . . . Sister . . ."

"Yes . . . ?"

"The money that was to have bought your little house barely pays the burial and stone. You have no money."

Silence, as Luigi flexed his thick fingers. ". . . But fear nothing, for you are not alone. These hands shall be devoted to the needs of my sister and hers."

Annunziata reached for Luigi's extended hand, and kissed it.

Paul kissed his other hand. Luigi raised his eyes, and sobbed softly.

5

In his boardinghouse bunk, Luigi had not slept at all that night. Fifty cents the hour, nine hours the day, brings four dollars and fifty cents. With six days the week brings—six by four brings twenty-four. One-half by six makes three. Twenty-four add three brings the final count twenty-seven dollars. The variables of the weather will make the twenty-seven less—and add the

fare and lunch. . . . But I shall prepare for the weather
and work through it. Of food I will do with less—I am
forty-five, and no longer growing.

Six by four add three brings twenty-seven . . . ? Yes,
twenty-seven it does bring. Say that three dollars shall
be expense—leaving twenty-four. Say perhaps four—no,
better three. The eight little ones, Annunziata and myself are eight—nine—ten. Ten Christians at twenty-four
dollars. . . . First, where to begin. . . . And he turned his
great body restlessly from side to side in the narrow
bunk. Suddenly, he swung off the quilt and arose in his
heavy underwear and thick socks. He let the faucet run,
drew a cup of water, drank, and went back to the bunk.
From his old second-hand sheepskin hanging on the
back of the chair near the bunk he secured a black
twisted di Nobili cigar, broke it in two, put one half in
his mouth and lit it. He lay back and puffed profoundly.

Let us to begin with the beginning . . . With twenty-
four dollars to be parted by ten—but no, one must begin with the food and then there are the calculations for
the rent and then there—But first we will better take—

He turned, spat on the floor, and once more puffed
thoughtfully . . . staring to nothing through the cigar's
glow.

With ten to consume twenty-four dollars, it needs
that first we are to consider what is to be considered
first. So, considering . . . He paused, the figures snarling
into a discordant mass in his forehead just between the
eyes. The alarm rang. Luigi arose. There is only one
way . . . and that will be managed with the aid from
above. . . . It may be my fate to win the lottery—one
never knows when Fortune deigns to visit.

He made his simple prayers, ate his stale bread in watery coffee, dressed, lit the other half di Nobili at the
doorway, and departed for Job.

Racing up floor cubed on floor into the uncertain
April sky, leaning toward sight a many-windowed con-
strained solid of sharp sheer expanding angles, towered

a building over the large foundation excavation into which Luigi descended. The hole was half a city block square, and went down over fifty feet deep into hard rock. Pools of grayish water, high derricks, piles of cable and twelve-by-twelve timbers, large boulders, steam shovels, compression machines, shanties, tool sheds and endless pipes filled the space between the walls of jagged rock. Luigi received his brass work check and proceeded in the line of laborers to the shanty. He carefully hung his sheepskin on a nail, sat on a box and removed his shoes to don hip-boots.

"To part four and twenty, brings for each, two . . . and—perhaps a half—"

The men nodded.

"With sleep in his eyes, Luigi talks to his mustaches."

"Signifying there is gold in the hidden strong-box . . ."

"Gold of another nature—hiding under his bed—in the piss-catcher-ino—"

Whistle shrilled Job awake, and the square pit thundered into an inferno of sense-pounding cacophony.

Compression engines snort viciously—sledge heads punch sinking spikes—steel drills bite shattering jazz in stony-stone excitedly jarring clinging hands—dust swirling—bells clanging insistent aggravated warning—severe bony iron cranes swivel swing dead heavy rock high—clattering dump—vibrating concussion swiftly absorbed—echo reverberating—scoops bulling horns in rock pile chug-shish-chug-chug aloft—hiss roar dynamite's boomdoom loosening petrified bowels—one hundred hands fighting rock—fifty spines derricking swiveling—fifty faces in set mask chopping stone into bread—fifty hearts interpreting Labor hurling oneself down and in at earth planting pod-footed Job.

With April morning breaking down in slanting rain—and up Luigi's pick—ten into twenty-four considering first the food for the children—down shivery hard in wall-boulder's crevice—up pick—down into slowly dislodging boulder from wall. Twenty-four parted by

ten—up pick—but we shall manage with strength—
down pick hard—miss aim—slide slippery boots in
puddle—down Luigi—down swiftly certain *stone*—but?!!
my leggssss . . .

With April's rain and ten *not* into twenty-four.

A nurse tendered Paul along the hospital corridor,
into the men's ward, and to Luigi. Luigi lay with pain
cut on his face.

"Here he is. And leave when the third bell rings."

Paul and Luigi looked at each other.

Ah, how stupidly I am sensed. I know not what to tell
to him . . . I know not how to excuse this failure.

He took Paul's hand in his hard, sweating palm and
said huskily, "Little Paul . . . uncle mine . . ."

And Paul asked, "Ci Luigi . . . when did it happen?"

"Fresh with the morning."

"Did it hurt very, very badly?"

"It hurt my heart more . . ."

"Are you in pain?"

". . . Much."

"A stone fell?"

"And ruined my legs.—They . . . now walled in plaster."

He tapped the large casts, and was silent.

"How feels dear mother Annunziata, and the
Geremino?"

"Mama is abed and weeps for papa, and now you.
Geremino is well. He cares only to eat, yell, and sleep
all day."

"Benedictions-benedictions."

"Ci Luigi, mama says you are the greatest brother in
the world . . . and we pray for you."

Luigi rolled his head away from Paul; his tears dropping.

"Sister—" he called, "how I have betrayed you. . . .
The stone has fixed my legs, and now I shall be your
stone . . . sister mine."

Paul embraced him, and they did not speak until the third bell.

"I will see you often, Ci Luigi, and shall bring you home to us someday. Rest . . . and good night."

Luigi brushed the thin sensitive face with his mustache, and his twisted eye eagerly followed Paul's form out of the ward.

April night.

Luigi finds himself down in the foundation pit. The men are working. He does not know them all. When did the whistle blow and why isn't he with them as he looks here—there in the shed near the crane on the stones under the machines between the timbers—and he cannot find his pick and he knows the foreman blueshirt is watching him—but he makes believe that he Luigi doesn't see him and that he is on an important singular mission, and he tries to hem and cough like someone else until he finds his pick and when he approaches the men they look at him sideways and as he recognizes them and wants to smile greeting they lower their eyes and turn away as though they don't know him and there is no noise and they work stiffly like quiet zombies in a spell and the foreman's eyes are big black angry spots under the lid of his felt hat always staring at him and he puts his head down and wants to do *something* or run away but he can't find his way out of the pit when by a wall Geremio is smiling with that overtopping twinkle and motions for him and hands him a brick hammer so that he can break stones with the men and Luigi wants to feel and embrace him because he knows that he is proud and lonely and has done something and for some reason it is known that Geremio is not supposed to mix with people and Geremio glides away from him and shakes his head smilingly like a stranger and Luigi feels the blueshirt's foreboding black eyes and spontaneously swings the little brick hammer as though he were wound up at the big stone that he recognizes and the hammer handle becomes smaller and smaller and the big black eyes blow up bigger and bigger and he no longer has any hammer and is frantically beating the stone with his hands and the stony face looms larger*larger* and rolls over on him and does not hurt him and he starts to laugh to think that somewhere that he couldn't place that stone had frightened him and when he laughs louder the men break out in storms of high-pitched laughter. But what is Annunziata doing there holding all her children in her arms and looking with terrible hungry sad eyes at him and he whispers to her that he will find Geremio for her and will work all his life for her and the children for she has nothing to worry about and that she should laugh and teach the children to laugh with the men whose laughter blows in gales—but she looks at his legs and he becomes terribly fearful and afraid to follow her eyes and when he tries to jump to his feet he cannot move and his two legs begin to pump like engines and pump pain through him and she lowers her vacant eyes and her mouth hangs meaning that she expected him to fail her and he tries to beat the stone from his legs and cries above the laughing men sister dear sister it was not I who betrayed you—it was someone stronger than you and me— someone who does not tell why—sister believe me it was not I who betrayed you!

"There, there, Luigi, no one will hurt you . . . no one will hurt you. You must not try to move your legs. Did you have bad dream?"

". . . Nurse-a . . . I no spick—I no can-a spick . . ."

6

Annunziata arose before her time. The thirtieth of March had broken her blood and painted age in her face. With the dawn, there no longer were Katarina or the Regina or the other women at the bedside, dressing

Geremino or the children, or preparing food or washing
clothes. . . . Annunziata arose alone, and in weeds of
black. At the meager dresser where a votive light flick-
ered low in a red glass, she stood weakly and with
clasped hands.

God of my fathers, God of my girlhood, God of my
mating, God of my innocent children, upon your sacred
bosom I lay my voice: To this widow alone black-
enshrouded, lend of your strength that she may live
only to raise her children. God of my life, death and
spirit . . . Amen.

Her head reeled. Sitting on the bedside she felt balance leaving her. She lay back on the bed. She was drift-
ing off when Geremino's squall brought her to, and for
a minute she did not know where she was. She reached
for her breasts, but when she drew one it was limp,
empty. Johnny, awakened by Geremino, swung his bottle and called for milk. Annunziata planted her feet on
the floor and walked unsteadily toward the kitchen. In
the next bedroom the other six children were curled
closely in one bed. She held to the bedstead and blessed
them.

Through the dining room and into the dark kitchen
she dragged her feet. She felt in the cupboard and
found a loaf of fresh bread, half a loaf of stale bread,
two onions, a handful of old potatoes, and a can of
evaporated milk. She fingered the food mechanically.
She would not eat. And still that leaves eight. With
three meals each, the day requires twenty-four portions.
Who would bring into the house that great necessity?
What magic power would supply twenty-four portions
each day? And the rent? And the fuel? And the clothes?
Andand*and* . . . ? Geremino and Johnny yelled impatiently—enraged. Annunziata shook the grate of the
coal stove and fired it. She heated water, mixed it with
evaporated milk and filled the babies' bottles. Geremino
and Johnny pulled them snugly to their breasts and
sucked and gurgled with ogle-ogle-grumble-joy. For
breakfast Annunziata gave the children the rest of the

evaporated milk diluted with warm water, and dry bread.

"Mama, aren't you going to eat?"

"I am not hungry, Paul."

The two onions and few potatoes stood out on the table.

Mama does not eat for there is nothing to eat. The children will be hungry again . . . what will mama and I say to them? And even understanding, hunger would yet remain. How did these onions and potatoes come to our table . . . and where are father's hands . . . ?

Father's hands were our home. They gave to us food and warmth. They gave us love, and they gave us joy. From the buildings he brought us life . . . and now strange hands are pushing us down and I feel we are sliding and there is nothing to grasp . . . father-father, I am scared!

Annunziata sat with folded hands.

Two onions. Four potatoes. One-two-three-four-five-six large crumbs one-two-three-four-five-six-seven-eight-nine-ten-eleven small crumbs. Paul Annina Lucia Giorgio Joseph Adela Johnny Geremino two onions four potatoes. Who will tap on the door to put baskets of food on Geremio's table? Who will come in quietly and feed the family of Geremio day upon day week upon week month upon month year upon year until they are strong men and women and I join Geremio? Jesu-Giuseppe e' Mari . . .

Paul read her eyes and the working of her lips.

I cannot sit here. I must find those whom God has chosen to feed us . . . for the Lord will take these two onions and four potatoes and break them into portions to last until my arms are strong for work.

He put on his faded green overcoat and left the house.

Where shall I go first? And how shall I say?

* FINE GROCERIES *

Into the grocery.

Here comes the son of the dead Geremio. On his face I read that he has come to obtain for nothing the goods for which I have paid money.

Paul waited. When he and the grocer were alone he spoke. ". . . we have always bought here and right now we have no money—"

I have my own family. I sympathize. What would happen to my children if I undertook to feed the widow and her eight? . . . No. "Yes yes."

"I will work for you."

Thin arms—you'll die on my hand. . . . No. "Ahhh, if I only had that much business."

". . . Perhaps? you could? give us credit? until I went to work . . . ? The Sisters at school say that I am smart and shall someday—"

No no no no no no no no no no. "I would like to do that, but I cannot. In fact there is a bill here already, but tell mama not to worry about that now. You see, Paul, I only make maybe a penny on a sale and—"

We are Christians together—we go to church together—father in Heaven watches and will pray for you—we will pray to the Lord Jesus for every bit of help you give us and that He shall reward you . . .

"Father John should be able to do something for your mother. You might tell him that I suggested you see him. I make donations to St. Prisca."

But you have the food here. Please.

No.

Please!

No.

"Thank you. I'll go to Father John."

"Do that. Tell I suggested. —I make donations . . ."

And Paul soon found himself wandering along the crowded street.

* MEATS OUR SPECIALTY *

He hesitated before the window and waited until the customers had left. Big thick red hands pushed a wire brush over the meat block and did not notice Paul. Over him a cardboard poster said in gilt letters on black that:

IN GOD WE TRUST * * * OTHERS PAY CASH!

The red meat-face came toward him and asked loudly, "Well?"

Paul walked out of the store. He moved with the street world for hours not knowing where to present himself.

MUNICIPAL BUILDING
JUSTICE
EQUALITY

Into the big building he went, and from corridor to corridor.

ROOM 302
OVERSEER OF THE POOR

Yes, he had a right to go in.

"What building collapse? Never heard about it. Was he an American citizen?"

"He had taken out his first papers."

"But he's dead."

"Yes . . ."

"Well, then he wasn't a citizen."

. . . My children will dance for me someday . . . and in the American style . . .

Dogging thin feet along the pavements and big strong people coming out of food shops with great bundles and laughing with lit eyes and store after store choked and flowing with bread and steak and fruit and shoes and cake and clothes and toys and darkness pushing day over tenement tops and Paul's thin wrists getting thinner and thinner.

Shrill note, steam's blow, siren and bell sounded labor still and sent feet from Job. Endless living feet bringing message of tired bodies to someone, something, that waited somewhere. . . . And Annunziata waited at the front window. . . .

Feet-feet-feet to my ears like rain . . . and whither Geremio's? Whither the dark eyes and tanned face of beauty to twinkle love's greeting? Whither the Roman figure of man, the broad chest and curved back, the quick light step, and hands so strong? What do I here with only window ledge at bosom: the sight of many men stepping to wife and little ones, the rising-falling feet of husband-fathers on stairway, the opening and shutting of home doors, the shuffling legs of master and colting of little ones, the wonderful fantasy of eventide, of plates and bread and soup and spoons' clatter and sweet-sweet disturbing duties of table, of late evening's voicing twos and twos—fours and fours, of husband's pipe and smoke, of noddings, of husband's smell so precious, of husband's sanctified flesh of toil, of whispering between husband, God, and wife, of night . . . and husband-man. . . . What do I with only window ledge at bosom, and none to equal Geremio . . . ?

Paul had wandered to the hospital.

"Little uncle, you are white and tired. Have you eaten?"

Paul did not answer.

Luigi looked at him and looked, and then bit his hands and beat his casts until the nurse came. Between his tears Luigi tried to tell the nurse of trouble, great trouble and hunger.

On the way home, Paul paused in front of the police station. He went up the steps, opened the door, and as he went in he heard a live loud voice laughing. He stopped. He had heard that voice before . . . the wop the wop (yes! that was it!) . . . *The wop is out in the court-yard . . . under the wrappin' paper!!!*

He ran out into the street and toward home until his side stabbed him.

Bong bong bong bong bong bong bong belled Saint Prisca above him. He crept into the huge church. Candles were lit on the altar. Saints stood poised magnificently, beautifully, on their niches in the shadowed wall. Fluted gray marble pillars rose up high-high and disappeared in the ceiling that led to Paradise. Behind him, above the balcony, the organ was a pyramid of golden reeds. And up front was Christ nailed fast on thick crossed timber, His live blood pouring against His naked white athletic body.

Here in the church of worship I kneel, my Lord. You have taken dear father away for your own need . . . can you not send him back, O Lord? We love him—we are hungry—we need him. . . . Pleasepleaseplease, dear Jesus, may I not go home and find him seated with the children, and mama placing the hot food and macaroni on the table, and laughter, laughter of all our family, my Lord God and Creator of the earth and skies and all the living? It would be simple for you and I know you want us to be happy and we will adore you and sing your praises every-every minute. . . . Wouldn't it be glorious, O Lord, to bring father right here right now and I'll take him by the hand and up the stairs and knock on the door and then when mama opens the door I'll say mama here's papa—O Lord, don't you see how wonderful—?

A form came slowly and majestically from behind the altar. Through his wet eyes he beheld it approach, and his heart wanted to burst. His fingers tightened into each other and his lips dried. He wanted to go to the form. It came nearer, stopped, and then reached up with a candle-snuffer.

Paul walked out into the aisle, wet his fingers with holy water from the marble bowl, signed the cross, and went wearily down the stone steps.

He sat down on the bottom step and dropped his head on his knees.

The bell of Saint Prisca aloft rang eight.

Tell him I suggested . . . I make donations there . . .

A tall gaunt woman with a sack slung over her shoulders came swiftly along the street. She sighted Paul and stopped.

"Son of Geremio . . . ?"

Paul raised his head.

"Yes, it is you!"

"Dame Katarina . . ."

"Little son, how stung and pale you are. What do you upon church steps?"

"I came to the church to ask . . ."

"Something of Dio?"

"To ask Him to bring back father."

Katarina drew a red bandanna from her dress, blew her nose, made a quick pass at her eyes, put it away, and remained silent for a minute.

"You have not eaten."

"There is nothing at home."

Katarina drew a round loaf of bread from her sack, and from a little soiled bag tied about her neck and hidden between her breasts she took out its contents.

"Take this, O little son. It is all that an old gypsy woman possesses, but would to Dio she could bring this sack full with pure gold to you."

Paul said, "Please, perhaps I do not have to take it from you."

"And why not, boy?"

"I am going to see Father John."

"And the priest will give?"

"When I tell him our need he will help us."

Katarina muttered and then said, "I will wait for you."

Paul got up and walked slowly around the corner to the rectory. He rang the bell and stepped back. The door opened and an old-old face appeared through the half-opened door.

"What do you want?"

"I want to see Father John."

"He is at supper."

"I must see him."

"What about?"

"It's—Oh, I can only tell him."

"Does he expect you?"

"No, but I know he will see me."

"He is at supper. And then he has many duties."

"I cannot leave until I see him."

The door was closing.

"You will have to come back some other time . . . Next week perhaps, when he is not too busy."

Paul put his hand in the doorway.

"Oh, if you only knew how serious it is . . . !"

The old man hesitated.

"Is some Catholic dying . . . from this parish?"

"No. Father died under a building. We are eight and mother. We need help. We will suffer . . ."

"This is a *church*!"

". . . That is why I must see Father John."

"You are too young to come here."

"I do not understand."

"Let your mother come . . . next week when the Father is not too busy."

The door was closing.

"I must see him . . ."

"Not tonight!" said the old man.

From behind Paul a voice burst out in furious scathing Italian. The old man tried quickly to close the door but Katarina's long arm pushed the door and sent it wide. The old man doddered. She shook a violent finger in his face and yelled, "Whattsa matta you! Whattsa matta you bastia! Animale vecchia, catch Padre John subito!"

The old man fearfully followed her instruction.

"Antique rotted son of a whore! His decayed stomach is full!"

The old man returned and told Paul to come in.
"G-go, little son. I'll await you," said Katarina.

High severe chambers through tall heavy doors stout
walls warmth quiet thick everlasting wood trim smooth
crackless plaster lacquered floors soft dark red rugs solid
chairs and broad tables church shadow lighting rectory
smell of woodwork candle incense and clean clean
cleanliness . . . are there ever babies' voices and songs
and joy and cries of anguish and tightening stomachs
are there—?

"Well . . . why do you insist upon seeing me?"

"Pardon me, Father, but you were suggested—"

And through the great door from which he had come
out with napkin around neck of rich black cassock of his
round body was a long table reaching away beautifully
lit with slim candles throwing warm glow on shiny por-
celain plates containing baked potatoes and cuts of
brown dripping lamb and fresh peas and platters of hot
food cool food hard food soft food . . .

"What?"

Then pink hands placed a wide and high shortcake
with big perfect strawberries staining the pure white
whipped cream.

"Who suggested what?"

The live red blood pouring from the spike pierced
wounds against the naked white flesh.

"Well—why don't you speak?"

Paul began, and spoke with burning weariness.

"Ah—yes, yes," said Father John. "But tell me, what
can I do?"

Mother could sit at the head of that wonderful table
and hand to Annina and Lucia and Giorgio and Joseph and Adela and Johnny and Geremino the beautiful
food and no cold could come through these walls—

"Has your mother applied at the Welfare?"

"They say my father wasn't a citizen."

"No?"

". . . No."

"Your mother is entitled to workmen's compensation."

"That's what they say. We got a letter from them."

"Good. So?"

"But it will be a long time before the case comes."

"Has your mother tried to get up a collection among the neighbors?"

But you, *you* have food on that long table, wonderful food and clean white hands picking it and voices speaking low. Who is eating that wonderful food?

Paul could not answer and for a minute they were silent.

"Father ..."

"Yes?"

"Could you please help us?"

"... How ... ?"

"We need—"

"I have nothing to do with the Charities. There is a board of trustees who confer and pass on every expenditure. Do you understand?"

"... Yes ..."

Silence.

"... You have a nice little overcoat. Keep you warm?"

"... Yes ..."

"That's good."

Silence.

A stomach trickles hollowly.

And thin wrists getting thinner.

Then a head in the doorway and a respectful voice: "Dessert on the table, Father."

Without turning, Father John said, "Cut a good portion of the cake, wrap it nicely and bring it here."

"Yes, Father."

"Do the children like strawberry shortcake?"

"... Yes ..."

A soft package into his hands from a shiny round face.

"... Thank you ..."

"God bless you."

Out through tall doors and strong walls.

Will they ever protect me and mine?

The old man closed the street door, surely, firmly.

"So soon, little son?"

". . . Yes . . ."

"And?"

". . . He has no power in Charities. We are Charities. But he was glad that my overcoat keeps me warm . . ."

"Blood of the Virgin, did he expect that your little life should go naked!"

"And to me he gave a rich-rich cake . . ."

"Man of God?—Man of God? . . . bursting gut and sausage-in-mouth!"

She took his hand and put into it the money from the bag.

"We will pray for you, Dame Katarina."

"Pray not for me. Pray for the strength you now need."

"Dame Katarina, tell me, please, to whom shall we turn? What shall I do?"

Said she in strings of plaintive song, "Dear little son, we are the unfortunates under the skies of God. . . . There are none to help—but many to take from us. From the sweat of our blood comes the bread in mouth. Good night, little son, straight-straight your spine with hands into the heavens, and the poor carpenter Christ build strong the bread of your arms."

The kitchen was dark. Paul placed the bread, cake and money on the table, and tiptoed through the flat. The dining room was empty-still, in the bedroom the children were heaped in one bed sleeping the fraught sleep of hunger. In the bed of Geremio and Annunziata in the following room little Johnny slept, one hand clutching empty bottle and one arm above the head of Geremino, and at the parlor window in the April moon's ray sat Annunziata. She was whispering, her eyes half-closed and her right hand extended toward the moon: "In the home of Geremio the air has become hunger. In the home of Geremio stomachs have become wounds. In the home of Geremio senses have become famished mouths. In the home of Geremio hearts have become swollen vessels and eyes ceaseless falls. . . . In the home of Geremio the love of Geremio has become rising mountains."

Mother . . . mother forever.

Annunziata swayed and chanted: "But thine and mine shall not want. My soul shall consume hunger; and my body, their wall against suffering. On hands and knees shall I glean the earth for their food."

She became silent and remained staring up into the moon with unseeing eyes. Paul fell quietly in the corner. The room swooped up, sideways, and then down into darkness.

On the twelfth stroke of Saint Prisca Paul opened his eyes. Annunziata was at the window, still-staring at the moon. He arose jerkily and went to her. He touched her shoulder lightly.

"*Geremio!*"

He caught her.

"Mamamamamamamama—it's me it's me Paul . . ."

She held to him with vibrating tautness.

"It's me it's me oh mama it's me!"

Suddenly the veil fell away, reality whirled into focus, and she clasped him, weeping: "Paul little Paul the son of his father Paul Paul . . ."

He aided her to bed.

"Sleep mama—do not worry—sleep mama sleep . . ."

He removed his clothes and crept in among the five sleeping children. Under cover the sweetish steam of close child-bodies brought him comfort. He arranged his position to fit the gentle tangle of stockinged limbs, snuggled his thin hands between his legs and sighed.

Paul shivered awake. He tried to find a dry spot, but Joie hugging his back had wet his underwear and stockings thoroughly. He lay awake, trying to hold the wet underwear away from his chilled flesh . . . thinking and thinking.

Before the children awoke Paul lit the stove with a few bits of wood and a half-pail of coal. He removed his stockings and underwear and held them up to the heat until they were dried warm. He went into the bedroom, got the canvas bag from under the bed and went back into the kitchen. There were mason-lines, square-cut nails, thick chisels, long chisels, old canvas gloves, lumps of hardened mortar, chips of bricks, steel square, small hand level, joint slickers, marking pencil, lump-hammer, pointing trowel, brick hammer, brick scutch, and bricklaying trowel.

These were things he had seen when brought home new from the hardware store and things he had seen on Job the many times he had been there to bring to Geremio his lunch, or the message that "mama's gotta baby, papa," and though he recognized them they seemed different and heavy in his thin hands. The trowel had a long smooth wooden handle, high shank; the ten-inch blade of tough thin steel had a broad heel and tapered to a sharp point. Around the shank and heel there was a close hard layer of dried mortar, and cut in on the upper face toward the shank was H. L. DISTON. He revolved it in his hand, made scooping motions, and took the match box and imagined it a brick which he laid along the edge of the table over and over, tapping it and eyeing it. He contemplated the tools for a few minutes and then picked up the trowel and stuck it in his belt over his hip. He put on his cotton sweater, a baggy corduroy cap, and his faded green overcoat. By Annunziata's bed he said.

"Mama, I am going out. Do not worry, mama."

"Son of mine . . . to where, where?"

And as he sounded from her she implored:

Paul my Paul, be careful ... be careful for mother yours.

The trowel on his hip felt a shield, a sword, and as he walked uptown to where the jobs lay he felt bigger. After an hour's search he noticed piles of brick and sand down the end of a street. He crossed over to the opposite side and slowly approached Job. When he was near enough he stood in a doorway and watched for a long while. Job was a six-story apartment. Out in the street laborers mixed mortar, loaded wheelbarrows with bricks and mortar, and carried planks for scaffolding. Up on the second floor laborers threw their loads on the scaffolds where bricklayers were laying up the walls. He tried to learn something by watching but soon became bewildered. He continued uptown and watched three other buildings going up. He began to feel discouraged. Soon he was walking toward the hospital.

Luigi was sitting up. He was shaven, combed, pale and clean. He asked of home. And Paul told him of his quest for help.

How can I ask further, little uncle, when I know that I have failed and there are none to help? How can I, laborer ignorant and unschooled, tell you that this our world is beyond us ... ? What food into your stomach can any word of mine bring? What shall I to this boy say that he may bring back as help and use to the racked Annunziata? Nothing-nothing may I say ... and the future for these children of Christ is as a fog of stone ...

Ci Luigi, please tell me that I can be a bricklayer— please say that someone will let me lay bricks—please tell me that I shall grow swiftly ...

As Paul rose to go Luigi saw the bulge under his overcoat. He asked Paul to come near. Luigi opened his overcoat and drew forth the trowel. He wanted to speak, but returned the trowel, and covered Paul's hands with kisses and tears.

Paul recognized some of the faces that were chewing large sandwiches close by a job. They were faces he had seen at the great street feast of Saint Joseph, faces that had visited the house and drunk muscatel and alicante wine, faces he had seen at baptisms and weddings, faces he had seen at the Liberty Loan benefit in the Bricklayers' Local the time of the War with the Huns, the time they had beer and sandwiches and prize fights and where his father put him high on his shoulder and told him to sing *America I Raised a Boy for You* and *The Sunshine of Your Smile* and they threw pennies to him that glorious time he would never forget.... They were faces that had stood by and attended his father in coffin with severe eyes and lowered chins.

He wandered up closer to the men and sat wearily on a pile of two-by-fours. Mike "Orangepeel-Face" raised his wine bottle to his mouth and while drinking saw Paul.

"Son of Master Geremio are you?"

"Yes."

"Come, sit with us, little paesan, come."

Paul respectfully joined.

"The masculine first-born of the good spirit Geremio is here."

"How do you call yourself?" asked Salvatore "Four-Eyes."

"Paul."

Four-Eyes nodded his head significantly.

"Paul, Paul—ah, Peter and Paul ..."

A big handsome man with livid burn-scars across his right cheek, Nick "the Lucy," reared his head contemptuously, reached his fist over, and rapped Four-Eyes' skull with the accompanying yodel: "Pa-poo coo-coo, pa-poo coo-coo!"

Bastian the tongue-tied Calabrian roared through his horse teeth, "By the Ma-Ma-Madonna, 'tong-a tititittong-a' goes his head-box. It would go well in the grand op-op-opera!"

Four-Eyes stood his five feet up ferociously and cried, "Why do I get my top knuckled like that? Why do my brains receive this aggravation? Why?why?why?"

Salvatore cocked his straight eye into the air and muttered savagely, "All right! All right! It is understood that I'll have to trowel-ate some people to infinite bits or I do not call myself Salvatore!"

"*Pa-poo coo-coo!*" shouted the Lucy, and Salvatore sat down abruptly.

A bricklayer came from the job walking with a comical gait. He had large flat splay feet, a face of fat red cheeks pressing against a great nose, and eyes and lips that tried to assume important concern but were ever tickled otherwise. In his arms he carried shavings and split lime barrel staves.

"For pleasure, make way!" he commanded.

No one paid attention to him and he elbowed his way into the center of the circle and lit a fire in a mortar tub.

"Bravo," said the Lucy. "Nazone is what is called in truth 'Christian'!" And he knighted Nazone in the rear with his foot.

Nazone leaped up with a yowl.

"For pleasure, amuse yourself if you are so inclined by nature, but, whore of the Saints, do not violate the private properties of man . . . if you please!"

Four-Eyes tickled Nazone behind with a stick and as he jumped around another man did the same from the opposite side and they kept him jumping and yowling until he sat down breathing hard.

"Finished is the comedy!" ordered the Lucy. "A workingman has to eat!"

Nazone sat opposite Paul and opened his loaf-of-bread sandwich with a whole broiler within done in the hunter's style covered with stewed tomatoes and hot peppers, the sauce coloring the bread a reddish brown and dripping in its abundance. With the rest of the men he toasted his lunch on barrel wire over the fire. The smell of peppers, chicken, tomatoes, salami, fish, eggs, and thick fresh Italian bread over the wood flames in the tangy April air pulled Paul's stomach and squeezed it into aching. Nazone broke a tender drumstick, and

ate it with dancing eyes. The juice ran down the chan-
nel of his chubby dimpled chin. He scooped it and
while sucking his finger he saw Paul.

"To whom belongs the bambino?"

" 'Tis the first-born masculine of the departed
Geremio . . ."

". . . And son to the widow Annunziata."

"Such a sad little chippie is he," said Nazone.

He took the other drumstick and proffered it silently
to Paul.

Paul moved forward a bit and then leaned back
abashed. But Nazone read his hunger and came over
and seated himself next to Paul.

Paul ate of his chicken, bread and fruit.

How good, God! How good!

The Lucy took note and handed Paul a chunk of
dried goat's milk cheese and a slice of sweet red onion.
Paul thanked him.

The Lucy made a terrible face at Four-Eyes, Hunt-
Hunt, Bastian, and the others and said, "What cock of
Christians are you to let this child watch you eat!"

They all then gave to Paul parts of their lunch. Paul
gathered them into a paper bag and put it in his coat.
The fat bricklayer with the bulbous nose, loose thick
lips, and missing teeth whom they called Hunt-Hunt,
asked, "What do you here, Paulie?"

How can I tell you?

"Do you go to school?" asked Four-Eyes.

"Yes . . . but—"

But I can go no more. I must become a bricklayer!

"Who brings food to your home?" asked Nazone.

". . . No one . . ."

"How could there be anyone, when he is the first-
born—and so young?" said Hunt-Hunt.

"That is why I now no longer can go to school . . ."
said Paul.

Nazone said to Paul in under-voice:

"Would you wish to become a master-builder of walls
like the good spirit your father?"

"I . . . have his trowel with me."

"Bless God," said Nazone to the men, "and why shouldn't the son of a bricklayer learn the art and bring food to his family? Is the school going to satisfy their needs? The Police? The Army? Or Navy? The Church? Or the City Hall stinking with thieves?"

"Are you a fool, or is it my eyes," said the Lucy.

"Why?" answered Nazone.

"How do you expect him to lift a brick? The poor little one—my pingee is bigger than he."

"For pleasure, do not laugh," said Nazone. "The boy is man-child of master mason and born in the mortar tub. I beg you, this is not moment for comedy: the little one is son of Italian and paesano who left his blood under Job."

"Just!" said Hunt-Hunt.

"A verity misfortunate . . ." said Guido.

The Lucy assumed respect.

"It is understood . . . but who in his right senses will take responsibility for one so young and small?"

Nazone looked around to the men. No one ventured to say anything. On seeing Paul's anxious eyes, he motioned toward himself and said, "Vincenzo will."

O God, is it possible that I may work? That I may rebuild father's hands and the home to last forever?

Hunt-Hunt said, "Nazone as bricklayer may be a shoemaker, but he has a warm little heart beating under his arm. Eh, Master Vincenz, eh?"

"It is not a fact of heart," said Nazone. "It is the right of a bricklayer's family to live. It is the right of a bricklayer's son to follow the art of his father."

"What gr-gr-grand eloquence!" said Bastian.

"Nazone can even read and write," said Alfredo.

Four-Eyes pointed to the contractors' shed and said:

"There, there, Vincenz, is where you are to pour your oration: they are Jesu Christ and all the Saints on this job. They are the ones to permit the son of Geremio to become a bricklayer."

In the shed were the six who comprised the corpora-

tion; six bricklayers banded who took brickwork on contract and laid brick themselves. They were huddled at
the plan table, lunch half-eaten, fingers dirtied with
mortar, stubs of pencil over ear, gesturing, pipe and
sandwich in hand, arguing over blueprint interpreta-
tions and figures.

"Look at them!" mocked the Lucy, "American engi-
neers and scientists extra-orrrdinary." He shouted to
them, "Hey profes-ssors, what do the blueprints say,
'Rain' or 'snow'?"

Black Mike came out of the shed and blew the whistle.

The Lucy looked at his watch.

"Pig of God, he cheats us every time his stinking
mouth blows that peanut whistle!"

Conversation stopped dead. Hurriedly they left Paul.
Hastily, constrainedly, their bodily machines steered to
scaffold and wall.

Nazone said fumblingly to Paul, "To work must I
now go, Paul, but fear not, I shall speak to the corporation for you. You shall become a bricklayer."

The Lucy jammed his remnant pipe into mouth,
pulled his cap down toward the scarred side of his face
and deliberately waited until his watch registered one
o'clock. Before he sauntered to the scaffold he put his
hand on Paul's head and said, "Son of Geremio, do not
apply your hands for bread; better that you learn to
steal, become a priest or policeman . . ."

You shall become a bricklayer you shall become a
bricklayer—O dear God you have heard my prayer.

Paul clung to Job. He posted himself in position to be
visible to Nazone when he looked up from the laying of
wall. In a lull of Job movement Nazone beckoned to
Paul. "You have your father's trowel, yes? Then go near
the mortar box and advise old Santos the strong that
Master Vincenz sends you to practice the trowel on
mortar."

Old Santos wore a faded blue shirt rolled at the el-

bows, thick corduroy trousers with a wide leather belt
buckled in the rear, a cement bag apron, and heavy
work shoes. Shovel in hand, bareheaded, his clothes and
face powdered with lime and cement and almost as
white as his hair, he was an ancient mighty athlete of
Job. He shoveled sand from a great heap into the mortar box with timed wasteless grace, lifted ninety-four-
pound cement bags easily and spread their contents
upon the sand, shoveled both into even mixture, hollowed the mound, bucketed soft hot lime and water into
the hollow, and then hoed the sand-lime-water-cement
into warm greenish-gray plastic mortar.

Old Santos rested on his hoe. He smiled at Paul.

"See how it is done? It is so simple . . . and yet . . ."

Paul spoke and gave him the message. Santos gra-
ciously cleared a space behind the brick pile, placed
there a mortar tub, and filled it half-full of mortar. He
tempered the mortar especially smooth.

"Fine mortar for the fine little master," he said.

Paul looked at him hesitatingly.

"Remove your coat, little master, and build to your
pleasure. If you are truly son to Geremio, then you are
born artist of brick and mortar."

Paul removed his coat and pulled the trowel from his
belt. He stood nervously. Old Santos left him. No one
watched him now. He reached the trowel down into the
mortar. Slice down toward him, edgewise twist in quick
short circle and scoop up away from him. The trowel
came up half-covered with mortar—but how heavy! He
dropped it back into the tub and worked the trowel
back and forth in the mortar just as he had seen the
bricklayers do. The feel of flexible steel trowel in pliant
warm plushy soon-to-be-stone. The wet rub of mortar
on tender skin . . . the first fleshly sense of Job, Job who
would give living to mother Annunziata and the little
ones. He gathered straight unchipped red brick and
layed them dry in lengthwise string. Then he went over
to the building, studied the bond of a corner, and fixed
it in his eye.

At right angles with the string of brick he ran another string of six bricks. Standing back and surveying, he straightened it for square. Upon its corner he set a brick crossing lengthwise the head end of the brick below. He knew he was right and proceeded to lay the second course dry, and the third course and the fourth and on until the pyramided square corner was stepped back to the last possible top corner brick.

If we can only now build it with trowel and mortar . . . !

Oh, to lay it up really so that Mister Rinaldi could see . . . !

He took down the little dry wall. Puttering and swishing the mortar along the ground in as straight a line as possible, he spread the bed of his first course and set a brick at one end. Dabbing mortar on the head of another brick he laid it down and pressed it up against the end of the first brick and tapped it down into the soft mortar with the brick-cutting edge of the trowel until it seemed level with the first brick; and then did the same with four more bricks one after the other before the bed of mortar had dried. Bending low and running his left eye along the top outer edge, he tapped the bricks into line.

O God you have heard me—*I have laid brick!* He laid the other string of six bricks at right angles and then began laying up the second course, bonding it exactly as he had done it before without the mortar. One brick upon two, slowly one brick bridging across the joining of two bricks below, one on two, clipping off the mortar that pressed out from between the bricks, one on top of the two, slowly and with pained excitement he reached the last brick of his bonded, mortared, brick-pyramided corner. He stepped back. It stood almost as high as he. It was an actual corner. It was real. Though the corner bead leaned hard on one side and fell slack on the other, though the bed joints and cross joints were not full and uniform, though the courses were hilly for level and wavy for perpendicular, it was brickwork, real brickwork such as would harden into solid unity and resist elements ... such as in building of Job that would pay men to sustain life and home. He photographed it in his soul, and his eyes embraced it.... Then: What would these men think of it? Would it be all right? Is it possible that they would laugh? Was there something mysterious and unattainable that he had left out? But it looked real! It was real bricks and mortar and stood up without falling! He had worried and strained each brick into place; he had real gritty mortar on his hands and shoes and real red sharp brickdust on his trousers! He had built that.

The Lord had listened to him.... The Lord and his father worked with him to build it! Now he would wait until the men quit work and he would show it to Mister Nazone. He cleaned the trowel with sand and polished it affectionately. He washed his hands at the water barrel, dusted his trousers, put on his overcoat, and went to watch the bricklayers on Job.

When Nazone came off Job, tools in hand, Paul told him, "Mister Vincenzo, I have built a corner with brick and mortar."

"A *corner*?"

He followed Paul to the brick pile. But there was nothing to be seen.... A truck had dumped its four thousand bricks there.

That night his arms and back told him that he had laid his first brick on Job; but he did not mind the aches.... He told his mother Annunziata that he had been out in the street world seeking help and he was happy for something that would bring them food.

"And what may that be, little son?"

"Surprise, mama, surprise.... Sleep your weary self, and do not worry."

"Ah little Paul mine, would the will could disfact that which happens. Would that the heart's wishes could drink beyond sorrows. Would that the clouds of disaster

could disappear before the sun of desire ... would that
sleep could dispel fear and hunger ..."

Paul appeared at Job early. Nazone came to him embarrassed.

"I have spoken. But, they say you are much too
small."

Oh but you should have seen the real-real brick I laid
yesterday—

"... Oh ... thank you ... Mister Vincenzo ..."

Nazone could not bear Paul's eyes.

"By the Saints above, I shall manage to see you lay
bricks here! Do not go away. Have faith in me. We shall
manage! We shall open a door ..."

While Mister Giovanni Rinaldi mumbled to blueprints, Paul addressed him.

"Mister Rinaldi ..."

"Hello, Paulie?"

"... Mister Rinaldi ..."

"Yes?"

"Mister Vincenzo says that I ... can be a bricklayer ..."

"Ah Paulie, he told me."

"And ... please?"

"But you are too young. The school and police will
send us to Sing-Sing."

"Please, no, they will not. I went to them for help
and they were ... afraid to see me. They will not do
anything to you."

"Afraid of *you*?"

"I mean ... they told me they ... I mean they said
they had nothing to do with supporting us. Mister
Rinaldi, I am the only one who can work for mama and
the kids. ... I must!"

"See. You are a nice boy. Nice boy. That's too bad."

"Mister Rinaldi, I have papa's tools and I must lay
brick ..."

"I know, Paulie, I know. But you are too small. How old?"

". . . I am twelve."

"See. And how many pounds do you make?"

'I am not very heavy, I know."

"Do you weigh even a hundred pounds?"

"No . . . about seventy-five. But—"

"See. You are so small you will hurt yourself. In a few years—"

"But Mister Rinaldi I can lay bricks I *can*!"

Rinaldi retreated within himself and walked out of the shed and away from Paul.

You shall become a bricklayer.

And Paul would not go away. The men sent him for cigarettes and tobacco and gave him pennies. And Paul would not go away. Every time Nazone looked up from the wall there were Paul's eyes. Nazone thought and thought and thought and thought and pursed his lips and spoke to the bricks to the laborers and to anybody about the crime of corporations about the right of a bricklayer's son to support his family and what better than for an intelligent son of an Italian to learn the trowel art of building as an apprentice and that if the paesanos were afraid he wasn't—

"Little Paul!"

Paul flew to him.

He took off Paul's overcoat, put it on a window sill, brought Paul next to him on the wall, and whispered, "Stick yourself in by me, little master, and lay the bricks. Lay one, and lay it good. Fear no one. The trowel of your good spirit father is sainted and lays brick of itself."

You shall become a bricklayer!

Through drumming dizziness Paul pushed the force of his spirit into the handle of the trowel into the mortar-slice-twist-scoop-up over guide mason line and pull-drop on wall then down quick for red brick-up-quick down onto spread mortar on wall-press-wiggle-tap brick top edge with white guide mason line down over again and on this thin wrist and on for we cannot dare stop to ask where this strength springs from.

For I must become a bricklayer!

Nazone stepped back over the bricks and mortar of scaffold and beheld Paul with incredulous eyes.

"Father, Son and Holy Ghost," he exclaimed, "this child learned the art in good Geremio's seed! He is a terror! He will build us out of brick with his eyes closed in a few years!"

The men looked over. And Paul laid brick.

I am a bricklayer!

When Black Mike noticed from the other end of the wall how Nazone stood away from the wall, saw Paul working on the wall, and the bricklayers and laborers giving attention to Nazone and Paul, he raised himself on the wall and shouted until the veins stood out from his neck:

"Nazone shoemaking bastard what the cock are you trying to do to this job?"

Nazone folded his arms and hoarsed back:

"Lay bricks Sicilian whore's son and tend to your own facts for the first animal who disturbs the son of Geremio shall taste my trowel's point in heart!"

Paul laid bricks like one running from danger, like one struggling for air, like one who fights and must not fail.

When at last Black Mike's whistle signed surcease, Paul stood up straight, and as he did so the world rolled, hummed in his ears and whirled screwing points of light ahead of him. He leaned against the wall, closed his eyes, and determined himself back to balance.

"Mark you how a bricklayer's son inherits the art!" said Nazone to the paesanos as they left the wall. "Mark you!"

The Lucy squinted the eye on the scarred side of his face, looked at his trowel before he threw it into his kit, and said ruefully, "Inherits this tail. My blessed spirit father's hands should have rotted off the day he first gave to me his trowel!"

A tall slim girl with dancing ripe breasts walked past the job on the other side of the street.

Hunt-Hunt, who was removing his overalls, saw the girl going by. He stood up, rolled his sleepy eyes and drawled from loose lips in American, "Ahhhh bye-bee, you make-a me seeck. . . . uhmnnnnnn bye-bee you make-a me die-a . . ."

Bastian bared his horse teeth and stuttered ecstatically, "Ma-Ma-Madonna mine, what grapes she has!"

The Lucy said severely to them as he surveyed the girl, "Have you no respect for women? Put your tongue in tail or you'll go to Sing-a-Sing." And as his expression followed her with fierce delight he exclaimed, "Yes, little Nicholas, better a pimp than a bricklayer!"

Nazone admonished them incoherently about language and thoughts in the presence of the young; and twisting his neck to view the girl further he stumbled over his tools and fell into a wheelbarrow.

Before Nazone left, Paul spoke to him.

"What shall I do tomorrow, Mister Vincenzo? The corporation have not said anything, have they?"

"Present yourself positively in the morning. Lay bricks on the wall; no one can prevent you; you are a bricklayer!"

Yes O God and father I am a bricklayer and we shall not starve!

Before he left Job he smeared his shoes with mortar from the mortar box. His shoes must now be mortar-whitened!

O mother, home I come with father's hands . . . Mother, lift your heart and rejoice for father is in Heaven and we shall rise!

Along the already dusking street Paul walked toward Tenement home with the stiffness that spine called for—its rebellion against bend-bend-bend. Annunziata saw him from the window.

Where has my Paul been? . . . Why walks he thus— and why are his shoes so whitened? . . .

She opened the kitchen door and awaited. He came up the hallway hand on banister.

"Hello, mama."

—Cement on hands and shoes—smell of brick and mortar—

"O Thirtieth of March, what have you done to me?"

"Mama—nothing can happen to me—"

"Job!"

Late in the sleeping night world Annunziata arose and guarded the children as they slumbered close one on the other. She felt their foreheads, and brushed lightly the hair from over their shut full lids. She tucked the covers and kissed them, and to Paul whispered:

". . . Careful your every step, O love of Geremio and Annunziata, careful. . . ."

Paul was first on empty deserted Job. He studied the wall bonds and touched scaffold and brick and joint and stone of wall. Job was sharp with expanding fresh smell of lime cement, new-cut wood, iron's red paint and brackish night dew.

Though stiff the morning, sun was rising with tawny glow and told of warm workday.

Old Santos came, and opened the tool shed. He removed his mackinaw, rolled up his sleeves and prepared to create the mortar of Job.

"Early-early you have come, eh little Master Paul?" And he brought from the shed his roll of water hose, shovel, barrow, and hoe. Adjusting the sleeve of his smooth molded arm, he studied the sun.

"Today becomes warm. Shed not too many clothes, for this early heat brings with it the pulmonary woes."

Then, as one who goes on forever and quietly, he brought bag after bag of cement from the shed, stacked them by the mortar box, and prepared the mortary meal of Job.

The men had come, and Paul stood ready with trowel.

Why doesn't the corporation say something to me . . . ?

The corporation had not said anything. They came with their pained somber faces and instantly hurled themselves upon the laborers.

"But what is this anyway? Where is the mortar for this corner?"

"This is no comedy! We're spilling our blood to get the gold for this contract and where are the three-foot sills for the front! Bastian! Emanual! Amedeo! blood of the Virgin, am I distorting talk to myself?"

"Cock-o!" ejaculated Alfredo the Neapolitan. "He pours his heart out through his tail before he opens his morning eyes."

The starting whistle had not yet blown and Black Mike was already enfrenzied.

"Brick!mortar!brick!mortar! Bastian, never mind the three-foot sills for the front! I don't give a damn who told you to put them there! I want brick and mortar here right now! Bastian! Amedeo! not there! curses upon the one who permits you to breathe! Alfredo! Bastian! Amedeo! don't look at me! if you death-murdered cocks desire not to work then say so and go into the cellar and do the hand-job!!! God forgive me."

"Beautiful stuff," commented Nazone.

The Lucy screwed his scarred cheek and pointed to the corporation.

"That's what the America does for your peasants. Vomit your poison, you miserable bastards, for when you go to scratch the louse from your hungry faces you will not even possess the luxury of fingernails."

"Do not fear him," said Nazone to Paul. "He is in truth a bit fickle and difficult, but he is a bricklayer of the first class." Then whispering, he instructed, "Sh-sh, behind his back you will hear him named the Lucy, but for God's love do not ever let slip from your mouth that name!"

"Why?"

"Because his favorite opera is *Lucia de Lammermoor,*

and then he, like a woman, is mobile and goes insane asylum if he hears himself thus referred to. Attention, little master, for Mike the Black posts himself to blow into his whistle."

The ring tap and scrape of trowel on brick sounded.

Yellow-Fever Giuseppe, a short square-jawed jaundiced member of the corporation, called to Paul:

"Hey you, Philippe, come over and fill in between these floor beams!"

Paul noticed that he meant him, but hesitated because he heard him call for a Philippe.

"Yes you, down here, Philippe."

Paul hurried over to him and Yellow-Fever Giuseppe showed him how to fill in between the wooden floor beams that rested upon the concrete foundation wall. When Paul told him that his name was Paul, Yellow-Fever said, "That's all right, Philippe, go 'head fill the beams."

He worked for hours alone on his knees reaching down between the beams. Each time he bent there was a lightning-like splitting of his back right where it joined his hips. His trowel wrist began to feel helpless, the fine sharp brickdust bruised his fingers, and the hot lime mortar ate into his hands. He stood up to straighten his wrenched spine and as he sought footing on the beams one tired foot slipped and he fell upon the beams smashing himself up between the legs. His breath stopped and tears inflamed his eyes.

O God how it hurts—but I must not let them see I have hurt myself already—I must lay brick!

He bit his tongue and got to his knees on the beams, his testicles swelling and pulling the pit of his stomach. He leaned one hand on a beam and scooped some mortar with the other, dropped it on the wall between two beams, pressed a brick on it, and then had to cut a brick to fill up the remaining space.

Through smarting tears he tried to realize where he had to deal trowel to brick and then swung, the trowel catching his thumb against the brick and shocking him so that he huddled his hand to his mouth and tried desperately to keep from crying aloud.

They must not see me weeping O God—this is nothing-nothing, quiet my aches soft my pain please please I must fill these beams!

His thumb throbbed, swelled, and rapidly turned blue, but he would not stop, every beat of pain pushed him on, and when Black Mike blew noon, his cramped knees and toes could not lift him to his feet for a few minutes.

Noon hour was pleasant, with sun high up and soft licking breeze. Paul unwrapped his little lunch of a bread heel with dry tuna fish, but could hardly eat. When he winced upon handling the hard crusty bread, Nazone took his hands and examined them. The thin fingers of Paul's left hand were abrased right through the skin and pinpoints of raw flesh and blood showed, his thumb nail was swollen dark red and black, his right hand was angry-sore with mortar and his wrist inflamed.

"Discourage not, discourage not . . ." said Nazone. "I should have put a glove on your hand—it was my fault, but we will fix it."

He spat on his handkerchief and cleansed Paul's hands and gave to him the best part of his lunch.

The Lucy said to Paul, "Have you brought your titty bottle with the nipple?"

Before going back to the scaffolds Nazone helped Paul prepare his hands for the afternoon.

"First we will pee on your hands—"

"Huh?"

"I mean that you will pee on your hands, and then I, Vincenz, shall tape your fingers and the bricks shall not ruin them so."

"Do what first?"

"Pee-pee, urinate—"

"Oh . . ."

"—pass out from the kidneys the water. It is really the

best thing, little Master Paul; I am not joking; the pee contains nature's salt and heals quickly the bricklayer's finger."

Paul was embarrassed.

"Quickly now to my instructions, for I will tape your fingers." And Nazone modestly turned from Paul.

His own hot urine did quickly ease, close, and harden the raw skin of his fingers, and when Nazone taped them with adhesive they felt stiff, but safe from the grinding gritty brick. That afternoon Nazone insisted to the corporation that Paul be placed next to him so that the boy could learn the trade quicker; and with the walls flying up fast, Paul received his first introduction to sill-highs, scaffold-highs, arch-highs, and story-highs, eight- and twelve-inch walls, piers, pilasters, window lintels, flue-linings, header-courses, and backing up of front work. Building a course of brick over an iron lintel of an opening in a rough brick eight-inch party wall he dropped a brick from his stiff fingers just as the Lucy was passing underneath the scaffold tools in hand, and as the Lucy looked up to see that it was clear overhead he received Paul's brick on a point of his forehead. He dropped his tools, clutched his head and cursed madly.

Paul looked at him with open-mouthed fright.

The Lucy vowed murder, and then summoned Paul down in quiet voice, "Bricklayer in diapers, if you are to become a builder of walls, lay the brick where they belong or I'll lay your hands across the wall and chop them off with my trowel!"

"Yes yes—" said Paul, "yes I'm sorry yes—"

The Lucy rubbed his bump.

"Sorry. And the steamboat left Wednesday."

"Let be Master Paul," scolded Nazone, "for God above knows how many plumbers' and carpenters' heads you have ruined with dropped bricks. . . . And anyway, the brick Master Paul gave you served to make just a bit bigger your cornuted head."

The Lucy mimicked in falsetto, "If the shoemaker

Nazone says it is so, then it is so. . . . Pig of the scaffolds!"

"Whey, paesans, tend to your work," called Black Mike. "We are paying money!"

"Fricasee-fricasaa!" barked the Lucy.

In the tool shed Nazone told Paul:

"Wash your hands at the water barrel, but do not remove the tape; let it serve for tomorrow also." He studied Paul at his task, and decided to accompany him toward home.

As they walked along the city streets heads turned and looked curiously at the child in short pants with the cemented shoes and sun-wind-burned thin face. Nazone took Paul into a cheap clothing store.

"We must get you man's pantaloons."

They did not have his size, and after much fitting Paul came out into the street wearing boy's-size blue sailor pants with great wide bottoms.

"Little Master Paul, will you be my godson?"

"Yes please, Mister Vincenzo."

"Thank you, little Master Paul, you are now my godson and woe to him who harms you." Leaving Paul he hugged him and said, "Courage, little godson, and faith, and you shall be a great builder."

Walking happily along by himself, Nazone hummed through his large nose: ". . . Teer-ra-ree-rahrah we now have a godson who is sure to be famous . . . and someday my little Angelina in Abruzzi shall ride the steamboat to the America and wed my master godson and we shall all go to the amusement parks and I, Master Vincenzo, shall pay with American gold from my pocket—teer-ra-ree-rah-rah . . ."

In his corduroy cap, faded green overcoat, wide blue sailor pants and cemented shoes Paul walked with knowing pride.

With men I have competed and laid brick the long day.
And from Tenement window: *My Paul wears the pan-*

taloons of manhood. He walks sorely and belongs no more to the world of children, who play and laugh and sing.

Paul talked and talked and talked and said the men were good to him and that the work was not too hard and he told mother Annunziata about each and every one and what they said and what they did and what and how he did each hour of the day and told her that before the week was over he would be laying fancy brick on the front and that he would soon grow tall and strong and work on corners and they would have money for many wonderful things and that he could not fail. . . . Every part of his body flamed and before he had consumed his bit of potato and spaghetti, he slipped back in his chair and fell asleep.

Annunziata lifted him and carried him to the bed—he not even flickering a lid. She warmed him.

Now has begun anew my story with Job, now goes my heart with him to Job, now wards my spirit against each wind and rain and heat and cold of Job upon the head of my Paul, now rises my vigil of prayer for the son of Geremio in the weighting shadows of Geremio's fallen walls.

Thus, in dark cell, Builder's woman and Life's mother spoke to her carpenter Christ, her Christ of hunger.

The alarm ringing made Paul think it was Saint Prisca and that he had only gone to bed a short while, but the tinny belling insisted until it unsprung itself to a draggy stop and as he drowsed off the seven o'clock whistle blew and he struggled his eyes open to realize gray morning.

You are a bricklayer. You wear long pants. You *must* be on the scaffold when Black Mike blows a whistle.

He tried to get out of the bed quickly and without disturbing the children, but he could not raise his head.

What had happened during the night?

His neck was split and yet connected. He braced his hand under him and pushed, and his wrist crackled with pain. He rolled over on his side, his lower back shooting fire all over him and screaming of a spine of broken cords connected by a thread that would sever any second. He lay on his stomach and slowly pressed himself to his knees, stepped over Adela and reached the bed edge. He could not bend for his pants and shoes and he let himself down straight to reach them. His knees gave way, and he remained on the floor until he had put on his pants and shoes. O God how can I reach the job and then lay brick . . . ?

"Careful, Paul, abide your step, careful, my Paul . . ." And.

". . . By, mama. Don't worry . . ."

—While he tried to walk the street away from her window without communicating the awful, awful aches.

"Fill in beams, Philippe!"

Beams!

Paul got on his knees at the beams and blindly tried not to heed his back and joints.

"By your pleasure, Master Giuseppe, send him near me as I am his godfather and responsible of him," said Nazone to Yellow-Fever from the scaffold.

"Godfather this cock! I want him to fill beams. Lay brick!"

"Master Giuseppe, for my pleasure please—"

"*Philippe fills beams!*" And Yellow-Fever turned his back.

The Lucy scooped his trowel full of mortar and sent it flying clean from his trowel over a distance to catch Yellow-Fever directly in the back of the neck, and then he stooped over and eyed his corner concernedly with strict squint for plumb.

Yellow-Fever wheeled about with hand to neck.

"Come down here! Come down, Nazone traitor, and I'll let your head go rolling down the street like a carriage wheel!"

Nazone slashed his trowel about and yelled:

"You are neither bricklayer nor man! You are incompetent and cowardly! You are ignorant and lack the humanities! You reek with yellow sewage in your veins, you——"

"Lay brick! Lay brick! Lay brick!" shouted Black Mike while the laborers, carpenters, bricklayers, plumbers and other crafts meowed, booed, made train and boat noises, razzed and shouted "Shuddup Goddem yuh!" Nazone jumped off the scaffold, threatened Yellow-Fever with his trowel, took Paul back up on the scaffold with him; and Yellow-Fever bit both his hands in groaning rage. . . . The Lucy gestured to no one in particular and questioned, "May a gentleman bricklayer learn what is happening here?"

And laying bricks, he reflected aloud, "What imbroglio. What fracas. What a dung-a-fying of the noble Italian blood . . . Pa-poo e' coo-coo."

With how much money will I surprise mother Annunziata . . . how much money will the corporation give me . . . how much am I worth?

One bricklayer said he was worth four dollars a day, another, five, another said four and one-half, and Paul pushed himself into mortar and brick knowing how sweet would be the bread his flesh had earned, how mother and children would glorify with their appetites the good meat and fruit, how dear would be the week-end rest.

Saturday morning.

He could not possibly pause long enough to breathe normally. Job that day would never be forgotten: the day when Job would first give its holy communion of freedom. One-on-two-one-on-two-bend-scoop-swing-spread-tap-clip—and bend on for one-on-two—and now Job was no longer a bewildering corridor which one visited by chance and did not realize. Job was establishing itself in gray of stony joint and red of clayey brick, in smell of men's gray bones and wet red flesh.

Job was becoming a familiar being through aches and hours, plumb and level. Job was a new sense which brought excitement of men and steel and stone. Job was a game, a race, a play in which all were muscular actors serious from whistle to whistle, and he was one of them. It was pay-day, and in a few hours pay-check would sign short-short armistice. It was war for living, and Paul was a soldier. It was not as in marbles where he played for fun, it was men's siege against a hunger that traveled swiftly, against an enemy inherited.

Giovanni Rinaldi mumbled hours and figures, and Black Mike with cemented fingers thumbed dollars and stuck them into envelopes.

Yellow-Fever with stupid down-set lips of importance awkwardly handed out the envelopes. The men did not figure out their hours. They accepted, and hoped Rinaldi had blundered and put in five or ten dollars too much. The men were now smiling like foolish girls, and pleased. There were no more enemies, all were friends and Job a wonderful thing. They had received their money, all but Paul who stood alone with his jumping heart outside the shed.

"Haven't you figured something for Paulie?"

"Who?"

"The boy, Paulie."

"Oh, yes, yes the boy. . . . What are we to do?"

"What value has he? He throws himself well . . ."

"It is not a fact of value. . . And if we get into trouble?"

"Perhaps a serious complaint—from a trouble-making American, or jealousy-blinded paesan. We must watch ourselves, I say."

"Yes, we have woes of our own in abundance."

Giovanni Rinaldi called Paul in and handed an envelope to Yellow-Fever who handed it to Paul. He said thank you and it sounded as though he had said it in a foreign tongue. Everything seemed rushed and indistinct for he did not know what to do with the envelope clutched in his hand. Behind the shed alone he was afraid to open the envelope. Why was it so light and thin? Why did the corporation, so set and explosive, turn as though hands had pushed their heads down and around from him? When he finally opened the envelope he saw one papery five-dollar bill.

He ran through Job and came out the back way—to walk home alone. *Why why whywhy?* had they given him only five dollars? What could mother Annunziata and the children do with five dollars? What had he failed to do . . . ?

Saturday afternoon and the restless void and flesh of Job momentum that at home feels not at home and longs for the movement of wall and scaffold. Saturday afternoon in the pallsome fast world of Tenement, and Job's bruised rough fingers and crying spine remaining close. Saturday afternoon and Annunziata before the crucified Christ, votive light and glassed-in Virgin, kissing in tears the papery envelope. . . . Guard him, my Lord, guard him . . .

Sunday morning Annunziata and Paul visited Luigi. At first sight he looked better than usual, but he was flushed with fever. He followed raptly what Paul recounted of Job, and on hearing that they had given him five dollars he exclaimed, "They have spit into the hands of a boy. The son of the master who taught them the art and gave them the bread of work when there was none to be had, they have maltreated. They have bruted, widow's boy and one's kind. O men men you are cowardly blind and put to shame by children . . ."

Monday morning.
And men's tinged faces of spilled lust and breaths of undigested meat spaghetti wine garlic and sour tobacco lingerings and sleepy acid expression and ungraceful set of disconcerted lips and mean jerking of legs and hunched shoulders and slight smell of abused flesh and silence as pasty chill as morning . . . then . . . whistle and forced stilted push of bone-flesh into red-grays with

voices of men and Job organizing out of the cold into
action.

8

Luigi awoke fevered. A frightening heat had seized his
body and he saw the ward palpitating before him.
Something had grasped his right leg and was rolling and
trying to hurl him downward.

"Nurse-nurse, I sense badly . . . nurse-doctors, I sense
ill . . ."

On touching his hand the nurse summoned a doctor.
The thigh, above the plaster cast on his right leg, was
swelled out balloon-tight, emitting fierce warmth. They
screened the bed and commenced cutting away the cast.
His leg from above the kneecap down had a weird drop-
sical appearance, humid with swelling and raging green-
ish yellowish purplish reddish splotches. The doctor
ordered hot packs to his abdomen and spine, and called
in another doctor. The second doctor shook his head
disapprovingly.

"Son, we'll have to operate immediately to save his
life. Sorry."

"But how could that happen . . . ?"

"We didn't wish it that way. I'll try to explain. The
shattering of your uncle's leg interrupted the circulation. . . ."

". . . Yes . . ."

"If we do not remove his leg soon the poisons created
will—well, it just means we have to amputate his leg to
save his life. Understand . . . ?"

". . . Yes . . ."

"I'm sorry, son."

". . . But the operation—will he live . . . ?"

"That . . . is always a gamble—"

"Do they always die . . . ?"

"Oh no. Don't worry, son, we'll fix him up."

Annunziata sat by him, and the great Luigi rolled and beat the sides of the bed. There was fear, terrible fear, on his features.

"Sister, my life cries no no to my agony and my senses yearn hopelessly that I were not here. . . . Would that I were not born: ah, but I cannot recourse and under this drunkenness I am in pinned passage—"

"Brother dear."

"Who buffets me and breathes into my flesh this rolling fire . . . ? Who beats my ears . . . why?"

"No one beats you, brother Luigi . . ."

"Ahhh, my senses come and go, and I an earth held fast under the pounding ocean . . ."

"Brother-brother."

"Who deals me this verdict . . . And I as ball hurled from cannon and falling deeper into fear. . . . But tell me, sister, what have I done?"

"You have only done good."

"Save me save me, sister . . . I fear . . ."

"We are with you, Ci Luigi," said Paul.

"And running pictures in my brain tell me that my life is to be chopped apart like the lamb on the meatblock. . . . And always the butcher has his ax in hand—on the land—on the sea—one-two-three-one-two-three. But who tells me of what butcher? What am I saying? Where do I find myself? Sister, tell me!"

"You are ill, Luigi."

"But I pain—I pain!"

"We are with you, dear Ci Luigi!"

"I am alone terribly alone and I fear I fear and I will die . . . oh no no please I am feared of death!"

"Brother-brother, you will not die. Brother-brother, courage of Christ . . ."

"It is all too strangely and please this cross I *cannot* accept!"

His voice rose and pierced the ward.

"Mother in Heaven I will die *I will die Iwilldie*!!! . . ."

The interne stuck the hypodermic in his arm and Luigi subsided so that he lay looking at Annunziata and Paul with bright eyes and remote body.

Little quiet wheels over the waxed linoleum and the stretcher carriage was ready. Voices of ward patients through the dark of what was happening to whom. Luigi on the carriage through the open elevator door looked at Annunziata and Paul as one who had died but yet through live eyes contemplated them. The shut of sliding door and smooth whir-up-away of Luigi as Annunziata and Paul go to waiting room and sit close with restless exhaustion.

Out of the elevator into the top-floor corridor, light live soft-soled feet and quiet rubber wheels into the operating room lighted with bright cold glow as of winter's street lamp, with dome of frosted corrugated glass as of factory, with white tiled walls as of subway, with marble and smell as of public lavatory, with gleaming nickeled instruments as of cutlery, with white aprons as of slaughterhouse, with faces as of soap and water, with passionless expression as of school and career, with table as of bier.

The interne quickly shaved Luigi's thigh and coated it with iodine.

From where come these Christians to dismember me and do they know I am Luigi and will they take from me life? But tell me, you people whole and well, who holds me to this course and why is Luigi here? Might I not fly from you to a distant refuge, to a cave and as animal on hands and knees lick my hurt and eat roots of earth and fish of sea, and to wing to the Saviour from under a sky clean-clean and broad . . . without pain and fear . . . ?

Internes' professional groomed hands as of manly lady's and white arms veined blue finely and softed with shiny black hair place him upon the slab.

And fear unravels his stomach.

"Nurse. Bedpan."

"Yes, doctor."

White enameled instrument table approaching with settings of steel as of scissors, steel of straight razor on hone.

Hands as of barber sheeting him. Great spotlight lowered, and at left a man as of pharmacy with small can, cloth, and wire mask.

Doctor dear doctor do not do me hurt—

Mask on nose and mouth. Throat clutched and chest blowing up. Oceans roaring into the caves of his ears. Body severed and withered to atom.

Doctor let me live!

"What does he say?"

". . . Nothing."

Spotlight plowing into his brain.

Jesu-Giuseppe-Marieee*eeeeee* . . . . Voices vibrating. Voices enlarging . . . voices oscillate and electrify him into the sirening light of the sun encompassing eternity.

The ether mask was removed. Luigi wheeled out. Annunziata and Paul permitted back to the ward. And that which wore swaddling, that scampered in olive grove, that bore him on boat to America, that braced back arm and heart into pick and shovel, that footed Job, that would have pressed rude joy between sweet-sweet thighs, and that knelt him to God

. . . was expressed down to the basement, hastily wrapped in old newspapers, soaked in kerosene, and dumped into the incinerator.

The world returned to Luigi, and through ether nausea and gauzy focus he made out the tight tired faces of Annunziata and Paul.

I am alive. Jesu . . . Giuseppe . . . Mari, blessings to thee.

Tears of thanksgiving came from him, his lips parted and a small-small whisper labored the names of Annunziata and Paul.

Annunziata smoothed his forehead. It was wet; his
face was without expression and waxy blue-white, his
mustache seemed darker, and at intervals he inhaled
mountingly and sighed:

"Sister mine . . . sister beautiful . . ."

On city wind the seven o'clock whistle called.

Paul mustered himself up wearily, and kissed ethered
Luigi.

"Paul, son of Geremio. Paul . . . Paul of Job."

Paul huddled himself away.

And Annunziata held Luigi's hand as he weakly wept
himself into deep sleep.

In lusterless black from head to foot Annunziata
walked with simple nobility and widow's resolution. The
street was a via leading to Saint Prisca, and people and
noises she saw not nor heard. To her son, no one else
had her face of faith, her lips of courage, her pure
brown eyes that looked ever upward, her radiance of
will.

She is *my* mother . . . !

And Paul walked to Saint Prisca with the bricklayer's
bending backwardness and aches.

They sat in the rear pew where Geremio had been
wont to sit every Sunday. With the same thought they
dreamed of him and his delight in listening to the glorious High Mass. They retraced in memory how he sat
there looking so fine in his Sunday clothes and how
with joy he followed the *Ave Maria* and the ceremonies
dedicated to the Lord Christ up front on the Sacred Altar, and how even in the church women would glance at
him admiringly. Of how he came home from Saint
Prisca and officiated at the grand Sunday dinner where
he would hand out the plates and say with each portion:
"This is the best dinner in the whole world!" And how
when preparing for his Sunday evening diversion he
would scrub himself thoroughly, wrap a towel around
his head to keep in place the wonderful black wavy hair
and go through the drab flat humming the *Ave Maria*

and arias from operas, and when finished dressing how he would make proud eyes at himself in the mirror and say in his best American accent: "Card-in-dean, Card-in-dean, where the *hell* have you bean?—Where the hell have you *bee-an*?"

And how he would then josh Annunziata about meeting some mysterious "Blondy-Blondina—a real golden-haired American Spring Chicken!" To which she would poutingly answer: "Go ahead, see if I care. God bless you."

And then his stroll through the fashionable districts where he would smoke his Royal Bengals with luxurious dignity and make pictures in his mind of how his children would someday live in this or that fine house with electricity and steam heat. And of topping off the evening with Master Anilio the fantastically lazy Neapolitan, Ferdinando the redhead, and Master Antonio, in the little chamber back of Master Antonio's cobbling shop where they would play seven-up, eat good salted beans and drink thick-red wine and talk juicily of women.... And then back home to Annunziata as though he had been a bad boy....

After the beauty of choir and Holy Communion, they lit candles with prayers for Geremio's soul and Luigi's recovery.

The corporation had each his particular demeanor which Paul tried to fit himself to. If he did his work well they did not speak. But if he blundered they were quick with tongue and gesture, and their every shade of temper he took painfully. One of them commanded Paul in rapid chopped Italian and when Paul asked him over and over what he meant, he ejaculated in American: "No-stand! No-stand!" and finished off in Italian, "You are not son of Italian; you are a little cock-o of an American without salt!"

Paul was not Paul; he was Philippe, he was the diapered one, he was sill-high, he was the apprentice-boyo, he was the first-born masculine of the deceased, he was

the little master, he was the half-pint jerk-off, he was
godson, he was the titty-drinker, he took orders from
everyone, and each time they joked or had their tempers
out on him it was hours before he could forget—And
always, he felt he had to keep up with the men and that
that was what the corporation expected of him.

During a speed-up the shouting Mike-the-Black
called Paul and directed him to start a wall to a line he
had set, but did not say which side of the line. The wall
was up a few feet, and Rinaldi on rechecking the wall
layout discovered the mistake. Hundreds of brick had to
be torn down and the wall rebuilt. Black Mike and
Yellow-Fever cursed and frothed and yelled at Paul.

The few days before pay-day he no longer possessed
physical capacity. He thought he could convince his
body to accept the duty, but now everything within had
broken apart and was trickling away. At night the nervous exhaustion kept him awake, and fears clouded
through his mind.

What did they do after his error? Did they think he
was not doing his best? Did they think he looked so
weary because he was lazy? Did it cost them a lot of
money to repair the wall—and did they hate him or did
they realize it was not his fault?

Why could he not sleep, and what if he should get ill?

Ci Luigi—Ci Luigi—Ci Luigi—How could he accept
the operation knowing if he awoke he would be without
his right leg, and that perhaps he might never again
awake and see light and Annunziata and Paul . . . ?

He knew his mind was going to entertain the horror
of Luigi's amputation and the more he tried to push it
from his consciousness the stronger the picture of knife
and saw and blood decided. Acute pain stabbed his right
thigh, and he clasped his legs and sorrowed bitterly for
Ci Luigi.

Long, far, into his dreams he wrestled with the corporation, with bonded walls and Father John and un-
known forms and saw Luigi pushing wheelbarrows and
hopping about with one leg.

Pay-day was rainy miserable, but the mortar was mixed and the men went up on the scaffolds. The more Paul strove the more draggily answered his body. The rain soaked through his cap and sweater, wet his feet, and made the bricks' sharp crisp surface rub his fingers with disagreeable electricity.

"Quack-quack," mimicked the Lucy. "In good weather we pick our noses looking for a job, and now we lay brick in the rain up to our tails. Quack-quack!"

Paul knew he was becoming ill. Mortar fell from his trowel and slopped the wall, his shoes and the scaffold, and bricks kept slipping from his hands. When the whistle finally blew end of work-week he was so strained he did not care if he remained working on the wall until life left him.

After Rinaldi gave him the envelope with five dollars in it he wanted to speak at last and plead for more money but he was voiceless and his breast stuck with paralyzing emotion. Nazone remonstrated with the corporation, and they shouted back violently for him to mind his own affairs. Paul could not stay near the job and witness the grown men with their ten and twenty dollar bills; and he could not go home. He waited in the rain a distance from the job until Rinaldi came by. He walked beside and a bit behind Rinaldi, and Rinaldi did not speak once.

When Rinaldi stopped at a corner and waited for the trolley Paul forced from his lips:

"Mister Rinaldi, if you don't mind—I'd like to say something to you—"

Rinaldi bent his ear a little toward Paul but did not look at him.

"Mister Rinaldi, we can't do anything with my five dollars—oh, please, Mr. Rinaldi, am I not worth more than five dollars? Oh please, I can't go home with only five dollars . . ."

"You see, Paulie, I don't run the corporation by myself. Understand?"

"But, Mister Rinaldi, don't *you* think I should get more than five dollars . . . ?"

". . . . I—say you are."

"So, Mister Rinaldi . . . please . . . ?"

"I can't fight with the corporation."

"But they knew my father and worked for him—they *know* I am worth more than five dollars—why don't they help me? Mister Rinaldi, why?"

Rinaldi looked for the first time at Paul, and kindly, then said with a shrug:

"I'm sorry, Paulie. . . . That's the way the world is."

They looked to each other until the trolley came. Rinaldi nodded and climbed up onto the trolley. And Paul went sobbing aimlessly in the rain.

Annunziata held him in her arms and consoled him but his convulsive sobs would not cease.

"Mama, mama, they gave me only five dollars and I feel so small and everything aches . . ."

"Do not lose your precious tears, Paul my Paul—the young Jesu cast from him the power of wealth—weep not, my son . . ."

"But mama—I cannot help it—I cannot stop, mama—everything hurts me—Oh I worked so—so hard I thought I was going to die—and they gave me only five dollars—Oh they know I am worth more—Mister Rinaldi said so himself—"

"It is the Jesu who keeps us living and not their gold, my boy. I would rather starve than for you to weep."

"Please, mama, I cannot help it—And when I asked him why they did not help me when they knew we deserved it he said: 'That's the way the world is.'—Why is the world that way, mama? It is not—it is not—oh mama, I cannot stop crying—"

Annunziata held him fast until he fell asleep. She cried quietly, and while she removed his wet clothes and warmed him, his shivering body sobbed with quick starts.

At evening he awoke and came out into the kitchen in a stupor. Annunziata prepared him some salad, coffee and bread. After a few mouthfuls he could eat no more and wandered back to bed.

Sleep. And from out of unconsciousness flows a smooth level highway, a force all-encompassing with muted parallels of red; it flows on a plane whose extreme levelness leads to terror; the action is soundless and the stream broadens, heightens, and runs along the level faster and faster smoother and smoother and toward it heads a gray speck, an infinitesimal point, and when the stream hits it the forces of red whirl and curve and circle and explode and race and screw into each other larger and faster and larger beyond all control.

Paul's hysterical screams sent Annunziata from bed and to his side. The children awakened and crowded in one corner of the bed.

"I can't do it!—I can't pay—I can't pay it—" he screamed on and on. Against her arms his heart thundered and was tearing from him. She called for Saint Joseph to come to his aid. Annina lit the gaslight and its flickering glare showed Paul's screaming face and wild eyes. Without being told she ran for the doctor.

When through his hysteria he recognized Annunziata, he gripped her. "Oh mama mama, stop him—oh mama there's somebody chasing me—mama mama, I can't run any more—stop him, mama, stop him—"

"No no," wept Annunziata, "no one chases you, my Paul, you are safe at my breast—safe, my Paul . . ."

"Oh mama I can't do it—I can't pay it—oh stop him mama—mama mama my heart is going to explode—!"

Annunziata put the crucifix to his lips and kissing it he begged: "Save me from him Jesus—stop him—"

His stomach heaved and he vomited over the bed.

Annina brought Doctor Murphy with her. He felt Paul's heart, and then ordered cold packs to his chest.

"Strained heart, missus. Rest and quiet. More nourishment, and no more Cops and Robbers. Cut out coffee and exercise for a good long while . . ."

"Exercise, Doctor Murphy?" echoed Annina. "He has

been laying bricks on buildings with men for two weeks."

Doctor Murphy shook his head sleepily and left without asking for money. The children went back to sleep, some in the same bed, the rest in the bed of Annunziata with Johnny and Geremino, and Annunziata remained awake with Paul.

"But mama," said Paul holding her hand tightly to his heart, "someone *was* chasing me—like I owed someone a billion dollars and only had a penny—oh mama. . . ."

III

TENEMENT

1

Paul remained in bed for days. He slept heavily, and during the day. At night Annunziata would turn the gas-light on low and stay by him. When she left him he would hear her praying intensely at the votive light in soft Italian. He would stay awake listening to the snoring children, the cats moaning, the milk wagons over the cobblestones, the rattling Els, the whistle-rumble of the river boats, and the stirrings coming and going. Soon in the hollowness of night the sounds would not mean anything and fantasy rose. One night he lay looking at the wall ahead, and over the little singing gas-jet danced unceasing shadows that were never twice alike. He thought serenely of Job and Job's men of strength, and every brick he had laid in his two weeks of Job he laid over again ... And he thought how good his god-father Vincenzo was to visit him, bring home to him his tools and help them with money. He thought of Katarina and the Lucy and the shadows on the wall resolved into moving forms that were bending, lifting, twisting, toiling, and though he did not recognize them he lay there feeling he knew them. Was it that he had seen them in his history book? Or were they the men of Job? They became countless and were all the people in the world. His chest thumped-sumped slowly and unconsciousness began covering him, but he did not want to fall off. ... Here was the answer to everything. He felt like one who was never born and would never die, and as he tried to stay awake darkness was closing over him.

On the tenth morning a touch of May air found its way down the light-shaft and into his bedroom. It was dry and clean and suggestive of something that did not exist in the world of Tenement. His heartbeat was more regular, his bruised hands healed, and he felt no pains. When he got up from bed he was weak and heavy. After he had had his small glass of milk and the children had gone he sat at the kitchen window looking abstractly at back yards, clothes poles, and windows of other tenements; and when he tired of that he sought his tools and busied himself cleaning them. The wide thick sailor pants were heavy and he changed back to his short pants. He had a salami sandwich and an apple for lunch; after that he drank water until he was full. In the afternoon Annunziata arranged a comfortable place with pillow and quilt for him out on their side of the front fire escape. He lay down on his back looking up through the bars of the fire escape, up past the rusty tin cornice of the tenement parapet, up at a distant sky. His problems revolved until he forgot everything, everything but the faraway blue sky that fascinated him up and up closer to it. His eyes closed and he dozed off healthily. The homecoming school children woke him, and the sun was no longer there. Annunziata brought him his sweater, and sitting up he looked at the street and his interest gradually followed the gangs of children below in the gutter playing cat-stick, running, fighting, and shouting themselves delirious. From avenue to avenue the six-story discolored brick face was a cliff with sightless windows and crumbling fire escapes. Separating it from an opposite cliff was a narrow cobbled street bordered with cement sidewalks. And to Paul the third floor right in the center of the block was their little tunnel of refuge, their privacy and home.

"It is the month of May," said Annunziata. "Amuse yourself, and then you will take the beautiful rest on the fire escape when the sun comes in the afternoon." He would then wander about the building, going up on the roof and watching the men with their pigeons, the boys with their kites and smokes; sit on the stone stoop or on the curb and talk to the children of his own age and with the neighbors. He became spectator to the atmosphere in which he had always lived.

Tenement was a twelve-family house. There were two families on each floor with the flats running in box-car fashion from front to rear and with one toilet between them. Each flat had its distinctive powerful odor. There was the particular individual bouquet that aroused a repulsion followed by sympathetic human kinship; the great organ of Tenement fuguing forth its rhapsody with pounding identification to each sense. The Donovan's tunnel caught the mouth and nostrils with a broad gangrenous gray that overwhelmed the throat, but on acquaintance nourished into a mousey buffet. Missus Donovan, an honest Catholic woman, was old, cataplasmic, and sat for hours in the closet-small hallway toilet breathing in private heavy content, or at the front-room window munching her toothless gums. "Potatoes and hamburgers's what I dish 'em alla time," she would tell Annunziata. "If they squawk, I say, 'Make your own eats.'" Whenever she saw Geremio's children with a hungry look she would call them in to bread and baloney. The large Farabutti family in one of the upper flats had an oily pleasing aroma—the Maestro carrying with him a mixture of barbershop and strong di Nobili tobacco—and the children savoring of the big potato-fried-egg sandwiches which they chewed while shouting at cat-stick. The Hoopers had a colorless moldy emanation that hung and clung anemically but drily definite. The gaunt woman on the top floor who wore the gaudy old-fashioned dresses and brought men home with her talcumed herself stark flat white and left an insistent trail of old bathrooms littered with cheap perfumes. The top floor right—Lobans'—gave off a pasty fleshiness as though the bowels were excreting through the pores. Their breaths were revolting, and everyone in the family had snarling lips ready to let go profanities.

The Olsens drew Paul.

"Come up, Paulie, an' we'll put somethin' on your bones," Missus Olsen often said when meeting him. She had a booming Ha! Ha! laughter and wallowed in bawdy tales. And then there was Gloria, Gloria twelve, who broad and shapely looked sixteen. She had blunt features, full ripe lower lip, and blonde hair. Her eyes had a smoldering semiconscious manner, rolling open slowly and presaging a charged disturbing smile. At times she would come up to him when he was sitting on the stoop and stare at him through her peculiar veiled eyes, and he would not know what to say. She would swing and push forward her hips and breasts, then light up and say in a vibrating off-tone: "Whatcha doin' . . . ? Play with me?"

He would give her some reason for not being able to; she would not understand and turn away from him swiftly. He felt distant, but silently gazed when she was near, and drank in her clean-washing maiden scent.

And the Jewish family who lived silently on the opposite side of the thin shadowy light-shaft—from there came the smells of cabbage soup and chicken fat. Paul would watch them come to the table: the somber-looking boy of his own age with the shaved head and heavy features; the old man's long black coat and skull cap, his beard and his rising-falling fervent monotone of prayer; the old mother with her shawl, constantly rocking her head; the other son with his mustache, hooked nose, and huskiness, who sorted newspapers on the table and whistled; the heavy drinking glasses of steaming amber tea, the black bread—and they each in his studious and contemplative world.

Then the winding staired passage of Tenement hallway gaseous in its internationality of latrines, dank with walls that never knew day, acrid in the corners where vermin, dogs, cats and children relieved themselves; the defeated air rubbery with greasy cooking and cut with cheap strong disinfectant.

So different were people, thought Paul in his bedroom darkness. After the show of day, after all the incidents and faces and voices and smells, what was he to think? Did they not all live one atop the other and feel and taste and smell each other? Did not Job claim them all? With what all-embracing thought could he bless Amen today?

They, like me, are children of Christ.

2

In the third week, Paul, feeling able, visited Luigi with Annunziata and Cola. It was a wonderfully happy time. They cried and laughed with joy on seeing Luigi, for he was well. His bison head was as shaggy as ever and he needed a haircut. He was wan, with the large bones of his face showing, but his eyes were clear and he wept joyously with them.

"The good Dio has heard my prayers. I am getting so well that you will soon see." He wiped his eyes with his huge hand, and inquired of the children one by one.

"They are well with the protection of God."

"Benedictions, sister."

"Benedictions," affirmed Cola.

Luigi had Paul sit on the bed by his good leg, and hugged him.

"And how goes our Master Paul?"

"Very well, Ci Luigi. In a few more weeks I shall lay brick."

"Paul-Paul," said Annunziata, "we can sit at home and cut embroidery, we can eat one piece of bread instead of two."

"Don't worry, mama, I'll grow."

"We'll live, we'll live," said Luigi excitedly. "They tell me the job insurance is to pay me with five dollars weekly. In a month I shall come to live with you. I shall have a little bunk in the parlor. I will help, I will help."

They were silent for a space. He rubbed his hands.

"Sister . . . I feel in my heart the storm has come and gone. Life will change. The bambinos will rise to men and women.—Geremio is above . . . and we are on earth."

Before they left he told about the ward and that the doctors were good to him and the nurses called him Louie.

"And you cannot conceive how peculiar I feel when the nurse undresses me and I am a big naked thing in her hands . . . Madonna, but I do say!"

Cola caught her big breasts and laughed until tears poured from her dark-circled eyes.

"Now then. A night I lay here as a prostrate ox, and calling for the pot. I might just as well been singing out for a bag of gold. Was I to poison my insides?—So I let go!"

Cola screamed and giggled so that she went out into the hall to recover. When she left, Luigi whispered to Annunziata, "Sister, I shame to say it, but I am overrun with lice."

"Lice? But the sheets appear clean."

"Ah, the sheets are clean but God only knows how many Christians have decayed on this mattress, for the lice have grown big and bold in my hair and walk down my face. They do keep me awake, sister."

Annunziata sent Paul down for a fine comb. Cola came back and soon behaved with matronly modesty. She took it upon herself to arrange Luigi's bed. With womanly touches she smartened the mattress and sheets. "Your position does not look too comfortable," said Cola. And she swarmed her breasts over his face to reach behind him and adjust his pillow. He tried to draw himself back but could not go back any farther and for a moment her heavy warm breasts brought him intoxicating consternation, and Luigi felt hot blood sheet his face. But when she noticed his unkempt hair and began searching her purse for a comb Luigi became terrified and mumbled that she should not put herself out of the way for his sake. She insisted it was her Christian duty and what was a "woman for, anyway?" Until she discovered neither she nor Annunziata had a comb, Luigi remained frozen. When Paul brought back a comb Annunziata stuck it under his pillow. They left, and in the street Cola hugged her breast with one hand and sighed to Annunziata: "Even big strong men are like children."

At home awaiting Annunziata was a letter from the State Compensation Bureau. It advised Annunziata to attend a hearing at the Death Claim department the coming week.

That night Cola, who had also received a letter, the dame Katarina, the Regent Govanni and Grazia la Caffone were with Annunziata and Paul in the kitchen.

"Sign nothing!" advised Katarina.

"Yes," said the Regina, "your cross made on a thin paper will bring ruin to you and your children."

"When you present yourself there, demand bread for your children!" said Katarina.

Grazia sighed: "Ah, but how can a widow without the American tongue tell her needs to men whose guts do not know which way first to burst forth?"

"Listen not to these peasants and potato-diggers, Annunziata," said Katarina. "Cart your eight hungry little children to this official post. You need not speak, for if they belong to our Christ, these men will know their duty when they look upon the faces of Geremio's children."

"Yes, but I, this stupid Grazia who counts with fingers on nose, tell you that the full gut sees not the hungry face."

"Nor sees God nor Christ nor Saints and company beautiful," affirmed the Regina.

Cola raised her eyes and said:

"Yes, but the wheel goes round."

"And we 'neath it," muttered Katarina.

"How shall I bring all my children there?" asked Annunziata.

Katarina thought for a moment.

"Head-of-Pig shall bring you and your children with his ice-wagon."

"Right!" affirmed the Regina.

And the women sat in circle, full breast to breast, and settled for the evening—the workers' women, the poor with the poor in conversation of this life.

3

The next morning Annunziata prepared to go out.

"Paul, dress and come with me." And her face was excitement.

"Where are we going?"

"We are going to speak with your father."

Paul got out of bed immediately.

"Last night the paesanos told of one who communicates with the departed."

"But who is it, mama?"

"An American woman who is called 'the Cripple.' And she lives not far."

"The Cripple?"

"Yes, she is real, and truly marvelous."

"And what is her name?"

"I do not know how to say it, but I have it upon a paper—which Theresa gave specially to me."

Paul dressed and quickly had his glass of milk. On the scrap of paper Annunziata handed him there was the name "Nichols" and an address written in a painfully worked Italian hand.

The building was an ancient sagging two-story frame structure. The first floor was a junk shop, and over it lived the Cripple. At the street entrance Paul turned a dilapidated bell-handle. For a few minutes there was no answer. Paul carefully pushed the door open.

"Who's there?" cried an arrogant voice.

". . . Me . . ."

"Who?"

"Somebody for Missus Nichols . . ."

Dirty white muscular legs in shabby black high-heeled shoes appeared at the head of the stairs.

"Awright, wait a minute." And a girl of fifteen clattered down the dusty stairs. She wore a soiled ragged white petticoat that revealed her dirty bony breast and muscular arms. Her face was square with pointed chin, her eyes circular and hard, her teeth rotted and almost black, and her long bobbed hair a dirty platinum that hung leadenly. She stopped by Paul and inquired in a wantonly guttural but naïve voice, "Who yuh wanna see?"

"Somebody sent us to Missus Nichols . . ."

The girl looked at Annunziata's weeds.

"Awright."

An undersized wizened grown-up girl stood at the top of the stairs and inquired:

"Who is it, Margie?"

" 'Sawright Florine. Some Eyetalyuns to see momma."

Annunziata and Paul followed her up the stairs and into a wretched kitchen. Margie motioned them to some chairs by the coal stove. They sat and remained with extreme respect. Opposite them, and sitting by the washtub, were three other people waiting to see the Cripple, a nervous dignified middle-aged man, a Negress, and a woman dressed in furs and silks. The kitchen was large, dark, and low-ceilinged. Three half-naked children with the same faces, voices, and hair as Margie played in the center of the floor with dirt and water making mud-pies. At the table near the lone window sat the father. He was holding the baby and looking dumbly out. On the wall over the table was a dirty ornamented "Home Sweet Home." Margie made herself some coffee, and a sandwich of bread and baloney. The children saw her eating and clamored. "Give the kids some, you!" commanded the eldest girl Florine, who was not only humpbacked, but paralyzed on one side so that her neck was stiff and her head twisted to the left. "Give it to them yourself! What the hell d' yuh think I am?" They argued and swore, while the children squalled. The father did not turn from the window. Florine limped about the kitchen making coffee and sandwiches for the baby and herself. The coffee and baloney smell mingled with the kitchen's oppression of unwashed bodies and dry sewage.

Four hours had gone by while Annunziata and Paul waited. The dignified man, the Negress, and the well-dressed woman had all gone nervously through the door over which hung a sooty wooden lettered sign, "Jesus Never Fails." Each had left with the same relieved, inspired expression. At last Florine limped to Annunziata.

"Whatcha name?"

Paul told her and she scribbled it on a pad which she held in her useless left hand. She went into the Cripple's room, and soon returned. "Awright, momma says to go in."

Seated in a small rocker at the window was the Cripple. She smiled to Annunziata and signed her to a cane chair facing her. She looked at Paul, and questioned in an iron adenoidal voice that ran up:

"Do you want the boy to stay?"

Annunziata pulled Paul to her side.

The Cripple rocked, looked out the window at the passing elevated trains and completely forgot Annunziata and Paul. They received an immediate impression of her positive voice, her wide neck's hard bulging goiter, and the short withered steel-braced leg that dangled from the rocker. She was short, and her muscular body and limbs were fatted with the appearance of tough tubular lard. She wore a cheap purple silk dress, and a corset barreled her torso burstingly.

The trains had banged past and the Cripple still stared out the window. Suddenly she shouted, startling Annunziata and Paul:

"Florine! Bring me a glassa water!"

Florine limped in with a glass of cloudy water, handed it to her mother and watched her as she globbed it down.

"More?"

"Nope."

Florine stood for a moment and then said:

"Margie's gettin' too Goddamn fresh in frunna the people!"

The Cripple waved her away. She settled herself once more and asked Annunziata, "Missus, have you brung the flower?"

Annunziata nervously brought out the single fresh rose from its tissue wrapper. The Cripple fingered its petals, and put it to her nose with both hands. With a rasping inhale she nosed it and then let out a sigh of satisfaction. Next to her right side was a small three-legged table bearing a rusty phonograph with a dented horn. She cranked it, and sent the needle scratching over a record. From the horn quavered the *Indian Love Call* in a tremulous, seeking, evangelical female voice.

The afternoon sun lighted the room as the Cripple rocked back and forth, staring hard at Annunziata. Her every breath and gesture were strenuous, and she seemed pent with a starchy electricity. Her face came back and forth to the clinging Annunziata. It was a durable death's-head face larded over; with small beaked nose, popping circular eyes, and stony forehead. The red moist lips folded bottom over top, and her chin ran to a point. Her lifeless yellowish platinum hair was bobbed short. She chewed her lips, sinking two rotted teeth with every chop up in between her upper gum and lip. When the *Indian Love Call* had run its course she put it on again.

Paul glanced about the room. It was crowded with old and incongruous furniture. Behind him was a piano

with the front lid missing and all the strings exposed.
On top of the piano and facing the Cripple directly was
a large plaster Indian chieftain's head; and in disarray
beside it were dirty kewpie dolls with torn spangles,
starfish and dusty photographs. Above and behind the
Cripple was a lithograph in heavy colors of an Indian
maiden atop a mountain peak, her arms upspread toward a dazzling pink heaven. The room was close and
musty, and rankly disinfected with chloride. The phonograph stuck and kept repeating:

"Calling you-ooo-hoo—calling you-ooo-hooo"

The Cripple turned it off.

"Lemme have your wedding ring, missus."

When she received it she fitted it onto her left index
finger, dropped the rose in her lap and began revolving
the ring with the fingers of her right hand. Her hands
were round, full, hard, the short thick fingers running
off to thin bony ends.

She began straining her entire being and shut her
eyes fast. Her face reddened and perspiration formed
about her lips. Annunziata and Paul felt uneasy. She
stopped rocking and her right hand went up to her
forehead.

"There's a voice from the spirit woild . . ."

Annunziata and Paul reached forward.

She rocked once more.

"It's the voice of a woman. An old woman. It seems to
me she passed away in the old country—some time ago.
She's saying something. And it's in the Eyetalyun language."

The elevated trains went by. She opened her eyes and
stared at the anxious and slightly perplexed Annunziata.

"This party reaching out from the spirit woild is on
your mother's side."

Paul looked inquiringly to his mother. And
Annunziata was pushing herself terribly to understand
the difficult American tongue. Who could it be? Why
do I not know? Why am I so stupid when the spirit
world wishes to communicate with me?

"Wait!" requested the Cripple. She fell back again into the rocker and shut her eyes. She swayed her head about.

"There's interference—there's another party trying to push this old woman—he's trying to force his way through the spirit woild—he's a man—how he pushes!"

She shuddered forcibly. She ceased rocking and leaned forward as though seized with cramps, and clutched her great bulging throat.

"Oh how strong he's comin' in. He's so eager!"

Annunziata and Paul clasped each other's hands and held their breaths.

The Cripple stiffened, choked and writhed.

"My God in Heaven—he's so anxious to break through and embrace you! He must have died not so long ago because he's trying to reach out to you from the spirit woild before his time.... The force is grippin' my neck and paralyzin' me! Now tell me, who is this man that passed away not long ago? He must be very dear and lovin' to you. I get a pitcher of him. He's about your age and is Eyetalyun and looks so healthy with dark hair and red cheeks and dark beautiful eyes—" She reeled as though hit. "Oh God, I've gotta use all my strength to receive him—I can't rest—he won't stop ... He reaches right out from the spirit woild with his arms open wide and a great big smile on his face—and he says—he says ... He's comin' so strong, I can hardly make it out—"

The door opened and Florine stuck her head into the room.

"Momma, Margie's actin' like a reg'lar bitch, and there's people out here!"

The Cripple, with her eyes shut tight, and straining, waved away in Florine's direction. She shuddered violently, and nodded to some distant realm that she was heeding. Her face broke out in kindly smile and enjoyment.

"He says, I kiss my wife and children—"

Annunziata softly cried: "Geremio!" She reached out from her living world and up to the spirit world.

The Cripple opened her eyes and compassionately permitted Annunziata and Paul to rejoice and weep.

"He stands before me and says to me that he wants to tell me somethin'." With closed eyes she listened and nodded.

"He says for you to be happy 'cause he's livin' in Paradise—"

Annunziata whispered, "The richest treasures of Paradise to Geremio . . ."

". . . He opens his arms and takes you endearing to his breast. He wants for you specially not to weep too much—for I see him holding his chest, and that means it hoits him when you cry."

Annunziata and Paul wiped their tears and smiled.

". . . There, now he takes his hand away from his chest and his face is shining like the sun."

Annunziata wanted to speak from her overflowing heart but the Cripple raised her hand.

"He's not ready for questions—he has a message and if you talk I'll lose the connection with the spirit woild."

For a minute all were silent, and the Cripple listened on to the spirit world, nodding that she understood.

"Oh, what a beautiful message!" And tears came from her eyes. "His face comes through and he's speakin' right over my shoulder and facing' you and your boy. He says that he never left you, and never will. He says he's watchin' you with his endearing love every minute and that he's doin' all in his power from the spirit woild to protect and help you. . . . Now he stands back and wants you to make a wish to yourself; the wish of your heart's desire. Don't let me hear it!"

Annunziata and Paul clasped their hands and closed their eyes. They prayed to God. They forgot themselves and their troubles. They spoke to God and prayed:

O God, our wish is for the peace and happiness of him who is in Paradise, our Geremio, our father and husband who is in Heaven . . .

And while they prayed the Cripple pressed the rose to her lips and aided them.

"He says he heard your wish and blesses you for it, and tells me to tell you that it will be taken care of. Now he says from the spirit woild for you to ask questions before he goes away; for he came in so strong he's worn me out. Now open your heart an' don't be afraid to ask. He's listenin'."

Annunziata molded her comprehension to the Cripple instinctively. She spoke to Paul.

". . . My mama wants to know if papa . . . is happy."

The Cripple shut her eyes, pressed her forehead, and rocked for a moment.

"Yes. He says he's happy and poifectly content. He says there's only one thing he wants—but not now. He wants your mother to join him someday in Paradise. . . . But not now! Someday when all the children grow up, and she is old. . . . Oh yes, he shows me all his children—ah I see—there's around five or more, and they all have his face. He has his arms around them. He says: 'See, these are my children, and I love them.' Yes, he's very extremely happy. Any more questions?"

Paul hesitated, and then wistfully said, "There is one thing I want to ask father more than anything else . . ."

"Don't be afraid to ask, sonny; that's what he wants you to do."

"Missus Nichols," he began, "when the building fell apart and came down . . . when he died . . . did it frighten him terribly—did it hurt him much? . . . What did he think of . . . ? How did he feel . . . ? What did he say?"

She closed her eyes and rocked.

"Sonny, he says he's glad you asked that question. He has his arms out to you and is pleadin' for you to put your mind at rest, for when his time came, he says, he knew he had to go and that God needed him. When the accident happened, he told God he was ready, and just asked Him to take care of his family, and then he went to his Maker just like that!" And she snapped her fingers sharply. "No, sonny, he shakes his head and says there wasn't a stitch of pain, and that he went to his Lord God with a clean soul and a smile."

The weight of the world lifted itself from Paul. Tears dropped soothingly from his eyes.

"That was a wonderful question, sonny," said the Cripple softly.

"Is there anything more you want to ask him?"

"Yes. Will Ci Luigi's leg get better?"

"Your father shows me a man's leg. There's been a lotta trouble. I see a horspital—I see a big number four. Now, it's not clear, but anyway it'll be four days or four weeks or maybe four months when this leg trouble will be cured—if he takes care of himself and prays, your father says. Anything else you want to know?"

Paul asked slowly, and in low voice, "Ask father if my heart will get better . . . please."

The Cripple rocked. She stopped.

"Your father says for you not to strain yourself, and all will be well. I see him putting his strong hand on your shoulder and helping you. I hear him say proudly: 'This is *my* boy, and while I help him he will be the champion of my family!' And how wonderful he looks when he says it! Now ain't there anything else?"

Paul thought. And slight fear passed over his face.

"Missus Nichols, I just thought. I thought about how little money we have . . . and I was thinking . . . about the children home—will anything happen to them—will they be all right?"

"Hmmnn . . . your father says not to worry. . . . He does say though, that if one should pass away, it'll be 'cause . . . he was lonely and wanted one of his dear little children. But don't let that worry you 'cause I don't see anything like that. He does say that he can help and pray for them only if they try to take care of themselves. Now he's kissing you, missus, and all his children, and says, 'Do not worry, my endearing family, for I am always with you an' have never left you!' . . . Oh missus, this has been the best communication with the spirit

woild I've had in years! See, now he's left me, and look
at me ... I swear I'm like a rag."

Annunziata kissed the Cripple's hands. And Paul did
likewise in his heart. When Annunziata timidly asked
what she owed, the Cripple sniffed the rose and studied
its petals.

"You an' me's poor people. . . . And I'll only charge
you one dollar."

Mother and son thanked her.

"Florine!" cried the Cripple.

Florine stuck her head in.

"Are you ready for the next people, momma?"

"Florine, bring a nice cup of tea for me and the missus here, and her boy."

"But momma, you promised these people two o'clock
and now it's past three ...?"

"Never mind, Florine, tell them to come tomorrow at
eleven, and make a note of it. Got the name?"

"Yes."

"Well, bring us the tea and do as I tell you."

As Florine prepared the tea the Cripple became very
amiable with Annunziata. She told of her two sons
killed in the War and pointed to the photographs on the
piano. She told of the sickness in the family. She told of
the police trouble and the bribes they grafted from her
because it was against the law to contact the spirit
world. "So you see, missus, we all got our troubles.
What good's my husband to me? He doesn't bring in a
cent, and drinks every dollar I make." Annunziata felt
for her, and in return passionately unburdened to her of
her Geremio, her Paul, and her children.

Florine brought the tea in thick, soiled cups—the first
time they of Geremio had ever tasted tea.

"Momma, Missus Schaefer says it's very important,
and she'll wait until you're ready."

The Cripple sucked her tea.

"Is it a matter of life and death?"

"I'll ask her."

"Yes, do that, Florine, 'cause this last communication's worn me out. . . ."

". . . And momma, about Margie—"

"Don't bother us now."

Florine soon limped back from the kitchen.

"Missus Schaefer says for me to tell you, 'You can call it life and death.' "

The Cripple settled back into the rocker.

"Awright, tell her I've gotta have my tea here with the missus and I'll be ready for her in fifteen minutes."

Home. And hours were wings of fantasy to a mother and son. They gathered the children. They told what father had said, and they kissed them. They told of a father who had never left them, a father whose love surmounted the distance of death, a father who held their hands by day and cradled them in the sleeping dark. Never now would living be without Geremio. No force could harm them, no filth could soil nor sicken them, no circumstance could discourage them, and no discord could displace their faith.

That night Geremio was present in the two narrow bedrooms. Wan, happy Paul could not sleep. He lay at the foot of the bed, and spoke to the wavering votive light that hovered from Annunziata's room.

O papa, forgive my tears. . . . For I weep with joy. And papa . . . why can't we all be together? Can't we go up to you, and never separate? Doesn't God need us? We could help . . . And papa, there's something I want to tell you . . . When the job fell down on you I felt every pain. But now that I know you did not feel the wounds, now that you told mama and me that you were not frightened and that you went when you had to go . . . I don't feel the building on you, and me. . . .

The votive light burned its delicate fire of devotion beneath the crucifix, and in the dark dust of dreams came a vast pressure to blanket the senses of mother and son; a force coming from afar and stealing their breathing, a sucking breath upon their own. And through their breathless world a consciousness told them that . . . the living do not die.

4

Paul wandered the waterfront on the bright May days. One warm afternoon he followed the street gang to the docks. Felix Farabutti headed them and shouted through the streets: "Yow, Yow, Bare-rass-beach here we come!" Christy, Chicken, Benny O'Gahtz, and the others chased after him, upsetting everything before them. Paul came upon them later. Felix was already stripped naked. He stood on a pile, ready to leap. He hastily signed the cross, and kissed the scapular that hung around his neck. Holding himself between the legs with one hand, and holding his nose with the other, he shouted and jumped in feet first. "Cold's a bitch!" he cried when his head bobbed up out of the water. Soon, the dozen or so boys were naked and slapping through the river water.

Watching them, Paul saw himself swimming in the cold bubbly water and threading it like a fish. But he knew he was afraid of the river. He knew if he jumped in or fell in he would sink hysterically. And he wondered how it would be. It would probably be like being overwhelmed again in that dream he had the night of his heart strain. How was it the other boys swam and were not afraid? And he thought of the story the boys told him of a man who dived off a wharf and never came up. He was a good diver and swimmer, but when he dived he cut the water swiftly and his head got stuck in the top of an old milk can down on the bottom of the river. He shivered at the contemplation of mysterious river. Would he ever learn to swim? How would it be? Would it ever be that he should drown? No. No, he had duties, and God would never permit it. But why did He make rivers? He automatically backed away from the wharf edge.

"Whatcha thinkin' about?"

He turned. It was Gloria Olsen. The sun, river, and May, brought her broad milk-sweet person to him in a flame of flesh. He stood dumfounded.

"Dontcha swim?"

Bare-legged and in clean-washed pink gingham dress, and smelling of blonde hair and broad freshness, she was before him, standing taller than he, her dull smoldering eyes lighting slowly, her broad soft lips smiling, her breasts and hips swinging.

He felt a slight cramp in the stomach, and his heart pushed faster. He moved backward.

". . . No."

"Why dontcha?"

Chicken climbed up on the wharf. "Hey guys," he called, pointing to Gloria, "look what's here!" They scrambled out of the river, their naked bodies white and dripping. Gloria ran; but not too fast. She wanted to play.

"Yow! Yow! meat for the monkeys!" cried Felix as he chased.

They formed a circle and danced about her. She dashed from side to side, swinging her hair and pushing them. Paul felt ashamed for her. He walked away, and not without knowing that the big Gloria did something to his stomach. She left the boys and ran to the avenue.

"Where ya goin', Paul?"

". . . Home."

They walked along without speaking. If she had spoken to him he would not have known how to answer her. He was older than all those children of his own age. He was a bricklayer. He was the father of his father's family. And her pushing soft presence beside him brought a nervousness. Girls were creatures referred to in many ways that he did not understand. He always saw them at a distance, and above him, for God made them finer and gentler and sweeter than he and the other boys. He had had many warnings. He had seen close panting and jerking bodies in hallways and cellars and on roofs. He had seen eyes hypnotically ablaze in tensed flushed faces of men and women, and their silent signalings. He had heard big boys and men conversing in hot trembling voice about what they did to "Her" and what they intended to do to "Her." He had heard the paesanos whisper and then roar, and it was about men and women.

Paul was curious about the Jewish family on the opposite side of the shaft. He watched them each night before going to bed. The old father prayed, the old mother made tea, the husky brother sorted his newspapers, and the somber boy with the shaved head studied profoundly. Paul wanted to know him. The week before Decoration Day it came about. Chicken, the tough boy of the neighborhood, had repeatedly made fun of the boy with the shaved head. That day he stopped him.

"Hey, Jew baby, what's yer name?" And he pushed him in the chest.

The boy with the shaved head looked at him coldly, and attempted to get by.

"Lissen, Sheeny, I'm askin' ya what's yer name an' why!"

"Let me pass."

Chicken swung and hit him in the face. The boy with the shaved head charged him head-first and threw him back against the circle of boys. Chicken cursed and swung both fists, but was sent back again violently. Chicken screamed: "Killdejewbastard! Killum!" The circle closed in on the boy with the shaved head. He said nothing. He backed to an electric pole and kicked with his thick-soled shoes. He caught Chicken in the stomach, and then Chicken lay on the pavement screaming that he was dying. That stopped the assault, and the boy with the shaved head walked away, his face red and swelling but his gray eyes as cold as ever.

Paul smiled to him as he approached, but the boy

lowered his eyes and walked up the steps of his tenement. Yet, he had done it respectfully. Paul had a feeling that he would be up in the room visible from the lightshaft. He went up to his bedroom to look. Across the shaft and by his window the boy was settling to a book. He realized Paul was watching him. He put the book aside and looked out into the shaft. They studied each other. Paul saw a round blunt face; the gray eyes and contemplative lips of a thinker; the serious lowered blunt chin of a quiet somber personality.

"What are you reading?" asked Paul.

"The Economic Theory of the Leisure Class," answered the low gray voice.

"Who wrote it?"

The shaved head looked down at the book.

"Thorstein Veblen."

"Is it good?"

The shaved head nodded.

"Can I come over and talk with you?"

"Yes, if you wish."

The boy with the shaved head was taller and broader than Paul. He led him through the bare rooms and into the room that looked out on the shaft.

They talked of school. He also was in the eighth grade, and was two years older than Paul.

"My name is Paul. And I'm Italian."

"I know it. I hear your mother now and then."

They were silent.

"I wasn't born in this country."

"That's what I thought," said Paul.

"We are Russian Jews. My name is Louis Molov."

"Is that the way it is in Russian also?"

". . . No. In Russia it was Lazare Molovitch."

"That sounds nice."

"But here in America it was changed by my eldest brother."

"You have another brother?"

"Yes. He has a stationery store uptown. He's married."

"When did you come to America?"

"Three years ago."

"Is that all?"

"Yes."

"Did you come on a big boat? How was it?"

"It was all right."

"Were you afraid the boat would go down?"

"I didn't think of it."

"Loiy—ee," called his mother from the kitchen; and then she spoke in Hebrew. He answered her in the same tongue. To Paul it was incomprehensible, but it sounded ancient and rich. Missus Molov came in with a small samovar and poured tea for the boys and herself. She was an old woman with Louis's face, only it was line-worn, her mouth toothless, and her gray-blue eyes watery.

Louis spoke to his mother, and Paul knew he was talking about him, for he looked at Paul and said: "Italianisch." The mother smiled and offered Paul a thick slice of pumpernickel. The tea was not like the tea he had at the Cripple's. It had a tan dry hot savor. It was good. And the black bread tasted of brown moist nuts. The only furniture was the table where they sat and the chairs beneath them. In the corners of the room were thick wooden trunks bound with tough leather straps, and on the trunks were piles of books. These people smelled of earth, with their quiet strong blunt selves, coarse dark clothes, wooden trunks, books, tea and bread. And Paul knew Louis would be his friend.

"I have a brother Av-rom. He has a newspaper route, and studies law at evening college."

"I saw him from my bedroom."

"Av-rom is a good student."

"He looks very husky."

"He is strong. And he is good-hearted."

"Is your father a—rabbi?"

"No . . . but he is very religious. He cuts chicken's throats at the Jewish poultry markets. And on the side he teaches Hebrew."

"I'll bet they like America. It's the best country in the world."

Louis did not answer. He looked into his tea.

"Don't they?"

Still looking into his tea, and without emotion, Louis said, "Father and mother are old."

Oh if father were old and alive! Whether he were old or young, or whether he were armless or crippled or legless so long as he were alive and they could hear his voice and laugh with him and weep with him!

"I had another brother," said Louis.

"Is he alive?"

Louis shook his head.

"He was shot by the Czar's soldiers."

Evening was now falling, and Louis's mother left them. Louis began the story in the darkening room. The gray of his voice was changing as he spoke of his dead brother Leov:

"And he was the most brilliant student in Minsk Gubernia. He was a poet. He wore his hair long, and he sang and danced like the Russian winds. He loved everyone and was loved. He was quick and sympathetic. . . . He was a genius."

"Why did they kill him?"

"During the World War he tried to organize the peasants against war. I can still see him. I was very small. Thousands and thousands of people from all over Minsk came to hear him in the city square."

The room was now dark, and Louis's voice lighted it.

"He made a great speech against the Czar and his war. He made the people cry. He did it even though father was making a lot of money by the war. He hated money and war and cruel people. The crowds carried him on their shoulders. I'll never forget."

They were both quiet but the beat of Louis's voice hung in the dark.

"Then one day after the big snow father received an order for merchandise and he sent Leov to deliver it. When Leov got out on a country road the Czar's sol-

diers arrested him and brought him to a little prison.
We did not know what happened to him. We were told
later that the soldiers got drunk and he had a chance to
run away, but he refused to because he said he had done
nothing wrong and was afraid of no one. The soldiers
later took him out in the woods and made him dig a
large hole. They stripped his clothes from him and shot
him. Soon after, the revolution came and these soldiers
passed through town: one of them was wearing Leov's
clothes. Mother recognized the suit. Father lost everything. Brother Max uptown sent for us and we ran away
from Russia. . . ."

"How is it now in Russia?"

Louis rose and lit a match.

"Do you want to look at Leov's picture?"

Paul followed him into a bare bedroom. Over Louis's
and Av-rom's bed was Leov's picture. Louis lit another
match.

Leov sat on a chair that was sideways. His left arm
rested over the back of the chair and he held his left
hand with his right. He looked right out from the picture. It was Leov at Paul's age. He had large dark eyes
and rich dark hair. He was all that Louis said. The
match died out, and they left the room. Louis spoke no
more of Leov.

"Go for a little walk?" asked Paul.

"If you wish."

Paul took him along the waterfront.

They sat on a dock. A water-logged crate floated by
slowly. It struggled to stay afloat, but it would soon sub-
merge.

Louis's lowered chin contemplated distance. Paul
watched the crate.

"Water is a strange thing."

"Water is an element. A chemical composed of two
parts hydrogen to one of oxygen."

"Where did you learn that?"

"Av-rom has a book on physics."

"Oh. . . . I wonder if a person who studied physics

would think of that if he were drowning. What do you think?"

"I don't know."

"Did you ever see anyone drown?"

"Yes."

"You did! Where? What did they look like?"

"In a river. In Russia."

"A river like this?"

"Yes. The spring before we ran away from Russia, three other boys and I made a raft. We floated out. None of us could swim. Some distance from shore the raft came apart."

"What did you do?"

"In the water I kicked and fought until some men reached me."

"And the other boys?"

"They weren't found until days later."

". . . Dead?"

"Yes."

"What did they look like?"

"Dead; swollen, blue."

"How did it make you feel?"

"I just looked at them."

"Weren't you scared?"

"No."

Paul did not know what to think. He remained silent.

Louis spoke. His voice was level; yet there was a cold fire.

"Every day people died about us. Starved. Killed. They were workers and peasants. Families were cut to pieces by the Czar's sharp swords."

"You saw it?"

"Yes."

"You knew the people?"

"Yes."

"Why were they killed?"

Louis's gray eyes searched the river depths.

They walked back. Paul told Louis of his father Geremio.

Louis held his head down.

Paul said so much, and could not go further. He held his lips.

"What does the doctor say about your heart now?"

"He says I'm almost better, and that I must not strain myself."

"When are you going back to school?"

Paul could not find his voice. He watched his feet stepping along the pavement.

". . . I'm not going back."

Louis turned to him.

"What do you mean . . . ?"

Paul did not answer.

When they arrived at Tenement there was a heat in the gray eyes.

They stood by the stoop.

"Are you going to the cemetery on Memorial Day?"

"Yes."

"May I come with you?"

They clasped hands tightly.

5

Head-of-Pig brought his ice-wagon the morning Annunziata was to appear at the Compensation Bureau. He had cleaned the wagon floor and spread it with newspapers and burlap. Annunziata and Annina had prepared the children, and when Paul at the window saw Head-of-Pig's horse and wagon he cried: "The wagon's here, ma!"

Head-of-Pig wasn't one to talk much. When Katarina commanded him to bring Annunziata and her children to the Compensation Bureau he blubbered through his thick lips, "With pleasure. Yes, with pleasure."

The children, thin from undernourishment and shabbily dressed, were scrubbed clean. Annunziata carried Geremino; Head-of-Pig carried Johnny. Paul and

Annina guided the four other children. Missus Olsen, returning from her morning shopping, set her bundles on the stoop and helped Head-of-Pig lift the children up into the wagon. Annunziata sat up front with Geremino in her arms while Annina held Johnny, and the other children sat in front of them. Head-of-Pig asked Paul if he wanted to sit up on the high driver's seat with him. Paul climbed up by him. It seemed high and insecure. He sat back as far as possible and held tightly to the seat. Missus Donovan opened her window and called to Annunziata, "Good luck, Missus!"

Head-of-Pig snapped the reins, clucked his tongue, and the big white horse started. Missus Donovan blew a kiss to Geremino. Annunziata waved back. The iron-tired wheels bounced over the uneven stones and jounced Geremio's family about in the wagon. After a few blocks Paul relaxed his tight hold on the seat and enjoyed his perch.

The great building of the Compensation Bureau was a thick-walled forbidding ten-storied structure. It had the discouraging semblance and overwhelming morgue aspect of Institution. Head-of-Pig got down from the wagon, tied the reins to a telephone pole, and went into the building. From the third story of the building projected a flagpole and from it hung a huge blue flag. On it in soiled white letters was the State emblem and the words: "Workmen's State Compensation Bureau."

People, poor people. And their faces pulled at Paul's heart. Their eyes and lips said, we are the battered poor, poor stupid poor, we are the maimed and crippled and bandaged and blind workers who can not speak and are led and pushed through these corridors like subway corridors and into chambers where we understand nothing.

INFORMATION. INFORMATZIONE.

"Mister, will you please tell me where the toilet is?"

Head-of-Pig suggested Annunziata prepare for the hearing.

In the building she became bewildered.

Is it here that they are to repay me for my Geremio? But how can they repay me for my Geremio, my beautiful Christian? Corridors and stairways, chamber after chamber, and floors paved with hard little octagonal white tiles of undetermined cleanliness. Corridors. Files of human beings went past her and her children. They were as herself. They were wounded and sought the helping hand of Christ's Christians.

They were the roots uptorn, the stalks bent and shattered. In their meek faces of hurt and hunger Annunziata saw herself and her children. But those who led them and carried leather cases beneath arm—who are these fine-looking men, well-groomed, daintily mustached and casually opulent? What do they here? They look not anguished and tightly pressed. They look not humble and at sea. They look not part of grief, and seem masters. They bear transparent distant eye of policeman. They seem not of Christ.

O Geremio, guard our children!

The children were afraid to enter the elevator, and Annunziata had to walk them up to the sixth floor.

Up the stairs, twists and turns, and more corridors. Room 100. Industrial Board—Room 101. Disability— Room 102. After-Care Dept.—Room 103. Interpreters—Room 104. Clinic—Room 105. Adjustments— Room 106. Board of Appeals—Room 107. Death Claims. Referee Parker.

The attendant at the doorway put on his glasses and looked at Annunziata's letter. He advised her to take a seat on one of the rear benches. When he noticed the children behind her he said, "Are these your children, lady?"

Paul stepped forward and asked: "Why?"

The attendant mumbled, "All them kids."

Paul and Annina respectfully herded the children into the rear benches.

When Annunziata's name was called, her breath came fast. Holding Geremino to her breast, she went through the little gate in the railing and sat in a chair assigned by the attendant. The children stood up to watch her.

Referee Parker, pink-toned sixty-five, snowy hair, spectacles, wearing a rough tweed suit, was a gentle masculine American grandmother. He did not lay bricks. His flesh had never built. He did not know how bricks were laid. What did Annunziata and Geremio's children mean to him!

Referee Parker read out the names of the Baldwin Insurance Company, and Fred Murdin of the Murdin Construction Company.

At the mention of Murdin's name Annunziata looked about to see the man her Geremio had spoken of as boss—padrone. Mister Murdin was a broad-shouldered six-foot man of clean-shaven beefy countenance. He was businesslike and cocksure. He was accompanied by Norr, his attorney, a tall judicious-looking man with pince-nez, high white collar and immaculate white starched cuffs.

Paul and Annunziata gazed at Murdin. They could not remove their eyes from him. They stared and searched him. He was Boss, Padrone . . . and he did not turn once to look at the family of Geremio.

Referee Parker greeted attorneys Norr and Kagan: "Hello Pete. Hello Bill."

Bill Kagan, the corpulent urbane representative for the carriers, smoothed his dark mustache and nodded. Referee Parker smiled and chatted with them. They smiled and chatted with him. They knew each other. They respected each other.

Referee Parker read from a paper, and asked Mister Murdin if Geremio had worked for him.

"Yes," said Murdin, "he was one of the laborers."

Paul raised his hand and cried, "That's a lie!"

Everyone in the room turned.

"My father was the *foreman*!"

Referee smiled charitably, and ordered Paul to be seated.

"Was he the foreman, Mister Murdin?"

"Those Eyetalian names are quite confusing."

Why are they smiling?

Referee Parker asked Annunziata how many children she had.

But why couldn't she answer? Why did her breast catch? What crime had she committed? A short swarthy round-cheeked interpreter with oily eyes and thick glasses hunched near Annunziata and asked her Referee Parker's questions. Then he would turn and relay her answers to Referee Parker with unction and over-respect.

"Mister Murdin, what actually was the cause of the collapse?"

"Your Honor, I've been in business for years—and I've always had the same difficulty with Eyetalian laborers—"

"Yes—"

"But I'll be hanged if I can prevent them from hurting themselves!"

"Just how do you relate that?"

"I gave this Geremio definite orders to proceed safely with the work; especially the demolition—"

"In just what way?"

"I ordered him to remove the demolished walls from the floors and chute it down to the yard to relieve any strain on the floors. I also ordered him to double the bracing and underpinning. He was a good foreman, but he was stubborn, and I feel he was directly responsible for the—accident."

Why why why didn't the building fall also on Murdin? *Why?*

Referee Parker had the interpreter ask Annunziata if she knew anything or remembered anything that Geremio had said concerning the job he worked on, and if she knew of any witnesses who could refute what Mister Murdin had said.

"My man was buried alive—my man was crucified—here are his children!"

Upon learning what she said, Referee Parker nodded.

"Your Honor," continued Murdin, "I speak from experience. The Eyetalians are good workers, when you watch them and take care of them like a wet nurse. But when not personally supervised they get themselves into all kinds of trouble. They're careless like children."

Mister Kagan of the carriers was not interested in anything Murdin had to say. He stated and proved that Murdin had not notified the Baldwin Insurance Company of the existence of *that* particular operation, and that they only found out that he had not listed that job and its payroll when they were summoned by the Compensation Bureau. "Furthermore," he added, "the Murdin Construction Company carried a policy covering demolition work done by laborers; and at the time the structure collapsed the major operation was construction, not demolition!" He asked the court to adjourn the case for their further investigation, permitting the Baldwin Insurance Company "fully to substantiate the disclaiming of all or any liability."

"Granted," said Referee Parker.

The lawyers smiled. The Referee smiled. And as Murdin was leaving Annunziata rushed to him with Geremino in her arms. She touched his coat sleeve. Murdin turned.

"Mister Boss—Mister Murdin-a, my man—my Geremio, he die on your job!"

Murdin withdrew his elbow.

"*I* didn't kill him."

The ride back in the ice-wagon was harder to endure. What had these men said? What had been done?

The children, tired and hungry, wondered why they had ridden to a great building to watch men talk and make faces, and then come home again ... without eating.

At Tenement Annunziata asked Head-of-Pig up for a cup of coffee.

"But how said they of my Geremio? And he builder's blood of centuries. Who looked toward me? Who is to pay me?"

Head-of-Pig shook his head and said it would be a good thing if one knew the American tongue—"for without it we are dumb and blind."

Back again in the sanctity of night's cave Annunziata and Paul lay communing with the poor's Christ. As they spoke to him the ghostly army of maimed shabby humans with the seeking faces filed humbly past them in the corridors of the vast prison where there were numerous chambers, and signs sticking out over the doors that said: "Clinic"—"Disability"—"Men's Toilet"—"Adjustments"—"Death Claims." And they saw the sleek flaccid state employees, and heard the correct American voices of Parker, Murdin, Norr, Kagan and other passionless soaped tongues that conquered with grammatic clean-cut: "What is your name? Your maiden name? How many children? Where were you born? This way please. Sit here please. Please answer yes or no. Eyetalians insist on hurting themselves when not personally supervised ... directly his fault ... substantiate ... disclaim ... liability ... case adjourned."

And they saw the winning smiles that made them feel they had conspired with Geremio to kill himself so that they could present themselves there as objects of pity and then receive American dollars for nothing. The smiles that made them feel they had undressed in front of these gentlemen and revealed dirty underwear. The smiles that smelled of refreshing toothpaste and considered flesh. The smiles that made them feel they were un-Godly and greasy pagan Christians; the smiles that told them they did not belong in the Workmen's Compensation Bureau.

Where did these men come from? Who are they?

Where and how do they live? For whom do they weep, and to whom do they pray?

That night was passed in uncertainty, in the feeling that for some reason, *some* reason the family of Geremio was wrong, that the meek fearful faces in the corridors of Workmen's Compensation were wrong, that the people who lived about them in careers of fits and starts were wrong, that the men who sweated and cursed on Job were wrong, that they were cheap, immoral, a weight of charity and wrong to the mysterious winning forces of right.

And Paul clutched his pillow.

O God above, what world and country are we in? We didn't mean to be wrong.

And toward dawn Annunziata also went into sleep wondering of her wrongness.

Born in sin, said the walls. Born in sin, said the dark. Born in sin, said the air. Born in sin, said fear.

IV

FIESTA

1

Annunziata, Paul and Louis stood by the mound. The cemetery was on the side of a steep hill that ran down to a great marsh. It was the burial ground of the Poor. In different parts of the slope lay Tomas, Julio the Snoutnose, Nick the Lean, Lazarene Tobacco-Eater and the other men of Geremio's Job. Job had arrested each, and as their widows and children surveyed the earth that cluttered them hard, how felt they? Their crushed bodies huddled in hole wrapped of dirt, but whither their laboring spirits? Did they soar about their comrade-worker Christ, or did worker return to Job and press ghostly self against scaffold and wall?

Annunziata and Paul kissed the glassed-in picture on the stone.

Did the cold bulk warm lips against their own?

Memory. Remembrance cruel and beautiful. Black, deeply shrouded widows with tear-bleeding eyes asking from stone and earth what they cannot give. And bright sun and blue sky watch. A new spring sends forth between the graves fresh blades of grass.

This is cemetery. This is underground where Job has sent worker to dwell with soil and worm while above them the hungry press breast and electrify God's earth with desire of their return. This is living where none may transmit the unwritten melody of warm blood's grief.

"Good morning, Annunziata."

"Good morning, Master Fausta."

Fausta removed his hat. He looked at the tombstone and shook his head.

"Who would think it? Ah, Geremio, we laid many a brick together."

Then with a twinkle in his eye: "Listen, Annunziata, the paesanos say when my time comes the Devil will catch me by my crooked nose and put me to work laying brick inside the boilers. Ahhh, is it true that even in the bad region I'm to deal with brick?"

Annunziata smiled.

He playfully tapped Paul's head with his hat.

"And how is the little American?"

"Well, thank you."

"Benedictions. Are you still as smart as the good spirit your father used to tell us about? Are you jumping ahead five grades at a time, or six grades?"

Paul smiled.

"I do not go to school. I lay bricks."

"By the Madonna, you don't mean!"

Annunziata looked up proudly.

"My Paul lays brick on the *front*."

Fausta placed his hand on Paul's head.

"On what job are you working? You must come to work for me!"

Paul told him of his experience with the corporation.

"The greedy greenhorn carrion, to treat the son of Master Geremio thus! Come to work for the old major-general and you will get not five dollars the week but five dollars the day!"

Paul's eager eyes sought those of Annunziata.

Mother! We shall live!

He became incoherent in his gratitude, and kept repeating the job's location in his excitement.

"Monday—yes, tomorrow I'll be there! I'll bring all my tools with me! I'll be there!"

"This job is just starting, and you'll be one of my first bricklayers."

Fausta's eyes glinted.

"And do you know what I'm doing to the corporation? I am taking from them all their men! A *boom* is coming and I shall pay more than they can afford! The cor-por-ation . . . bahhhh!"

A group of paesanos joined.

They spoke of the Dead, and of Luigi, and of the facts of their world. Paul and Louis left them and wandered the paths among the tombstones.

"Louis, is it not wonderful that I am to earn five dollars a day?"

"Is that what the man told you?"

"Yes, I am to start tomorrow. And it's a big job!"

Louis nodded. They came to an old grave at the end of the cemetery and rested upon it. Louis picked up a twig and made circles in the dirt.

"Louis, every year, no matter where we may be, we'll meet here on Memorial Day. And we'll think of my father and your brother Leov."

"Yes . . . and of the many others like them."

Paul opened his mouth but the question stopped where it began. He saw the armies of seeking faces in corridors and the endlessly bending figures of his dreams.

Louis contemplated the ground and spoke.

"Do you think that your father and these other men buried here will someday rise from their graves and cry for revenge?"

". . . Revenge . . . why?"

"Why? Did they want to die?"

". . . Want to?"

"My brother Leov did not want to die. They shot the life out of him against his will, but he sprang up from his grave and destroyed the Czar and all his soldiers!"

"He was dead . . . ?"

"They killed him—but his spirit threw the grave aside and paid back the murders of centuries!"

". . . That was the spirit of God."

". . . That was the spirit of my brother's ideals."

"I don't understand. Your brother was dead. Only God could have punished his killers."

Louis's gray eyes studied Paul.

"What God?"

"Why ... God ..."

"Whose God?"

"Whose God? There's only one God."

"Where?"

"Everywhere."

"You have seen your father."

"What do you mean?"

"You knew your father?"

"Yes ..."

"And you know your mother?"

"Of course."

"And you love them."

"Why, yes."

"Have you seen God?"

Paul felt something weakening him.

"Louis—haven't you—don't you believe in God?"

The gray eyes turned full on him.

"There is no God."

They walked toward the marsh. A large black bird flew out of the tall grass and flapped its wings over them. They looked up. When they looked down their eyes met.

At Tenement stoop the three were silent. Louis wanted to speak.

Annunziata waited. She smiled.

"Paul, aren't you coming with me to school tomorrow?"

Paul could not look at him. Louis sought his face.

"Paul ... isn't there some way?"

"We must live. I am going back to the job."

"Must you? Is there no other way? Some way?"

"No one brings us food."

"Paul ..."

"Job is freedom ... for us."

"Missus," said Louis, "must Paul go to the buildings? Missus, he has a fine brain; he must study!"

Annunziata looked to Paul helplessly.

"Missus, we'll study books together. I'll help him. Don't you see?"

He took Paul's hand. And his voice was tears.

"Paul, the job is not freedom. Your wonderful brain is freedom . . ."

Paul shook his head. And the three wept.

2

Job. A great mass of interwinding stone foundation walls lay waiting to bear building on its rubble shoulders. Out in the street along the sidewalk were shanties for the various trades. Hills of new red brick were side by side with mounds of sand, neat piles of lumber, fresh red-painted steel girders, and stacked piles of cement bags covered with tarpaulins. Men stood about in small groups; some were waiting for the whistle, and others were looking for work.

Fausta, perched upon a foundation wall, was jerking his arms about and shouting orders to the laborers in violent professional rage.

He blew the whistle and Paul was down in the open cellar laying bricks on a wide wall.

"Now then," cried Fausta, "make love to it! Push into it, my children, for this is the money wall!"

Fausta is a man, a paesan, a bricklayer and father of ten children. He himself has been goaded for years by other foremen and will again be shouted at and pushed by foremen. These things the men know. Fausta shouts and imprecates. He leans upon them and they sway and lend themselves. Men lower their eyes and submit to the unwritten law.

"Mortar! Brick! Scaffold here! Scaffold there! Tubs! Put up the line, this is the money wall!"

Before the grace of morning properly rises over earth, before Christians can gather their senses and stretch upward to God's heaven in joy of living, they are bent and twisted into unfeeling reds and grays of Job.

"Beat against it and give it for what! Beautiful-beautifuls, this is the money wall!"

Stab into tub—scoop—swing around—up—swish down—press and push, with bricks and pieces of brick underfoot, stumbling, fighting to keep balance, bobbing, hooking, curving, and praying like a soldier.

"Now it can be seen who are champions! Let it fly," called Fausta. "Knead those sweet little bones in the back, sons of whores!"

Paul laid brick for brick with some of the men. He worked next to the Lucy and at one time kept up with him for a few courses. He ran his stretch of wall right up to the Lucy's part, and it thrilled him. It felt like one of his dreams where he had raced an incredible distance at terrific speed on a road that stretched beyond earth. Quickly he sweated, and human water commingled with lime-mortar and brick. This is the fresh stink of Job, this is the eight-houred daily duel, this is the sense of red and gray, and our bodies are no longer meat and bone of our parents, but substance of Job.

Job became noisier expanding organism—banging, groaning, thudding and pushing UP.

Brick and mortar was to become for Paul as stuff he could eat, and the constant cycle from brick pile and tub to wall was to become a motion that fed upon itself.

With the beginning of each job men, though knowing one another and having raised Job for years, wed themselves to Job with the same new ceremony, the same new energy and fear, the same fierce silence and loss of consciousness, and the perpetual sense of their wrongness ... struggling to fulfill a destiny of never-ending debt. These men were the hardness that would bruise Paul many times. They were the bodies to whom he would be joined in bondage to Job. Job would be a brick labyrinth that would suck him in deeper and deeper, and there would be no going back. Life would never be a dear music, a festival, a gift of Nature. Life would be the torque of Wall's battle that distorted straight limbs beneath weight in heat and rain and cold.

No poet would be there to intone meter of soul's sentence to stone, no artist upon scaffold to paint the vinegary sweat of Christian in correspondence with red brick and gray mortar, no composer attuned to the screaming movement of Job and voiceless cry in overalls.

Sugar and shine would ride high in state and wave a wand . . .

And blood and stone would go on creating World.

Unseen would be the pushing hands and driving shoulders, the ripple-strained stomachs, and gripping feet.

Unsmelled and untasted would be Tenement and manger of worker.

And Paul was now bricklayer-worker . . . welded to the hands whose vibrations could shatter the earth.

That week came summer. It came from afar as soft call of shepherd's horn over long hill. It came a hot sirup to the senses. It brought heavy balm, and men stripped to waist, each giving out his personal manly smell. As they made labor's love to Job, walls rose swiftly, rising into position fast, and to remain thus for generations.

Paul learned with each brick, and no longer had to be told of heights and bonds and lintels and measurements. He did not have to be directed. He moved from wall to wall as bird from limb to limb. It was so hard. It was so heavy!

His back ached from morn to night. It broke and never seemed to come apart. The bending point severed and became a gap connected with trickling, shocking electrical flashes. His thin arms and shoulders blistered and tanned in the baking sun. At night he smelled his arms. They smelled of brown sun and of the lime-flowery flesh of Patsy and the Lucy. It was nourishing and good. And as he lay back in bed among the children his aching joints unloosed to let the hot blood thrill through, leaving him to recede on drug of strain into heavy physical fantasy. . . . That was labor's reward.

Summer's Job was hot and clean. Under season of warmth men were children. They gloried in the bronze of their bare flesh. They bathed in sweat. And the body's dew caught each breeze deliciously. They played pranks and sang. Alfredo the Neopolitan would pause at wheelbarrow, put hand to mouth and joyously lift rough voice:

"Ahhh, lovely is the hour of summer, where
  One beholds the gull freshly fresh in ocean air . . ."

And the men reveling in Nature's joy would join, and midst ring of brick and steel, and glow of sun and dust of building, sing from their hearts about "white breasts like hills of sand on shore of sea."

3

Luigi dressed himself carefully. He sat on the bed, and nurse helped him. In his breast was a newness and a sublimination. Today Annunziata and Paul were coming for him. Home would he go now. Something had hurled him through a strange cycle of hurt. An invisible car had borne him in position of pain and made him cry many times. Now the force had stopped, and he was to alight. Why thrills he when nothing awaits? These big hands no more are protected with callous, and feel empty.

Nurse had had his suit and tie cleaned. She fitted his trousers. Gently and understandingly she flapped the right trouser up and pinned it. She brushed the one shoe and fitted it to his foot.

Even summer's sun had come into the ward and delighted with him.

"Nice day, isn't it, Louie?"

"Too much . . . !" he sighed.

"Glad you're goin' home?"

A mist came over his twisted eye. He wiped his nose.

"I be much-a happy . . ."

She stood up and surveyed the great rough man.

"Comb your hair, Louie. I want to see if you need a little trim."

He did so.

"Just what I thought. Hold still and we'll clip those long ends."

Luigi bent his head respectfully. Nurse clipped quickly around the edges.

"You've got to look right. Isn't that so?"

Luigi nodded.

"Comb it out now. Feel the difference? Of course!"

Nurse was a good woman. She was a worker.

"And you're leaving us just like that! Ah, you don't love me any more, Louie."

"Yes, I like-a you. You be too good-a by me."

His voice lifted.

"I like-a every peoples."

She smoothed his hair and fixed his tie.

"You are a good man, Louie. I wish everything will be all right with you. Honest, Louie, I wish you have no more trouble in your whole life."

He rubbed his hands and thanked her with his eyes.

She set the crutches up under his armpits, and he hobbled off to the toilets. Above the washstands were the big mirrors.

Yes, that was he: tousled hair parted on side, face pallored but shining and fuller now, and the ragged mustache trimmed a bit.

With his rough brown suit pressed, and white shirt and black tie, he admired himself unknowingly at first; but then:

How strange I seem with sticks beneath arms to uphold me.

He stared.

Staring, the figure before him changed.

Before him was a rugged Luigi in great sheepskin, heavy cap, hands in coat pocket, di Nobili cigar in side of mouth, head askance, and twisted eye cocked on right. He looked at Luigi and tried to read him. His large calloused hand came out of coat pocket and reached forward in questioning gesture.

What do you thus? Who separated us? Where go you now without leg where leg should be? How shall it be now, when before with grace of whole limbs you barely gave bread to mouth . . . and now with what courage do you present yourself?

The figure shook its head, and melted away.

The hospitalized Luigi remained. He sighed and hobbled out. In the ward he sat at the window.

There is motion without. God's Christians are ever in the streets. No, the world lacks not legs. But, where belong I rightfully . . . I, man disjoined? Air of Job will no longer nourish me. Only upon pity will I now feed . . . and my lack cannot be measured.

He felt his great square hands. He held them in the sunlight and looked at them closely. He fisted his right hand and slowly hammered it into his left palm. There is strength. There is yet the strength of years against rock. But am I to be carted in wheelbarrow? Or am I to be left squatting on boulder pile to crack stones as nuts?

Ah, would that I could laugh with myself. But O myself, tell me, tell me, how came I thus? How came I thus? And he muttered the question over and over and listening to his voice.

Annunziata and Paul come to claim Luigi. In a moment as this the poor enjoy themselves. One of their own has been freed from pain. They rejoice in meeting. They kiss and embrace. Heart beats to heart. And the tears are as clean showers over the burst of sun. The other poor in the ward wave from bed.

"Good-by . . ." "Stay away from this place." "So long, Louie!"

At the main office a young interne gave them instructions.

"You've a dandy stump there, Louie. Now it's up to you to take care of it."

Luigi did naught but nod.

"See that he rubs it plenty and keeps it clean," said the interne to Paul. "He's got to exercise it. You know, slap it around—but not too hard at first. The pad over the bone requires plenty of blood; therefore it's necessary to watch the circulation. He's got to exercise the stump—well, anyway, just tell him to use his common sense and everything'll be all right."

The three left the vast hospital. Out in the street Luigi feared to look back at it. Paul summoned a taxi.

"A taxi for me?" Luigi's mouth opened.

"Yes," said Paul, "especially for you, Ci Luigi."

They helped him in, and Paul asked the driver to go slowly.

Luigi drew Paul to him and kissed his face.

They rode, and Luigi held his dear ones.

Good, greatly good is the Lord who gives my sister's little Paul to earn. . . . And I have lived to see him bear me in taxi-car . . .

At home Luigi took the children to him and wept. They received him wonderingly. What has Ci Luigi done with his leg? Where is he hiding it?

That night the paesanos came. They brought wine, biscuits and stogies. And Cola brought proudly the cake she had made. By midnight the kitchen floated in tobacco fumes and smelled goodly of wine. Luigi drained many glasses of wine at mouth and wiped red drops of wine from mustache. When one stogie smoked itself down dangerously near his mustache he would stamp it beneath foot, put another in mouth, light it, throw back his head and puff with all his lungs.

Mike gulped his glass, contemplated, and then suggested, "Is it not miraculous how they cut the human animal apart and fix him up again!"

Bastian held out his glass.

"B-bu-bu-but *how* do they finish off one's leg?"

The Lucy answered, "They cop it off with a sharp trowel and then patch up the end with mortar . . ."

"Yes," quested Mike, "could one know how they tie up the end of a living thing . . . ?"

Mike's curiosity became the curiosity of the paesanos.

Luigi, heady with wine and stogie, opened his fly to unloose his trousers and exhibit his stump. The women squealed.

"Ey!" said the Lucy, "What is this romance? Will one's wound bite you? It is not such a wound as you ladies have! If you pigeons desire not to look, it's your own pleasure! Fricassee-fricassaa?"

The women put hands to face and held their breath.

Luigi removed his stump from trousers. With head cocked to right and fuming stogie jutting upward from mouth, he unwrapped the gauze. He did it with a familiar and nonchalant air, and when undone, he laid the stump bare.

The men bent forward. They instinctively put hand between legs. Mike squirmed. "By the Madonna," he said, "it gives me electricity in the intestines."

Bastian waved the tobacco smoke away from the stump.

"S-S-Saint Michael, butchered and s-served up as a meat roast!"

The cicatrix was a concentric vermilion scar through the face of the stump. The joining was two long thin livid lips stitched tightly together; and the head of the stump was tinged a slight blue.

The men pursed their lips and sucked in their breaths. Luigi puffed up smoke to the ceiling.

Gentle old Santos shook his head sorrowfully.

"Does it not pain?" he asked.

Luigi spoke with stogie in mouth, rolling his great head about to evade its burning smoke.

"Ah, dear Santos, whenever the weather changes one degree, I receive the news.—Pins and needles—needles and pins. I am now a Christian thermometer of meat and bone. Ask me the weather, and you shall know." Rolling his head and nodding:

"A curious fact. At the hospital I was informed I would sense pain in the toes that are gone. . . . And by the Madonna, without leg I feel pain in the toes!"

The women could not hold their squeamish pose for long, and soon they lowered hands from face and gazed upon Luigi's stump. Many an "ooh" was sucked in and sigh of pitying "ahh" let out.

Said the Lucy: "The good Lord made the women when he was drunk or asleep, for they are all pa-poo coo-coo!" And he rapped his knuckles on his head.

"And why, Signor Nicholas, why?" asked the Regina.

"Is it wrong if we changed our minds and decide to view the leg of Luigi?" asked Cola. "Are we not Christians?"

Luigi removed stogie from mouth and said respectfully, "And why not? Do not be afraid to look."

He slapped the stump good-naturedly and the women gasped. Soon, the paesanos one by one touched the stump and ran light fearful finger along cicatrix. When Cola placed her plump warm hand on Luigi's stump he caught on fire and shivered all over.

But with night and wine the paesanos found themselves clapping hands and singing. From song to song went they and sang:

"Whey Mari, whey Mari, much slumber have I lost
    for thee . . .
Oh let me once sleep . . . Whey Mari, Ohhhh Mari!"

The Lucy winked at Luigi, nodded toward the joyful breasts of Cola and sighed:

"Ah, mother mine, your nursing habit I yet have not lost . . ."

Luigi's twisted eye danced.

"Now is the tamborine needed!" He lifted full glass to lips, and drank gustfully.

4

Paul's awakening alarm would start Luigi from sleep. Instinctively he would sit up in his narrow cot in the parlor and almost leave the bed for Job. But instantly the realization would come, and he would lie down again, and twist in thought. In hearing he would follow Paul. The squeak of bed, the rustle of dressing, the stiff walking telling of tired back and legs, the distant noise of breakfast in kitchen: Paul's "By, ma," Annunziata's "Abide thy step, my Paul, abide," and his reassuring, "Yes, 'by, ma. Don't worry," the door softly closing, his feet down hall steps, and then Annunziata to parlor window to watch her Paul away.

"Brother, why suffers your spirit?"
Luigi shook his head.
"Sister, the holiday of my accident shall never leave me. And not only my limb has been dismembered. It was not enough that you have to bear the tragedy of Geremio . . . and now my woe should press your heart."
"You are ours, dear brother. Let no burdening thought cloud your breast. Did you not yourself say we shall live, a way shall be found, and our Christ ever with us?"
He nodded.
"Brother, hearten thee for we shall be as sticks bound in union. We shall divide our loaf. We shall warm each other and be as one . . . as is our Christ at one with us."
The great Luigi became a background of help and understanding. He occupied himself the day long fixing, adjusting, cleaning about the flat, and minding Johnny and Geremino. They, the little ones, quickly learned to

love him and tug at his mustaches. At night he would listen eagerly to Paul's tales of Job.

"And how went it today, little uncle? Did you prove the son of Geremio?"

"This afternoon I laid front brick next to Master Nicholas the Lucy. It was a Flemish bond, a wonderful bond. And I didn't make any mistakes! Tomorrow we'll be story high with the first floor."

"And how much does your back hurt? Shall I rub it? Come, I will tingle it for you."

". . . No, Ci Luigi, it does not bother me very much."

"And who said what of whom?"

"Well . . . the Lucy told Godfather Vincenz that a Chinaman married an Eskimo, and that was how Godfather was born—"

It smote Luigi to see Paul's thin arms and the flushed tiredness of his face.

God above, why cannot I give to him my useless great arms and might?

The afternoons were dull and fearful. They brought a conscious emptiness followed with boiling restlessness. To whom could he say: My muscles strain for Job. My mind distempers me, and these bowels burst for woman?

I have ever myself with me. I cannot forget myself. The streams flow about and go by, and I am damned. I am now a race of man apart.

I have lost my small place in world, and it is not in the heart of men to know this hunger within, as even I do not love Luigi for his fate. But who pursues me? What nemesis feeds upon such poor beasts as I? Why ask I, when to these miserable brains a voice tells that no gesture from the living can reconcile my questioning?. . . Alone am I . . . He would suck hungrily on his di Nobilis and try to lose himself. I must work!

It was not long before he sat at the kitchen window cutting embroidery. Cola had become a frequent visitor, and she suggested it. She had been earning her existence since her husband's death by doing home work on textile goods from the mills.

"It is simple," said she to Luigi. "Run the scissors along the edge of the embroidery and separate it from the plain cloth. See, upon the plain cloth is stitched the embroidery, and we must—well here, like this—"

It was something for him to do, and it would bring in a dollar or so each day!

Annunziata's kitchen became a small gathering place where the widows sat in circle busily cutting through rolls of embroidery. At first Luigi was slow. His great fingers worked the tiny scissors tremblingly for fear he would mar the material. It was Cola who patiently aided him, and after a few days he was able to steer his scissors. He looked forward to each morning when the widows, aided by some of the children, would bring the large rolls of embroidery from the mill. Cola's warm dark voice in the hall would send him hobbling about nervously in search of comb for hair, tie for shirt, or soap for hands. In the hours when fingers maneuvered swiftly and scissors' edge sliced through embroidery, much was said. Conchettina's second masculine had mumps; two barrels of Octavio's wine had soured; it looked like matrimony for Passwater's first feminine; the next hearing to be held at the Compensation Bureau . . . these and other news and opinions, the while Luigi remained silent and respectful. It was always Cola's voice that sounded most and richest. She was quickest to mirth and tears. There was a succulent dark womanliness to her that kept Luigi in continual condition of faint. She was an excellent worker, and generous. She was the first to bring out from oilcloth shopping bag the bottle of wine, the bread, or cake. Delightful were the afternoons when hands moved fast, and flagon and hard peppery biscuits and salted yellow beans in water stood by. And it was thrilling to Luigi when the women would sing in their soprano voices (Cola's always warm and dramatic) the old canzonettas of Abruzzi: there be-

ing the songs that told of "That little peasant mine,"
"The coffee cup tête-à-tête," "The heart tick-tock alike
to clock," and "The wheel of life that went round and
round." Luigi's shy presence lent to the gatherings a
moral tone. Whenever they spoke of facts sexual they
went about it in delicate manner which they employed
with certain joy. And if Cola forgot herself and came
out with hearty indiscretion, Luigi would lower his head
and profoundly study the embroidery.

"Yesterday came a vendor of sacred things. I pur-
chased from him a new crucifix. I did not need it. He is
an old man. I would never send him away without
something."

Angelina said it significantly.

"And if you had not money to purchase?"

"Ah, then I would charge. But never-never would I
send him away."

" . . . And why?"

"Why? Beautiful Madonna mine. I will recount a fact.
Know you the tale of the woman who cast a vendor of
holy things from her door? No? Well, it so happened
that a woman told to people there was no God above."

"A woman said that?"

"Yes. She believed in nothing. It came about that she
was with big belly. One day an old man came to the
door. He was a good soul who went about from Christian to Christian selling pictures of Our Lord and the
Saints and articles of the Church. 'Who are you and
what do you wish?' asked she. 'Will you not help me
and buy from me a beautiful thing of God? See, good
signora, here I have the Virgin in glass.' 'I care not if
you had her and all her relatives in gold. Go!' Now this
good soul said to her: 'If you have not the money, I will
let you have it as a gift. Here, I present it to you. And
God bless you.' What do you think she did? She pushed
him from the door and with breast of beast said: 'I do
not need God in my house!' Said the poor old man at
her door: 'If you need not God, whom do you need, the
Evil One?' 'Yes!' answered she."

Angelina paused, and then proceeded in voice of doom.

"Came the day when she took to bed. Now mind you, she had forgotten about the vendor of holy things. All right. Then with midwife doing her duty, and husband near by, that which was in her belly began to come forth."

She paused and looked from face to face.

'And what do you think came out of this woman who denied God?"

The scissors stopped for Angelina.

"Out leaped a real baby Devil, horns and all!"

The woman gasped. They signed the cross against the Evil One, and then repeated it upon their bellies.

—Although they had heard the tale many times.

5

The day before Christmas was brilliantly cold. The streets were enameled with frozen snow. The hard air hurt the temples, and a sharp light wind transparently sliced the cheeks. On the scaffold noses burned and eyes watered.

"Pork of the Messiah," gasped Nazone, "my ends are turned to sticks!"

He blew his hands and kicked his feet against the wall.

"Put your head between your legs and lay bricks!" shouted Fausta as he hopped about for warmth.

"Eskimos wouldn't work in this temperature," complained Nazone.

"Dig!"

"It's too cold to lay brick!"

"Dig, jackass, dig!"

"Look villain, the scaffold planks crack with cold 'neath footstep, the bricks weep with frost, and the wall is swollen crooked. . . . But tell me—what are we Christians, men or not?"

"Twist that female tongue around trowel-handle and lay brick with it! Blood of Saint Break-your-neck, don't remain gazing at me! Dig into the wall, pantaloon full of manure!"

Nazone cast his trowel to scaffold.

"Bad luck on the Troywhore of a mother who spat you forth to plague honest fathers of family—curses to the day I set forth on your job forsaken by the Saints—"

Fausta tore his hat and threw it down; kicking it madly he yelled, "Maledicted is the Jew Christ who allowed your germination!"

A minute later he was conversing genially with the architect who had summoned him about the freezing brickwork.

Said Bastian, "M-m-mother mine, if we do not stop working soon—if we do not stop working soon they will f-f-find us stuck to wall open-mouth and rigid as breeches on clothesline . . ."

Paul was blue and stupefied with cold. His head and limbs felt artificial, breathing pinched his lungs, and his marrow was coursed with needling shocks. The mortar iced and clung encrusted to his trowel, and when he dumped it on the wall it crumbled. The wet mortar in the wall froze hard. It froze rapidly, and in expanding bulged the wall dangerously. At noon the men quit.

Surcease from relentless wall—escape from cold. Men fumble down the ladders tools in hand—release speaks not in words, but with slight sheepish grin. At first-floor level they push against wall to urinate; stung bloated red fingers struggle through the buttons of stout overall, trousers and underbreeches. Small clouds of steam from wall as in stable—Men shake themselves and sigh. "This shanty is a tomb!"

In quick half-hour bricks and mortar into shanty— here, there, ho-ho and the sure hands of Fausta and the Lucy send up a tight brick stove from floor and through ceiling . . .

"Cocko! in the old country style—with compartment for baking lunch!"

"Paper—wood!—Jump!"

"Flame and smoke for the love of God!"

Cracked mortar-stained hands drip with juice of hot spicy lunch, and reach toward stove with warmth-hungry stretched fingers. "Cocko, *this* can be called *Life!*"

Anxious flaming fire. Warmth good warmth for backs hands feet heads to unjell and tingle ticklingly. The confined shanty barely contains the leathery brick faces, but—with its rough dusty walls and floor, the friendly stove, the strewn tools, the thick clothes, the strong-muscled chests and emphatic arms, the smell of tough bodies and full-throated voices—is Paradise . . . at the foot of Job who stands alone—austere—colder than the cold.

"Who will go for the wine?"

"Send Octavio!"

"Yes!"

"Get at least two gallons—"

"What are we to do with two gallons, wash our eyes?"

"Five gallons!"

"What'll I get it with, this salami? Talk to me with money!"

"All right, cockos," commanded Fausta, "throw up half a bean each." He collected the money. "Go to Gennaro's, instruct him that if he gives you the bottom of the barrel as he did last time—we'll take it out on the fat behind of his wife!"

"How am I to carry five gallons? On my head?"

"Fetch it in a wheelbarrow—bundle it with paper and cement bags—make sure the police catch you! Now, fly!"

Paul was sent on errands for tobacco, di Nobilis, hard biscuits, and roasted chick peas. When Octavio returned Fausta let Paul partake of a sip, gave him a bagful of biscuits and beans and sent him home.

From healthy, ready mouth to mouth and soon the jugs were forlorn—empty ... squat rusty teeth ground bean and biscuit ... fist resounded in palm ... bellow-lungs consumed smoking tobacco ... red-eared dark heads tossed ... shoulders swayed ... neck veins bulged ... cannon shouts shot the shanty air:

"Yes! ... No! ... One at a time! ... Shut up!!! ... Octavio! Scaffolding dog! Wine! Wine! *Wine!*"

The third time Octavio went for wine the short winter afternoon had slipped away unnoticed, and he went careening through the streets, jugs exposed and bawling:

"Take me to that home—erino of mine—ine, for I no
    longer see ...
Carry me to that little house and drop me in court-a
    number three-e. ..."

Two kerosene lamps lumed the tobacco fog.

"I'll lay brick for brick with any son-of-a bum in this state! In this nation!—Anybody in the cylindrical u-niverse!"

"Who ever even hinted you were a bricklayer?"

"And are *you* a bricklayer?"

"I? I am the flower of the art!"

"Excuse *me*! ... The flower of *this* art!"

On the floor of the shanty imaginary buildings were built, recalled, and kicked around. Finally one said:

"Cocko! My guts are full of bricks. I wish I had never seen one—ooph-phah!"

"Just!"

"Curses on the dear spirit of that departed old father who first took me to scaffold ..."

"—and not to go to school I picked up the trowel. To this day I cannot sign my name."

"This is the worst trade under the sun!"

"I should have taken a good physic instead of disfiguring myself with matrimony," lamented Octavio.

"Ah—the wife—a squishy squid that veritably swallows one whole . . . !"

The Lucy spat in his hands, slapped them and exclaimed savagely, "Yet nothing better has been invented for the human beast; nothing delights the spine, nor sugars the bones better than *she.* . . . Ah, I could see myself right now!"

Nazone finished a long drink, reeled into the center of the shanty and proclaimed eloquently with hand over heart, "In this world there is no animal more beautiful than the Woman." He rolled his eyes upward and kissed his fingers.

Hunt-Hunt shook his head.

"Now look at this schoolboy poet; are we Englishmen who talk-talk and sport caramel in eye? 'Bye-bee,' I feel like a tasty bit of whore proverbially now!"

Alfredo put finger to mouth and winked.

"Happy thought! . . . Only around the corner," he whispered, "a Polish woman and her two daughters—ah, specimens of femalia—very fine! Polite, and character sympathetic! Very fine! The mother even wears silk stockings—sometimes a veil, like a noblewoman—fine! First-class!"

Nazone's huge nostrils went up; the Lucy's fierce eye gleamed. Alfredo puckered his lips.

"And as clean as a whistle, I tell you." He pushed back his cap, placed palms on knees. "What's said—make we this little voyage?"

Sturdy spines bent forward, molars clamped, horny hands clutched jug handle, wine rivered, knees pressed together, and lust spread as scalding enema in bowels.

Near midnight the nineteen of them headed back to the shanty arm in arm, stogies blazing against the night, cap a-jaunt, footstep slack and manner philosophic.

"We should not have gone," muttered Santos.

They filed into the shanty. Orangepeel-Face heaped the stove with wood and warmed his front. "Ah she kissed me with a sentiment—mother mine, what a mouth! what a feeling!"

"Hush," said Nazone. "There sound the chimes of the midnight service. . . . For pity that we are like rabid swine and not with knee in pew . . ."

They became silent.

"And Our God Jesu the Son of Mary," continued Nazone, "is now born. This is a sin, really a sin."

"Cocko," said Fausta softly, "you know, it appears our dear little Nazone should have donned the cassock. . . ."

Remorse is a precious instant and then—no more. Praise brought the nod to Nazone's chin and flickering sparks to eye.

Said Alfredo: "Put a finger in his mouth."

"Ah, sweet is our Nazone . . ."

"Patron Saint of the whorehouses."

Nazone struggled to keep somber.

"Face of priest . . . veritably," remarked old Santos.

"Look at him," said the Lucy, "the shamefaced Tartuffe." And he jammed his finger into Nazone. Nazone howled, and each way he turned another fingered him.

"Blasphemy! Animals, you'll roast forever in Purgatory!"

Hunt-Hunt measured Nazone dreamily. He whispered to Fausta. Fausta's eyes opened, and he twirled his mustaches.

"And why not?"

The Lucy heard, and grinned, "He merits it."

They motioned to Octavio and instructed him on the side.

"Sure-sure . . . it will only take five minutes." He gathered his tool sack and left the shanty.

The men paid special attention to Nazone. He gloried.

"Man," he lectured, "though of the basest class, should observe the spir-it-tual. . . ."

Fausta feigned tears and wailed raucously, "He is a good man—nay, a sainted one . . . oh oh—what a man beatific!"

Nazone lifted the jug and drew heavily.

"Ah, paesans, this is not subject that one jokes with, for—"

The shanty door opened and Octavio lugged in a clumsy timber.

"What has he there?" asked Santos.

It was a large stout cross made of two cement-studded scaffold planks.

"J-J-J-Jesu G-Giuseppe e' Mari," exclaimed Bastian, "what have we . . . a c-c-crucifixion! Who is to adorn the scaffold cross?"

Nazone clung to his jug and looked about.

"Nazone sonofabitch!" cried Fausta, "prepare your-self, for only the good are crucified!"

They fell upon him and began undressing him.

"Stop! You do not realize—for charity's sake—I'll die of cold—oooh—bastards!"

They soon had him down to his long red underwear and shoved the cross upon his shoulder.

"Please, for the love of those children who depend on me in the old country—do not permit this outrage—this is immortal sin—let not your souls be soiled with this sacrilege—I say enough is enough—I shall lose this patience and blood will fly!"

They pushed him around the shanty and followed in drunken procession. He protested, then compromised that for each length of shanty he be refreshed from the jug. They did likewise. Through besotted tears they fixed the cross to the wall and roped him to it. The Lucy fashioned a crown of rope with nails pointing up-ward and placed it upon his head.

"I am dead of cold . . ." Nazone wept maudlinly. Orangepeel loaded the stove with dry timber. It roared, and the shanty became thick with smelly heat.

"Now I am dead of fire . . . oh oh this poor Christ," wept Nazone. Fausta pulled the long red underwear from him and left him tied to the cross plump naked and wearing only shoes and socks. They held the jug to his mouth and he drank and drank. Near the blazing stove, belly round with red drink, Nazone looked about at the revolving faces and then dropped head to breast.

They forgot him and gurgled wildly from the few remaining jugs. Alfredo opened his mouth wide and sang *Without a Mother!* As he sang he wrung his hands and cried with rending woe. They sang and fell against the shanty walls. One sang a bawdy tale, another a hymn.

"Allay! Our Nazone makes the slumber-ell."

"Let's awaken Nazone, our dear Nazone!"

"He doesn't move . . . perhaps he is gone!"

Octavio emptied a jug over Nazone's head. He raised heavy head, shivering and gasping, "What has happened? What goes on? What is this?"

Fausta tickled him. They all tickled him and he laughed and cried and wriggled and moaned: "Stop—I am dead—my arms are broken off—hahaha—stop I am sick . . . He he ho haha—police!—oh, my death on your heads—ha ha ha—ooooh—"

The louder he bawled the more they laughed. His nose dripped and tears rolled all over his shiny flush cheeks. Fausta dipped biscuit in wine and painted circles on him. He yelled unintelligibly until he gulped and vomited gushes of sour wine and lunch into Fausta's face. Then tight reeling muscles pushed out storms of open throated laughter stomach kicking laughter fist clenching chest shaking laughter that made the stove laugh and the cross laugh and bulged the shanty walls with crazy laughing laughter.

6

Annina had hunted in many stores before she found the small tree. Luigi set it up upon the washtub in the corner of the kitchen, for the other rooms were frigid.

Paul had planned excitedly with Annunziata about presents for the children. Fifty cents each! He spent hours in the five and tens, and Louis accompanied him.

Geremino and Johnny snoozed in the old baby carriage. Joie, Giorgio, and Lucia cut tissue paper and sorted tinsel while Annina carefully hung the fragile Christmas balls. Annunziata busily mixed flour, yeast, milk and eggs while Luigi at table gave the dough thumping blows; the dough that would be rolled into strips and fried in sizzling olive oil.

"Children mine, do not cast eye upon them."

"Why not, mama?"

"It is a sin. . . . And they will not come good!"

They fry, sending out a golden oily fragrance, and brown into thick and thin bubbly misshape.

Tonight, after Church, the little ones will make believe they sleep so that "Sondy Glause" will race over tenement roof tops with his reindeer from the North Pole and leave the children of Geremio wondrous presents—who knows, perhaps the billion-dollar electric trains Joie saw in the store window on the Avenue—and until then their hearts will grow as big as their chests with anticipation for why shouldn't their dreams come true!

Tonight the family will go to Saint Prisca and under lofty Gothic arches they'll be awed by a great magic organ. Hearts and souls will tremor forth in "Silent Night, Holy Night." Incense will reach the tongue like smoking brown spice. Tall yellow candles will burn generously and smell of tallowlike butter cakes. Father John will perform sacred ceremony of Mass and as he calls in Latin tone, from choir's heaven will wave back his call. In majestic silk and gold vestment he will deliver a beautiful story of the coming of the King of the Jews. Something will withdraw harsh strength and bring lit melted faces. The Donovans, the Farabuttis, the Lobans, the shabby, the debtors, will gather at the right of the altar and kneel with gentle tremulous touch to the Child Jesus in manger with outstretched baby arms. Mother Mary and Joseph will stand absorbed in understanding respect. The wise men will behold the star, and the beasts of stable will remain in position of content. They will file to the large white body whose carpenter's muscles strain and weep blood from greedy spikes, and mingle their kisses upon his foot. And Annunziata will pause before him. "Oh, my Christ—on this your natal day I come without him ... my Geremio ..."

7

Paul, wearing man's clothes and having broad brick-flattened hands, now looked no more than his slender fifteen. Brick in left hand and trowel in right, he had cherished them as Saint to Faith:

The faster better bricklayer I become the more I earn.

Strength in the thin arms and fingers commanded red brick into wall with sure note ... and he was respected by men of Job.

Job's measure of seasons brought tar-pinked hue to cheek. Constant plumb and level's plane set eagle's gleam to his eyes and developed precision sense. But never did spine forgive wall's hunger, and at whistle-blow when Job sent him home to Annunziata and the children he arched back and walked column straight. He was proud that God had given him hand, back, and eye to bring home food, proud that he earned almost as much as the thick-wristed men, proud that he studied blueprints and construction, proud that he felt beauty in his form and soul, proud of his wonderful family.

Three nights a week he went to school. Often while listening to the instructor his world would float from him and an indistinct pressure stood by him whispering: Walls—bearing—job—twenty-inch footings—upward thrust—diagonal tension—yes you are listening Paul—electrolysis—bending moment—concrete contraction—the job—that Job garage job apartment job brick job job *job*. ...

Riding home late in the subway the tunnel would humble-bumble-rumble: sliding resistance—bond stress—transverse elasticity—live load—dead load . . .

And the faces about him looked like this kind of a job and that kind of a job . . .

Nazone had long proved a godfather to Paul. He always did his best to make Paul's work less strenuous by helping him lift the heavy cement blocks, building footscaffolds for him, lending him tools and doing many little favors. He also tried to shield him from the men's broad tongues. "Remember," he would admonish, "he is a child and widow's son; soil not the purity of his mind!"

Paul had come to hear much, but it all seemed talk and a thing distant.

This sultry week in July the men moved as though clubbed. The mouth of every little pore distended helplessly, and when one man accidentally touched another's wet body he was repelled.

"Touch me not!"

"Who desires to feel your stinking meat anyway?"

"*I*, stink?"

"All right, all right, leave me in peace. For pleasure, do not work too close to me."

"Then each hound smells his own."

The Lucy wrapped handkerchief around neck. Down in the street old Santos toiled at the mortar-box, sprig of peppermint plant in mouth and mane of white hair cresting in the sunlight; while Alfredo wore striped mariner's undershirt and fashioned a hat of newspaper with lining of green leaves for his bald head. The younger men worked stripped to the belt. The men called for water and blasphemed halfheartedly: "Water-boyo!" . . . "The soul that morta-lizes you! Where is this water!"

"Observe, godson," said Nazone, "the sweat off my nose has wet out my cigarette."

He stood up, wiped his dripping forehead, and placed his handkerchief back in his cap. Paul noted that he did not have his usual gustiness.

"Is it too hot for you?" he asked.

Nazone mumbled, "Veritably, I am scalding—the sun has plumbed its fire directly through my head—" He lowered his eyes and busily re-engaged himself laying brick.

Waves of amber white simmered through Job. Steel gave off painty metal rance, scaffold breathed of growing forest ash, brick sent out crusty red bake of clay, from mortar traced gray flower of virgin sand, fresh lime and cement, and workers smelled of flesh brownly.

At noon they rested under the only tree in the adjoining lot.

Bastian removed his saturated shirt.

"A-a-and now it is the f-fiftieth time I hang this sheet to d-d-dry."

The Lucy balanced his lunch in one hand and contemplated it disgustedly.

"That polyp of mine has given me peppers and eggs again!"

He raised his arm to throw it away.

Alfredo fanned his bald spot and remarked:

"I would do me a bathe in mid-ocean." As he thought of it he closed his eyes. "Ahhh, how I could throw this Christian pelt into the sea so cool and green!"

Nazone fidgeted constantly. Often, he rubbed his groin and left to urinate.

"What ails this Nazone?" asked the Lucy as Nazone disappeared once more behind the job.

Octavio stuck out his lower lip.

"I don't know, my boyos . . . but he walks like a camel!"

The entire week, day lapping day, the heat glowered. Perspiration oozed from Paul's palms and oiled the trowel handle. When rubbing his wet palms on his work trousers the glassy brick dust abrased harshly. The sun stared with brutal insistence, and at night the great hot sphere reflected explosively through Paul's dreams.

An American bricklayer, "Hicky Nicky the floatin' bricky," scooped up a streamlet of sweat from his navel and said to Paul, "These flats break your hump; you're either laying bricks down on your face or a foot over your head. You oughta work on the steel jobs—at least they jack the swingin' scaffold and keep the wall waist-high."

On the very hottest day, at starting time the temperature read ninety-five.

"I am fatigued before I pick up the trowel . . ."

"Madonn, what a potato I have!"

Fausta stood in the shade and canted: "Now then . . . this life requires a little volition—allay!"

The men lugged themselves about dopily. Nazone's face read the annoyance of pain, and as he bent for brick and mortar he winced and groaned. Paul worried about him.

"Nothing at all, godson . . . just a slight distemper of the a-kidneys . . . perhaps the fried eggplants I ate for lunch a few days ago. . . . In reality, fried eggplants are bad with this unreasonable weather. . . . Work, godson, and do not concern yourself of me—'tis nothing—aie!" and punching his groin he muttered:

"Malcreance of pleasure!"

A fierce clinging stickiness closed the air and men's exudence offended greasily. Suddenly, from the pullulating heaviness burst spumes of mad whirling gnats. They pricked viciously, and the men beat and scratched with mortared hands and trowels against their dust-slimed bodies. Nazone's great nose swung about as he dodged the wild gnats, and he slashed the trowel through the air at them.

"Combined torment! This woe in bowels—this heat that broils Christians—and now these added thousand furies! Ouchouch—aie—one hundred thousand evils of inferno. . . ."

Fausta set Alfredo to smoking away the gnats with burning tar-paper.

The water pail was passed and the men drank copiously. Nazone drank and was about to hand the pail to

Paul when suddenly he withdrew the pail and emptied it over the scaffold.

"The water was a-dirty, godson—full of cement—" He sent Octavio for a pail of fresh water and told him to wash out the pail thoroughly. But Paul had seen the water and knew that it was clean.

The Lucy winked to Paul.

"Your godfather washed his feet without his socks on and now has a dirty nose."

Nazone threatened the Lucy behind Paul's back, and Paul caught the grimace.

"A-godson, pay no attention to Master Nicholas . . . he is a clown—yes, haha he does say funny things at times. . . . Really, that water had sand or bits of brick into it . . . and then it was warm . . . yes . . . oy, this groin!" He took from his pocket a small bottle and drank from it, making a wry face. "See godson, even medicine I must perforce employ for this-a groin—"

The Lucy tapped a brick down with a flourish. Little cracks came into his face and he sniggered, "Your godfather is now an American, first-class."

"What—why?"

Nazone looked over to the Lucy and shook his loose plump cheeks furiously.

"You do not understand? You no fricasee-fricasaa? No? The Americans like yourself call it 'claps'!"

Paul looked at the Lucy open-mouthed. His eyes burned, and he wanted to blow his nose. Nazone glared at the Lucy and bit his lips.

Paul felt weak and saw his trowel wavily. He wanted to cry. The Lucy's face changed; he nudged Paul and said in low jocular voice, "Every man gets his papers sooner or later—. . . it's like a bad cold . . ."

Nazone turned to the wall. It was hard to see. He and Paul worked silently. Soon, the heat gathered into low black clouds. Lightning shot through them, and huge drops slapped down abandonedly. The men grabbed their tools and jumped down under the scaffolds; but Paul and his godfather were slow.

Leaving the shanty Paul heard his godfather's voice seeking him through the rain. After supper, though he did not want to see him, he wandered to where Nazone lived. Paul went to his room. The door was ajar and he entered. He realized there was no one in. He looked around. The room was quite dark but he noticed the bed, chair, and his godfather's clothes and an old tool bag. Over the bed were photographs. As he was leaving, the light from the hallway revealed them more clearly. He halted. He went back into the room and up close to the bed. Pinned on the wall fanwise were French post-card pictures. He gazed and could not move. The pictures came to life and held him with a substance that pulled up from his toes. Their obscenity gripped his eyes and chilled his senses. Something within drummed, his mouth dried. He backed to the door, turned, but kept staring over the bed until he had closed the door behind him. It was raining heavily. Through the pour he saw the voluptuous bodies signing to him in flaunting positions.

At the doorway of Tenement he bumped into Gloria. Her body breathed a blonde milky dampness to him. Something within waved up high. He shut his eyes and wanted to fly.

"Inna hurry, Paul?"

He pulled his jacket about him and raced up the steps.

In the kitchen he removed his wet clothes and dried himself. As he combed his hair in the little mirror over the sink Annina looked up from her ironing. She watched him.

"Mama, look, Paul is getting fuller . . . and muscles like a man."

Yesterday's skies rained July away and today was vivid in August splendor. Job lay under washed blue fields and dry sunniness. Men of Job were Nature, and health's exuberance was their joy. All was clean. In the sun Paul tanned deeply, and his breast muscles showed rounder. Day's richness surged him with feel of trowel brick and mortar along wall, and he gloried in his body's labor. Building took his effort but gave reality. Building possessed his mind, but gave Divinity. He played the instrument of his growing power. Quick! up goes this corner! Fast! in goes this arch! Up! up reaches this wall! There was a motion to living, a dazzling nourishing rainbow of earth and man's bone and flesh . . . a fusion within of strength into a propelling beautiful new desire. With the intermission of noon Paul turned the hose on his head, back and chest.

How good!

The sun quickly drank the wet from him and left the bronzed skin radiant. When Paul joined the men Nazone occupied himself with his lunch in silent embarrassment. Paul sat with Nicky, and Nicky told him he was lined up as shop steward on a big steel job downtown. The thought of working on skyscrapers fascinated Paul.

"What's it like? Can you get me on?"

"Come around when they hang the swingin' scaffolds and I'll give the gaffer a buzz. Yeah kiddo—big steel is *the* nuts!"

"Do you really think I should leave the flats?"

Nazone kept his distance from Paul and furtively looked over. Paul met his eyes and smiled kindly. In the afternoon they laid brick together on the same pier. Nazone attempted to do more than his share and relieve Paul as he had always done, but Paul easily did his half and laid a few for his godfather. They said little. And Paul knew there was not much they could say now.

At quitting whistle he decided that he would go to work with Nicky on the big steel job. He felt grown. Striding along the street he raised his brown hand to his nose and smelled it. It was like a man's. He went down into the subway and boarded a crowded train. As the train traveled the people shifted and he found himself up against a woman. He moved back, but as the train rolled along unevenly it became impossible to keep from being pressed against her. He held his hands up near his lapels and tried not to look into her face. He read as many advertisements as he could. When he lowered his eyes he found her looking into his face. She smiled.

Was she smiling for him, or was she thinking of something to herself? She was a buxom middle-aged woman with mascaraed lids and rouged freckled face. He maintained himself respectfully and held his head back. She kept finding his eyes. The painted mouth breathed lipstick and whisky. When the train bent around a curve she fell heavily upon him and remained there after the train righted itself. Her body brought him an immediate disturbing message. He shut his eyes. Spongy breasts pulsed against his chest. Galvanic trills enveloped his nerves. The French pictures surrounded him ... He opened his eyes. She was smiling with beady red-rimmed eyes. His breath was helpless, and he found himself smiling at her painfully.

The train roared. Tired faces lay one atop another. His throat dried and his heart stretched. He could not stand erect, and his stomach galled to break. The face before him panted swiftly in heightened set. The train slowed and tugged to a stop. His body shuddered—and he fought through the crowd saying:

"Pardon me—pardon me—"

Out on the street he wanted to walk and walk.

* * *

At home his appetite was not for food. He left the table and went down into the street. He could not rest.
He felt he had to clench his fists and jaws and run! By
the stoop a pink gingham dress ran by him. It was Gloria. He sat down on the bottom step near the railing.
Gloria. The clean scent of the Olsen washing. Pink
gingham. Gloria. Playing with Felix, brother Joie,
Chicken, and three other boys. She ran and threw herself about with lovely wanton strength. Now she let
Felix grab hold and twist her—she protested indistinctly
. . . then she laughed tonelessly, and sent him tripping.

"Gloria's it!"

Gloria! Gloria! Gloria!

The boys drew round to bait her. She tossed her
head, and remained still. Suddenly she lunged aside, and
then about; her dress swirled up and the smooth muscled limbs solidly thrust the ground. Wildly she
charged, the blonde braids tumbling and her lithe broad
hips impelling her in joyed momentum.

From above, Missus Olsen called, "Sis-ter! Sister,
you've jumped aroun' enough now . . . come upstairs,
sisssterrr!"

Gloria looked up obediently and came toward Tenement. Paul gasped within as she came to the stoop. She
stopped by him and scratched her stomach. He felt his
eyes staring hard. He wanted to get up and run. What
would she say? What could he say to her? . . . He was a
bricklayer—a man—he must not sit there! She presented
herself directly in front of him . . . her breasts heaving
slightly and her broad hips swaying . . . pushing . . .

The low-muted voice asked:

"Where yuh been alla time . . . where do yuh stay alla
time?"

Quietly he told her he worked on buildings and studied.

To which she echoed, "Ohh," and thrust herself
within inches of him.

"Dontcha like to play with us . . . no more?"

"Sister! Sister, come up! If yuh wanna talk with Paul,

bring him upstairs. . . . Hullo, Paul, come up with sister."

"Dontcha like to play no more, huh?" and Gloria wiped her damp face.

He suddenly found himself perishing in a great desert, and his senses crying for her milky moistness: Gloria! Gloria!

"Come up with me, huh?"

How could he talk with her when he wanted to call her name aloud and clasp her like tree to earth.

"You ain't mad, huh?"

"No no . . . I'm always busy . . ." And he felt his voice a stupid thing.

"Ohh."

A lucent drop of perspiration sugared down the sheen of her inside thigh and over the slope of knee. He watched it. Down along the golden spun little hairs it glistened, down the line of splendid calf, down the quickly tapering sturdy ankle, down into the white cotton sock.

She went up, and he followed her awkwardly.

"Hullo, Paul—ie!" welcomed Missus Olsen. "Sit on the couch an' make yuhself t'home. . . . And yuh sister, go take a bath—yuh're sweatin' like a pig."

"Aw gee . . . ?"

"Now sisss-ter! Do as I tell yuh. Yuh'll find the washpan under the sideboard—an' I'll bring yuh some nice hot water."

Gloria stood, legs apart, scratching her stomach and grinning. She swung about. Her mother watched her leave.

"Sister's gettin' nice an' big, ain't she, Paulie—eh, Paulie?"

He nodded. She noticed him for a moment and then lifted a large basin of hot water from the stove.

"Yuh're lookin' fine—nne Paulie." And she carried the basin to the dining room.

He heard Gloria undressing—the splashing water—Missus Petersen's hand wacking Gloria. . . . Then she boomed through the flat: "Poppa! Pop-ppa! come and scrub sister!" Paul and Missis Olsen were alone.

"Whew," she gasped, "it's gettin' hot as hell in here!"

She went to the window and pushed it up. The sun-rays illumined her great body through the cheeseclothy shift.

She is Gloria's mother—from that thick-limbed mound was issued Gloria—she was Gloria at one time—the broad clean stench, the grayed blonde hair, the great dark-brown nipples—

She chattered away in loud rumbling tones while she worked. He nodded and in sordid hypnotism followed the constant move of her elephantine proportions ... their roll and pull knotting him. That will be Gloria: thick-jointed, whelming rounds. His stomach was drawing the color from his face. He felt ill. Gloria older and expanded—Gloria a sprawling worked earth— His bowels were petrifying and reaching up through him ...

Gloria entered. She stood resplendent: bare-legged in pink cotton wrap-around—the dull laughing eyes, the level white teeth and heavy chin.

"Ahhh," exclaimed her mother admiringly, "come here, sister, an' lemme fix yuhre hair."

She combed the unwoven gold lovingly, and petted her.

"Does sister feel nice an' clean—hmn ... yes, sure she does—lemme smell yuh—hmnn ahhh—"

Why do I look dumbly at the floor?

Missus Olsen prepared the evening sandwiches, cake and coffee.

"Eat, Paulie, eat—yuh can stand a few pounds!"

The food tasted as healthy as the Olsens. But when swallowed it met his bitter stomach and remained lumpy—heavy-heavy in the startled flaming region.

Missus Olsen pulled Gloria to her side, kissed her ear, and told her to join Paul, for ". . . he looks so lonely."

Gloria's immediate presence made him drunk, tense. She chewed her liverwurst sandwich and licked her thumbs. . . . He could smell vividly the clean cotton

wrap-around—the blonde wine of her hair—the newness of her mouth and her eating . . . and her flesh that
smothered.

So near—so close—and his blood punching in raging
rise.

"Why're yuh not sayin' nothin', Paul—don' yuh like
t' talk?"

". . . Well . . . Yes . . . I was just thinking . . ."

"Thinkin'?"

". . . . Well . . ."

"What about?"

". . . just . . . thinking. . . ."

This is wrong . . . Lord forgive me—forgive me!

His senses had become single tongues of fire . . .
threatening to dissolve and consume him. And he sat
. . . a burning stone. She leaned her shoulder against
him.

O God in Heaven I cannot help it. I cannot!

Olsen sat on the other side of Gloria. He nudged her.
She shoved him.

"Ahh naow sisster tinks she iss getting sooo strong to
putsch me—hahh? . . . well, maybe she tinks dat—
sohh!" and he twisted her arm.

"Don't tease sister, poppa," egged Missus Olsen. She
winked to Gloria: "An' sister is so weak . . . eh,
sisterrr?"

Gloria squirmed in low protesting murmur. And Paul
knew she desired the brunting struggle.

"Ohh yah?" exclaimed Olsen as he gave way. "Sohh
yah?" He permitted her to get hold, and as she push-
mauled the couch shook.

"Py yimminy, sissster has got me. . . . Yah, she hass."
With vicious speed he twisted her about. Her white
limbs leaped past Paul and she threw her giantess self
backward to pin her father beneath her—her wrap-
around unfurling, and stunning upon Paul her heavy
torso's turmoil—the full white bath-gleaming legs
kicking—the quick churning entangle of father-
daughter, and his legs scissoring hers . . .

Did he not hear the mother laugh boomingly? Was there not a world about him and he in it and his family below and he a bricklayer?

He closed his eyes and bent his head. Gloria wrenched herself free and fell against him, pushing him from the couch. Strained and curdled he wandered to the door saying it was warm and he did not feel well. He blushed. He mumbled, ". . . Well, so long," and left.

He sat hunched and trembling on the wharf.

Has father seen? Is he watching? Has he been with me—does he know of my desire? Oh why am I tormented? Forgive me . . . The yearning vitriol within possessed his middle and sent distaste to his mouth. He rubbed his stomach, and then pummeled it, weeping and distressed. He tried not to think, to feel, or recall, but caught in his brain were Gloria's soft white thighs outstretched and rolling.

It's wrong O God!—

I don't want to think of *it*—of her—I do not! I do not! Dusty gray-brown shades overcame Tenement and river, and hid Paul, lying faceward on the wharf, holding his breath and gripping the planks.

With blind hunger he arose and walked the docks.

How could he face mother Annunziata and the children? How could he! With what courage could he wrestle Job . . . how could he straightly stand in supplication to God and father above . . . ?

Oh mother mother I have desire great desire for woman and my only will is for Gloria's fruits . . . I cannot tell you—I must never let you know . . .

Paul lay in the bed in the dining room that he shared with brother Joie. He wanted to pray but the thought of Gloria blazed to the center of his understanding like the burning bush on the mount and her white thighs offered themselves as the white hands of God thrust through celestial clouds in a blaze of glory on the tops of holy pictures.

9

Big steel was downtown. It straddled the city block and its metal skeleton shot up fifty floors to the sky. At street level was a ten-foot wooden fence, and protecting the street people was a thick timbered bridge that reached the first floor. Trucks pulled in and out of its entrances loaded with sand cement lime bricks stone lumber pipes and steel. Laborers stood about in groups seeking to enter and ask for work. High up were iron-workers walking the thin girders . . . and Paul afraid to watch them. At about the twentieth floor were concrete workers pushing the heavy big-wheeled buggies from the hoists and dumping the fresh concrete into the floor forms. Above them the scaffold hangers were fastening the protruding I-beams from which other scaffolders hung the swinging scaffolds for the bricklayers. From the very peak the hundred-foot derrick swung its steel latticed arm out beyond the building and from it de-scended a cable with an ironworker clinging to it. The man was small-small and grew larger as he came toward the ground. When he reached the street two other iron-workers fastened the cable about a five-ton girder. Soon the great steel body and the ironworker upon it were rising slowly up up; the girder seesawing as a ship on rolling water and the surefooted ironworker captaining it up through space. Paul's breast prided for him. Far up in the bone-work of Job he saw the riveting crew. A rickety scaffolding held the little forge where the smith fired his bolts. He drew them white-hot, passed them to the thrower who sent them bulleting up to the catcher on his precarious rope-plank scaffold who snared them neatly in his tin cone and then with pincers inserted them into the bolt holes that matched in the beams to be mated fast by his partner, who pushed his compres-sor-gun upon the hot bolt's unheaded end, and while

the sledgeman resisted from the other end of the bolt
the furious ra-tat tat tat—tat-tat smashed the malleable
hot pin into locked steel home.

Skirting the structure at the fourth floor were the
swinging cable scaffolds. The labor-foremen, a big
heavy-voiced man, shouted directions. He called for
tubs bricks and mortar, and under his command Irish,
Italian, and Negro laborers swiftly loaded the scaffolds.
Soon a gang of bricklayers appeared on the scaffolds
and went to work. Hicky Nicky went along the scaffold inspecting their union cards. Paul whistled and
called. Nicky leaned over the scaffold-rail and summoned him. He motioned with his hands that it was all
fixed. Paul crossed the street excitedly and went into
Job through the truck entrance. Inside it was cool and
shadowed, and in the half light was an activity that bewildered him. Great concrete and mortar-mixers chug-
ged their huge barrelbellies about with incessant
disturbance while ragged laborers made indistinguish-
able with cement dust fed the maw into the mixers with
broken stone, sand, water and cement. Men pushing
barrows and buggies from mixer to hoists—at the bell's
clanging the hoistmen throwing the cable reels in and
out of gear and the hoists shooting up madly through
the shafts, to hurtle down again suckingly in a few minutes, pull up short near the bottom and hit the floor to
send the barrows clattering—men in overalls begrimed
and shouldering heavy steam pipes and tools—watch
your head buddy—trucks' bodies racketing up and
dumping thousands of bricks and tons and tons of sand
and stone and men transferring with human strength
the dead weights—men seeming all alike in olympic
contest for living with Job.

Nicky met Paul on the fourth floor and sent him to
the construction office to sign up. Soon he had a brass
check, a number and badge—and then out onto the
swinging scaffold with the bricklayers. The swinging
scaffold unnerved him. The scaffolds on the flats were
all putlog affairs, but these were planks lapped into the

steel braces underfoot and overhead that were attached to the suspended cables, and to every brace and pair of cables was a pair of winches that when jacked pulled the scaffold up and wound up cable. As he laid brick along the wall he couldn't believe the thin cables would really hold the gang of men and the piles of brick and mortar, but in the speed of work he forgot about it. No sooner was a setting-up of five courses and header-binder laid than the scaffolders came along with their jack-handles and jacked the scaffolds, keeping the wall always about waist level. Within a few hours Nicky came to Paul and told him that the foreman thought Paul was a "dandy little bricklayer" and wanted him to take his tools and come in and work on the particular walls of the stair-wells.

He'll put his tools here—no—put them there ... workers up and down the stairs—then the battery of riveting guns let loose and reverberating the live metal air of Job—whang! whang! resound the ironworkers' sledges ... hey buddy dump some mortar here—I can't stretch to the other tub—and get me an armful of damn brick in this corner!—put it up!—what's the bond in this angle?—uorrrrhhhhhh sing the hoists—goddamn-damn sonofabastarddd I said brick on the hoist—not tile! Brick you dago screwball! *brick* ...

Hey Murrphpheeee ... !

Ratatatatatat—ratatatatatatatattt

Hal-lloooo?

Send up the fourfoot angleirons!

Noise! noise O noise O noise and sounds swelling in from the sea of city life without of pushing scurrying purring motors and horns and bells and cries and sirens and whistles and padded stream of real feet O noise O noise—O noi—se and through Job mouths stretch wide screaming:

I want brick!

I want tile!

I want the scaffolder!

I want mortar!

I want speed I want rush I want haste I want noise I want action

I want you all of you to throw yourselves into job!

With the midday sun the close stairwell became a hotbox, and Paul stripped off his shirt. Just before lunch hour, as Paul was working a wall up along the stairs, someone came slowly down. When the man neared him Paul felt drops plash on his sweated back. He wiped his back and saw his hand covered with blood. He was frightened. He turned and looked up. A Swedish carpenter was coming down slowly and holding up his right hand. It looked like a ghastly dripping rose. The four fingers had been shorn off to the palm and the mangled remains ran red faucets. He walked silently with white face down the stairs. Later, Nicky told Paul that the carpenter was greasing the wheel at the top of the hoist when the cable suddenly ran and caught his hand against the wheel rubbing off his fingers.

"Don't let that bother you, kid," said Nicky.

O my Jesus, guard me. I am not afraid—It's that I am needed . . . and I know O Lord that I shall work on Job unharmed . . . in constant prayer and thanksgiving to Thee—our Jesus.

The scaffolds rose a floor a day. With each floor the height and majesty of skyscraper fascinated him, but he never told mother Annunziata about the danger of falling or being pushed from a swinging scaffold forty or fifty floors above the street. Or of a derrick cable snapping and sending a girder crashing the scaffold to earth. It seemed so daring to lay brick at the edge of a wall that ran down hundreds and hundreds of feet to a toy world below, a wall that leaned out and seemed about to fall away.

This was steel Job where danger was ever present with falling planks and beams and bolts and white-hot molten steel from acetylene torch and breaking cable and unexpected drop of hoist—great dangerous Job who thrilled Paul.

10

I must win the award! said Dave the only Jew
bricklayer—said Frank the Scotchman—said Barney the
Irishman—said Tommy the Englishman—said Hans the
German—said Grogan the "real" American—said they
all.

I must win! prayed Paul.

The men ran away with the job; to the delight of the
foremen and the firm. Years of bricklaying sense were
amplified to a point of acute accuracy and speed, and a
man's spirit was mortified if he was a brick or cross-joint
behind the next man. Nothing seemed impossible. Difficult brick cuts were made without spoil or trail—stiff
mortar was spread neatly—soupy mortar was spread
neatly—one man became two men—perverse twisted
vitrified tile blocks were "humored" with darting
instinct—while a man's hands sleighted the quick mortar and brick into upping wall his eyes crosshaired
plumb and level—he twisted to let laborer go by and
let fellowbricklayer do his share—he shouted for material—his feet kicked brick and fallen mortar from scaffold planks—he measured the man's pace—he planned
immediately his following moves—man's flesh lent itself
completely to the balanced delirium of building.

Night and day they lived with the award and automatically trained to the task. Real men grown men
watched their habits and felt they could keep laying
brick and sawing wood and bolting steel through eternity without ever pausing. They cared little for lunch or
joke or woman; the smell and feel and action of building
was their in and out of living. They never mentioned
the award and became respectful strangers bearing each
other a wholesome terrible hate. Grown men real men
fell away to one blind dimension and suffered beauty

from their beings so that vision became the constant photography of rising walls from out of their bodies while foreman's morbid pall loomed over shoulders.

. . . And within minute's reach out in the street world passed thousands who never set foot on building Job who never touched a brick nor smelled mortar who never thought of Job and her men. . . .

The day of the award the men worked with unusual tension. Grogan especially was beside himself in endeavor and open smiling to the foremen. At ten o'clock the thin expressionless Mister Ross came along the line of bricklayers working on the parapets. He stopped near Grogan. Grogan smiled wildly and made an anxious move to step out. But Ross tapped Paul and quietly told him to come down to the office. Paul dropped his trowel in the tub and followed him, his head getting light and trembling. The men paused and watched Ross and Paul go into the penthouse door and downstairs.

Dave the fat Jewish bricklayer wiped his forehead and exclaimed:

"Vell, I'm soit'nly glad for Paulie—He's a crackerjack!"

The men slowed and worked like empty shells—the suspense over. They felt slightly bitter, but relieved.

Grogan remained standing. He clenched his trowel-handle and his eyes glittered. Then, urinating against the wall, he cackled: "This is more than the barber kin do to his woik . . . !"

He scooped up some mortar and deliberately dirtied the wall.

The frogface showed its ugliness and spat:

"So they gi'e it to the goddamn li'l Dago!"

At noon the men were summoned to a large space on the second floor. Upon a wooden platform was the committee; the dapper bright-eyed mayor, officials, a stenographer, a few newspapermen, and three richly dressed women. When the workers saw the women they removed their caps and hats. Speeches were made while

the men stared at the sheer-silked legs of the three rich
women. Speeches were made and Paul gazed in wonder
at the beautiful pink cheeks and fine tailoring of the
men upon the platform.

Even when his name was called and he was handed a
certificate and the men clapped it seemed a revelation
that these glaze-skinned, soft, white-fingered men who
looked like painted mustached women dressed in tai-
lored men's clothes owned the great building and the
city.

That afternoon while laying brick he marveled at the
memory of the dainty pink-cheeked perfumed dolls of
men who gave out the awards and spoke tired high-class
talk.

Could he ever forget that these hot-housealia owned
great Job!

11

The paesanos said it would be a thing if Luigi and Cola
formed in matrimony.

"One is cripple and the other cannot produce babies."
But did they have to suggest the thought to Luigi when
he dreamed of her second by second? The only paradise
he prayed for was to be man to Cola's woman! Oh tender he would be to her—respectful! He would carry her
as warm little bird to breast and she would be his lord
and master! Oh dreams dreams!

Life was sweet to him when sitting near Cola and cutting embroidery. Wasn't her voice the dearest instrument in the world? Wasn't her nearness the caressing
heat of happiness?

The scissors and embroidery disappeared before his
open eyes and there he was with her in their own little
flat waiting on her hand and foot and caring for her as
though she were more precious than King Emanuel's
daughter. . . . Cola my Cola—Cola here and Cola there

. . . and back came the scissors and embroidery as Cola's rapid chattering lifted gaily.

"Remember what Carlotta (may her dear soul rest) said how her man thrilled her while she bathed nude?—ohh aie, aie, aie!" Tears of laughter ran quickly from the dark-circled eyes and she had to loosen her corset.

"Aie—yes yes the departed Carlotta was a one—she did like a taste of the man-beast! aie aie . . ."

It came about that the matchmakers went brewing a matrimony. From paesan mouth to paesan ear traveled the confirmation.

"Ey Serafina, I have a thing to tell: Luigi One-leg is to wed the big-titted Cola."

"In truth?"

". . . and that is the way it was told me."

"Ahhh, even I this fool could sense it. 'Put fire near hay' said I long since."

"I smelled smoke when told she had visited him at the hospital!"

There is a time to prepare; and thus it was seen by gaslight in the parlor that Luigi, Paul, and the Lucy arranged the large box-vats for the grape-crushing while Nazone and Orangepeel-Face Mike unloaded the boxes of grapes from Head-of-Pig's ice-wagon and carried them up into the parlor two at a time. The lower vat was a heavy six foot square box with sides over two feet high and with a plugged bunghole at one end. It was held up a short distance above the floor by thick wooden legs at the corners. A smaller vat with many holes in its bottom was fitted into it. Annunziata and Cola emptied boxes of the full red grapes into the top vat. They picked out the few dried grape leaves and spread the heavy clusters evenly. Annina brought a basin of hot water, soap and a towel and set it on the floor by a chair. The Lucy sat and removed his shoes and stockings. He rolled his trousers up to his knees and placed his feet in the basin. Cola went to him, knelt, and washed and dried his feet.

Nazone was next, and after Cola had cleansed his feet

he and the Lucy climbed into the grape-laden vat. As their broad white feet met the grapes the lush rounds crushed cheek to cheek and their escaping mingled blood revealed to the narrow gaslit parlor and autumn night its secret sweet. The men jumped from foot to foot with easy rhythm and beneath feet's press the grapy pad gave way with hydraulic squish. The Lucy's corded legs and Nazone's round chubby legs soon were laved in the grapes' abundant juice. Cola and Annunziata busily emptied grapes into the vat, and the children took the boxes out into the kitchen where they broke them apart, pulling out the nails, and stacking the wood in the dining room. With every tenth box of the crushed grapes the Lucy and Nazone ceased stamping to let the women scoop up the mashed seeds skins and vines which they deposited in three old open standing casks. Then Head-of-Pig and Mike would drain off the pure grape-juice from the lower vat and pour it into large wooden barrels. Before the one hundred boxes were crushed even the women and children had tasted under flesh of feet vineyard's blessings.

The task was over with late night. The pressings were left in the open standing casks, and three fifty-gallon barrels were filled to bunghole with thick juice. When all was done and grape-drunk legs dried and clad, the family and good paesanos rested in the kitchen to eat and drink and talk of wine. This one remembered a wine black, dry, and saporific that left his senses crystal-clear after he had drunk two whole gallons. The other one had made a cask of muscatel that he swore was worth its weight in rare perfumes!

"Remember when Passwater's house was lightning-struck, the house behind the olive grove, and four casks of liquid golden wine turned to rank vinegar like that!"

Wedding day, home was a delicious chaos of activity. All the beds had been taken apart, chairs and tables borrowed—and the chamberpots put out of view.

The feet of the women clopped in busy eddy through

the flat that looked more like a grimy boxed corridor. Katarina gave orders and slapped fat buttocks about; Grazia filled flagons with wine; old Philomena and Annunziata hovered proudly over the steaming portable oil stove and the coal stove; Serafina, wife to the Lucy, waddled her balloon self about Cola with straight pins in mouth adjusting the folds of Cola's cheap silk wedding gown; and Cola made fun with broad remarks.

How respectful and obedient are these hard men of Job as they show themselves anxiously willing to be sent about on errands and duties like children, delighting with nervous play-acting concern over their helplessness; and do they not look so different with their faces painfully over-washed and wearing new-smelling clothes with a care as if they were of glass? But who can stop Philomena's many children from running through the rooms desperately and fighting with the Lucy's children and Orangepeel-Face's children playing cowboys and Indians with the Regina's children out in the hall and then in the flat and out again and why do Angelina's girls kick and scratch each other and shout with all their might—

"Quiet!" cries Angelina. "Good mother of God, even at the scene of espousal in the home of others in the heart of the winter these little ones fight and abuse each other like lost souls—Theresina, enough! enough! You are disgracing those who brought you into this world—*Ther-es-sinn-nnaaa!* Oy, this heart is poisoned!'" And with that falls Angelina's raged hand upon her Theresina who directly goes into sharp tantrums.

The Regina takes her Amelia in hand, Philomena attempts to discipline her many children and soon the flat is shrapneled with cries and squalling.

"Ah Dio-Dio-Dio," wails the flustered Cola, "what insane asylum . . . ! But what is the time anyway? Are we never to go to the church?"

Dame Katarina swung her long arms through the flat and frightened the children into silence. In the dining room the Lucy looked at his watch and said officiously:

"Now then, come is the wedding hour. What does one say—is there to be a matrimony, or have I brought myself here in undertaker's suit to pose as a tree stump!"

"Yes to be sure, he is correct," affirmed the Regina.

"Look to your children, Mike," called Mike's mate Maria, "they are beneath people's feet . . . !"

"Where is Luigi?" asked Bastian.

"Theresina, behave while we are to church. Do you hear your mother!"

"And where may this Luigi of mine be?" inquired Cola a-flutter.

"Luigi, come, where do you find yourself!" cried Grazia hand to mouth.

Nazone came from the parlor and pointed back to the doorway.

"And here is Luigi!"

The women shrieked in surprise. Luigi stood in the parlor doorway—on *two* legs! He was smiling and held a cane to the floor. He wore a new baggy black suit with a black and white striped shirt and starched white bow-tie; he seemed a clothed Atlas framed in doorway. The shaggy hair was plastered to one side and the thick brows and heavy mustaches were brushed to shine. He was not the one-legged Luigi, he was that humble smiling twitch-eye Luigi of old!

"How do I seem . . . ?" he asked huskily.

"You are . . . beautiful," said Cola, clasping her hands. "And what have they done to you?"

"We have stuck a leg onto him!" proclaimed Nazone. "A limb as perfect as mother gives to child, only—that this one can be oiled, set aside, and not know the travail of corns and rheumatism."

Cola spread her hands to the paesanos: "But surely, you must have impoverished yourselves for—"

The Lucy made a terrible face and said, "This one. Just look at her. Our own Christ cared naught for gold—now are we to change Christian semblance? Don't let me lose patience."

Luigi bowed his head slightly and said gratefully, "A

most wonderful gift they have made me this day of espousal. This heart has not tongue to tell how happy—"

Nazone blew his nose loudly and skillfully blotted an
insistent tear. "Come," said he, "what does one let himself live for—if not to enjoy! . . . Here, see—there sings
the bell of Saint Prisca—one, two— three— and
four . . . Dio! at four we were to find ourselves before
Altar, and here are we like sausages hanging in butcher
shop."

"Quick the coat for Cola! Aid Luigi with his new
leg—"

"Annunziata, leave your apron and keep us not
tardy—"

"But dare I leave the kitchen what with the food and
children and—"

"I will take you by force, sister—come, you must
hold my hand at altar . . . for the love that I bear you,
sister, you must stand by me."

"Annunziata, Annunziata, here are your coat and
shawl—"

"Bravo!" shouted Orangepeel-Face Mike, "we arm
and go!"

Where had the children left their hats and coats?
Who would hold whose hand and tend so that there
would not be imbroglios and fracas and then it would
be said that one did not know how to bring up one's
children—ah but children were made to let the heads
of their mothers go scattering—woe-woe but why
were they born straight from the Malebolge and Devil
came they and parents were wracked and ruined for
them—No no, O blessed Jesu-Giuseppe e' Mari, excuse these rabid thoughts—I know not what I say . . .

At the joining the paesan men wore their church
masks of confused severity, and the women lent themselves ever so ready to tremulous verge of weeping. Father John spoke the holy words and Geremio's people
drank to heart the sacred mysteries.

Luigi and Cola are man and wife. It is the desire of

God. The Regina takes from crack of breasts the handkerchief to pursue a tear, little Geremino must to the toilet badly, Grazia holds hands across bosom and nods blessing, Dame Katarina sneaks a pinch of snuff to her nostrils and sniffs in tone meaning "life goes well," the marriageable daughters push forth their tight pouty breasts and wish they were themselves with man at altar, the men hold themselves fiercely stiff and regard the wedding ones with righteous propriety. Annunziata bears herself finely for Luigi, she sips the wine of his joy . . . and does not her chin quiver in vivid sensing of her and Geremio clasping hand in hand in red-cheeked bloom at the altar? In this living can she realize he has left?

"They come!"

"Amedeo, the door! Anzolotti, shed that poisonous pipe and make music!"

"Blood-death and woe, grant me grace to remove accordion from box!" With sway and grand upswing of chin Anzolotti drew from his pearly-nickeled instruments the happy signaling that "Here—comes—the bride—ta-ra-dada—*Here*—*comes*—the *bride*!" and he Anzolotti is so importantly understanding and nonchalant, he knows the magic of his part—for, is it not he who shall give light to eyes and rhythm to hearts?

"Children, out of the path, children! My God, these millions of children are tangled in people's legs—Lucio! Pasquale! do not cling to the doorway—remove yourselves—ahhh, enter Cola, Luigi—Madonna, how beautiful . . . hmnn la lala here comes the bride . . ."

Luigi felt as strange as his artificial leg for happiness hit him hard and left him holding Cola's hand. This joy left him without will, and if someone had crept quietly up to him and shouted "Jump out the window!" he would have obeyed. They seated him in the parlor corner, the paesanos flooded in to greet them. Ardent were the embraces and kisses!

"Hey, are the hands that pass the liquors paralyzed? Now then!"

Mint and licorice and coffee, sweet liquors for the ladies, and dynamite drinks for the men.

"To man and wife!"

"Health . . ."

"Good fortune for a hundred years!"

". . . A thousand years!"

The rooms were crowded with paesanos face to face and back to back. Paul lit the gaslamps upon them in their heavy brown and black suits and thick red and green dresses.

How painfully polite are the men; they stand straight-backed as grand signores and delicately lift glass to lips with strong square hands; hands scrupulously washed but covered with soil cracked callus. And for the big-hipped great-breasted women:

"Does Maria desire another cordial?"

"May I place this chair for the seating of the Regina?"

It was found in the arranging that there was not room at the tables for the children.

"But how was one to know, after all, it is not the same as though one had blueprints in hand . . ."

So boxes, crates and stools were placed throughout the bedrooms and parlor for them.

"My, what pandemonium, what headache—I only this second fixed a place for Philomena's children and now who has removed the chairs—who has upset my work I ask?—Amedeo, cease chattering and look to your little ones or they will die of hunger while other people's children bloat!"

"Madonna mine, how smells that suckling in oven. If others look at it, why should I not also behold its beauty? . . . Ahh, lovely it is—lovely!"

"Come come, you women will gobble it up with eyes alone."

Annunziata and Cola passed the platters of antipasto as the paesanos found their seats. Bitter green Sicilian olives and sweet Spanish olives, whitings and squid pickled in saffron, Genoese salami and mortatel, pickled eggplants, long pointed peppers and cherry peppers ... of which the mere looking upon watered the tongue.

With unconscious desire the paesanos sat themselves near to those who gave with soft of eye or with word that which was relished. Nazone sat on one side of the Regina while the Lucy was on her right, next to him was dame Katarina, then came Hunt-Hunt, and beside him was Grazia, and around the end were Amedeo, Yellow-Fever Giuseppe, his daughter Susie, then was Passwater's son Patsy (who sought Susie for dishonorable purposes and proved a constant gall to her father), Fausta the Evil-Mouth, old Santos, the Lucy's wife Serafina, and at the head were Luigi, Philomena, and Paul; in the kitchen the paesanos at the other table sat jammed, and in the bedrooms the children were piled like refugees quarreling happily.

The chicken soup was rich with eggs, fennel, artichoke roots, grated paremesan, and noodles that melted on lips. They ate leisurely and with the knowledge that there was much to be had and plenty of time in which to put it into their flesh. The soup plates were removed and in were brought broiled fat eels garnished with garlic and parsley. Lemon juice was squeezed upon them, and tender white was their meat. The flagons moved about the tables without stop and every mouthful was aided with thick red wine.

"The flagon will tip, Susie—there it falls!"

"Now you have drowned the cloth ... !"

"Nothing-nothing ... Spilled wine upon the table of joy is blessing!"

"Yes, feel not badly, our Christ is happy when poor's table weeps red in laughter of wine!"

Hardly had the eels been picked clean when dishes of fried squabs and sweetbreads and golden mushrooms were set before amazed eyes. The Lucy picked a sweetbread and brought it to his mouth with: "Oh how good you are to little Nicholas!" and munched with closed eyes of delight. Bowls of escarol salad spiced with wine

vinegar, salt and olive oil were heaped, and hands dug in
heartily. Out in the streets it was cold January, but in
the house of Geremio his family and kind sat knee to
knee at table under gaslight and smiled to the loving
goodness of food. The tables were blooded with wine
and soiled with oil and salt and peppers, and plates
crowded spoons and platters and flagons. The men
opened their belts and top buttons of pants-fly and relieved bulging stomach from tables' edge; and even
though wives loosened corset strings, their yearning
breasts overflowed corset-top. Their senses spoke
through contented eyes and pleasant flesh-swell, and
words kept extolling the wonderfulness of eat and drink.

Wine was drunk as though it were breathed air, and
mouths coated heavily with its red grapy strength. Luigi
was once more familiar with smoking di Nobili in
mouth of lolling shaggy contemplating head and
drinking-glass of wine in giant hand!

The voice of Alfredo the Neapolitan rose from the
feasters in the kitchen to tell the world that: "Love and
wine . . . Love and wine shall lead my mother's son a
merry good time, a merry good time, a . . . merr-rry
good timmmme!"

Fausta joined him in song and the reedy throat of
Anzolotti's accordion patterned behind the incoming
gruff maleness and shrill breasty femaleness: "Love and
wine, love and wine. . . ."

Annunziata and Cola were drawing the roast suckling
from its snug oven berth.

Fausta lifted his nostrils and looked to the kitchen.
He put hands over heart and sang: "Mama, I smell the
special smell of my love!" Then downing a hasty glass
of wine he went off into the kitchen. Over Annunziata's
shoulder he beheld the glossy dark brown suckling, and
made a very eloquent sign of the cross by kissing his
fingers loudly with each move. The suckling was evenly
sprawled in a thick bed of truffles and potatoes, its back
and sides were stuck with cloves and covered with
spices, the hollowed-out eyes packed with figs, and from

the smoking hot pork flesh came a mouth-provoking
feminine savor. When Annunziata and Cola lifted it
high those in the kitchen sighed in admiration. But
Fausta would lead it in in the *right* manner! "I shall lead
. . . now then . . . allay!" And then, beating a dishpan
with a large spoon he preceded its entry to the dining
room singing with gusto the triumphal march from
Aida.

Everyone fell to, banging glasses, dishes, forks,
spoons, clapping hands and stomping feet on floor, tarr-
ump! tarr-ump! in time with Fausta to set the air shaking. When the suckling was placed safely in the center
of the table Fausta demanded surcease.

" 'Tention, paesans!" then he quickly drank a glass of
wine, wiped at his mustache and continued: "Before all
the world I declare this pure love, but what a love! for
the naked little angel who lies in roasted beauty under these very eyes."

"How? How?" cried Katarina.

"Because she is good enough to eat!"

"Buffoon! Buffoon!" called the Regina.

"Forward with your romance, Master Fausta!" en-
couraged Mike.

"May I be split six ways if I tell not the truth; I say
that I love this she-suckling with all the sincerity of my
golden heart!" and thus he amorously kissed the suckling's mouth.

"Why?" shrieked the women.

Fausta screwed his sharp little black eyes evilly and
wagged his pointed ears as the gaslight danced over his
pompadour, and he hissed: "Bee-cause . . . love wishes
to *devour*!"

"Eeeeeeeee!" answered the women.

"Love is a hunger!" sang Nazone operatically. "Encore! Fausta encore!"

"You men are terr-i-ble!" tittered the Lucy's fat wife.

Luigi with long knife cut into the suckling and revealed the luscious meat beneath crisp candied-like
brown surface. The ohs and ahs were ecstatic, and

Fausta only warming to his theory of "love" plucked a fig from the suckling's eye and before eating it held it up and said: "Perhaps I am taken up as fool or lying one, but tell me veritably, has that creature of my wife such a fig that I may eat?"

The stuffing of the roast was rich with pignoli-nuts, chopped squab-livers, figs, cheese, eggs, and peppers, and the hands that shoveled it between wide lips were soaked in its flavors. The bones were polished clean; the men sucked the marrow and teethed away the soft tasty gristle . . . A few mouthfuls of meat, and down with it goes a glass of wine.

Ostula, the paesano barber, arrived with his five feet of perfumed dandy, waxed mustachio, and mandolin. After much imbibing, he and Anzolotti lazily played at the table while the men smoked. In the bedrooms the children were quarreling and bawling, and many who had stuffed their little bellies hard, were falling asleep on the floor.

From song to song went the paesanos. First it was the *Marche Reale*, then *Santa Lucia*, after that, *One Needs Volition;* then Fausta got up and with huckster sentiment put his heart and chords through the lamenting melody of the youth who could not live "without mother." During the singing, platters of sea-snails, more wine, and fresh home-baked bread were brought to the tables.

The snails were cooked in sauce of plum-tomatoes, parsley, garlic, olive oil, salt, hot pepper, and basil leaf. The maddeningly good savor of the snails revived eating desire, and after the countless snail-shells piled over plates and onto the floor, they were removed from table, and then came bowls of bitter dandelion salad and steaming pots loaded with lobsters, hard clams, soft clams, razor clams, crabs, and black mussels!

Ah brother and sister, this is the life—cuddingly arranged close to the flesh and smell and joy of them who are your own people . . . yes dear heart and soul, without words I tell you, I would this night lasted forever and more!

Five hours had they been at table, and now they sat back and in the strong tobacco clouds that nearly obscured gaslight they talked of other days.

"Remember the orange groves abloom upon the hills of Abruzzi? Ah, right now comes to me a night pregnant with blossom and ocean grand . . ."

". . . the Campobasso where grazed the sheep of Don Pepe . . ."

". . . and the Basilica of Saint Michael on All Souls' Day."

They reconstructed the beautiful terrain of Abruzzi and tenderly restored their youths and the times of Fiesta and Carnival.

Nazone rubbed his legs under table and sighed.

Old Philomena recounted of Geremio's father, Pietro the wild, as men and women talked of men and women.

"Handsome and wayward was the father of dear departed Geremio, with ring in ear, long raven curls, and bright kerchief about his neck. He was the one ever wanting to eat and drink finely, arouse the village with bedlam prank, and do for people's ripe daughter."

And Paul, full and happy, laughed.

"At the Feast of Saint Mary, Pietro first saw the gentle Theresa. (Ah what a boyo!) Without ceremony he cast bold arm about her waist, while the fierce Xavier her father was near-by, and with face of rascal told her she was so good that he was going to give her 'for what' and plenty!"

"That is what one can call *Man!*" exclaimed the Lucy lustily, and his hand sought directly the Regina's knee.

Yellow-Fever Giuseppe was swallowing spleen for he felt Passwater's Patsy was handling his Susie beneath tablecloth. Every few minutes he attempted to spy in the dark tangle under the table; then he would rub two fingers over his brows and grind through clenched jaws that: "Certain snotnoses had better watch out—!"

Philomena told on: " 'My daughter,' bellowed Xavier, 'is the flower of my vision, and he who dishonors her gouges out my sight. The first cocko who comes within a street of her shall taste my cleaver!' "

"What a beef-faced humanity was the old butcher," brought in Santos. "He made me an open-handed beating (that I feel to this day) behind the Convent of Saint Rosario for throwing stones at him. With a stone I raised a potato on his bull-head; ah, but mother mine, what-he-gave-to-me!"

Philomena chuckled: "Finally, a night when the tempest threatened to blow Abruzzi out to sea, the wild Pietro managed himself down chimney (like the Devil himself) and did for the butcher's daughter!"

From that they went to why each one of them took steamboat for the New World, the America.

"Said I, 'Will you wed and away with me across ocean?' "

". . . and I cared not to bear arms, so when I was called I packed valise, kissed that old woman of my mother and boarded ship—"

"With me it is of such a time antique since I left the other side that even I myself do not know how I am here," sighed Philomena.

". . . Me, I made me a passage over the water; and now, where I find myself I find myself."

"I always wanted to go to the New World, in fact as a little one I set out in rowboat, and fortunate for me the mariners found me."

Fausta peered at a glass of wine in the gaslight and said:

"A sort of a 'business-ette' made it healthy for me not to show this knob around the old home town; so one shady night, with finger to lips and shoes beneath arm I took wings."

". . . I tried my luck, but what luck have I, I ask you?"

"Go to the America! Go to the America! cried every open mouth. I went. Here am I. And so what?" Amedeo answered his own question with: "So what? . . . I'll have me another little litre of wine-o and a can-zon-ellll-la . . ." He waved command to Ostula:

"Sing on, O guitar of mine!"

Eyes danced fast with the gaslight, hands wandered forcefully beneath table (even so that the Lucy knew not that it was Nazone's hand he squeezed), and for some balance soared with song. In fine voice the Lucy started the suggestive popular Sicilian song, and guitar, accordion and the rest quickly caught him up.

> "With high moon far out at sea
> Each mother's daughter desires mat-tri-mo-ny . . .
> And if to her we give the fisherman
> In-doo-ah in-doo-ay
> Forever more with his fish in hand she'll stay!"

While in the dining room they in-doo-ah-ed—in-doo-ay-ed, those in the kitchen lilted with high melody:

> "Peasant woman mine, peasant woman mine
> Barefoot sweated and bovine
> Spread on summer stack of hay
> I loved with you to play,
> Peasant woman mine, peasant woman mine
> Sweeter are you than princess fine
> Ey! Ey! Ey! Peasant woman mine!"

The children were set shivering awake and cater-wauling in the bedrooms while the Regina (by request) wrung from her breasts the dulcent *Rimpianto* as Paul's woman-adoring godfather Nazone ran caressing respectful hand up the back of her thigh.

Louis and Av-rom arrived. Av-rom asked Paul confidentially:

"Is there any good eats left? . . . Any vino?"

"All you can eat and drink!"

He fed them and found room for them at the dining-room table where they watched the paesanos play Seven-up. Av-rom laughed every time one of the paesanos lost out and slammed his cards to the table with knuckle-breaking force.

"You misrepresented, big-nosed porkface!" shouted Fausta.

"You are not foreman here!" answered Nazone, shaking a fat finger.

"And remember I come from the best strain in Abruzzi; not like yours who had to go in person under hiding of night to fetch water at the fountain, and cast contents of chamber-pot out of window upon clean Christian heads!"

"I'll destroy you with a spit!" screeched Fausta. He made as though he were going to spit and as he rose he sniffed, and then suddenly called to the kitchen:

"Whey! you who wear dresses, bring me a cup-a-tella of that so-good scented coffee!" When he sat he shook his head and remarked: "And bravo to the dear little females, they've piazza-ed themselves with coffee and pastry. . . . Come, pass the cards."

Cola placed a large tray of the liquored nutted pastries before the men while the Regina passed about the thick black java. Then rainbow-colored spumonis, and gelatis, and creamy tortonis! The women stand breast to breast and suck ices so daintily. This one says the cords in her thighs ache, the other one swears a bone of her corset has penetrated a left kidney, that one fans her throat and looks with big eyes at the grandeur of Maestro Farabutti as he propounds to the Regina the great need of opera to "the barbarian America."

The Lucy wiped his forehead and then slapped his stomach with: "I am hungry!"

"By the Madonn-erino," said Fausta, "I *could* make me an eating of spaghetti!"

"Oh dear," wailed Serafina, "at unholy hour of night—oh dear . . ."

"Quick," said Fausta, "I am pregnant for it!"

"You men—you men," said the women, "you will bloat with the colic of horses—you will die of the indigest-ion!"

"Remove yourselves!" cried Giuseppe. "Man needs spaghetti!"

Hunt-Hunt and the Lucy took aprons and proclaimed: "We'll conjure a spaghetti that will surpass even that of the house of Savoi!"

". . . With mustaches!" added Fausta with a flourishing twirl of his own.

The ladies persuaded Maestro Farabutti to perform. He placed himself near the window. Then flinging his arms wide:

"We are Italians! Know you what that means? It means the regal blood of terrestrial man! Richer than the richest, purer than the finest, more capable than an-y! an-y! race breathing under the stellar rays of night or the lucent beams of day!—"

"What a man so gr-gr-grand . . ." sighed the Regina.

"—the I-tal-ian-nne is the flower of Christians—"

The Lucy, preparing to put the spaghetti into pots of boiling water, paused and looked toward the parlor.

"Who the cocko is being death-killed now?" he asked.

"That head of hair who wears the 'bandages' over his shoes," answered Fausta.

"Ahhh," said Bastian, "if-if-if—only *I* had that t-talk-ability . . ."

"—and in the sacred realm of Arts the children of Italia beautiful have achieved the celestial heights—for are not Michelangelo and Raphaelo our own? Cellini!—"

"It is understood . . ."

"—our brother Dante Alghieri who has scribed all that need be read—"

"Ah yes," mused Orangepeel-Face Mike profoundly, "the *Comedy Divine* is said to contain all the verities mundane and spiri-tual . . ."

"—the bravest warriors! and—"

"Right!"

"We are the glory of Rome, *the* culture! By us the rest are scum! And it is the duty of us great Italians to—"

He calmed. "And now I shall give to you the superb Ritorno Vincitore."

He went the gamut of chest-beating, hands-wringing, forehead-slapping and finger-biting. When he thundered toward the end he leaned forward and outstretched hands and scathed his words in terrible fury.

"Marrr-velous!"

"More! Again!"

The rich tomato-y olive-oil cooking of the spaghetti sauce brought the paesanos to the kitchen. The Lucy ordered Head-of-Pig and Bastian to wash the table-top. Then he went over it with a cloth wet with olive oil. Taking the pots of white-boiled spaghetti he heaped two high rows of it from end to end of the table-top, and upon them he poured the pans of thick red oily sauce and handfuls of grated cheese and hot pepper, mixing the contents of the separate rows deftly with fork and spoon. On a box at each end of the table the Lucy placed a large wooden bowl of wine.

He stood up to his full handsome height and said: "The cockos who call themselves Italian line up with hands tied behind and eat from the table with only the face!" Head-of-Pig, Orangepeel-Face, Giuseppe, Bastian, Amedeo and Santos removed their coats and stood themselves along one side of the table ready to have their hands tied, while Alfredo the Neapolitan, Passwater, Hunt-Hunt, Black Mike and Nazone prepared themselves opposite. The Lucy and Fausta went along tying their hands behind with lengths of Paul's mason twine.

"Hey Paul," whispered Av-rom drunkenly, "can Louis and me have some? Gee."

"No, Paul," said Louis gaily, "we'll join your paesanos at the table!"

Anzolotti's accordionic *Funiculi-Funicula* sent the anxious mouth-open faces into the spaghetti. With eyes tightly closed they sucked and swished and swilled in the juicy wheat-strings, beard to beard, head to head, Av-rom swoggling it prodigiously, Louis spluttering,

Paul's features fricaseed saucely red, Hunt-Hunt inhaling it, while Fausta swallowing from a plate went about pushing their heads deeper into the spaghetti, the Lucy following and permitting the eaters to bathe their faces and lap up wine from the wooden bowls.

"... Is far from wrong, is far from wrong!"

"Quick, slap Passwater's back, he's choking!"

"Funiculi-Funicula, Funiculi ... Funicula!"

Old Santos' white hair was painted with sauce, Amedeo's bald head was crossed with spaghetti strands, Orangepeel-Face cried for someone to wipe his eyes of the hot pepper, the skinny Nina bawled to her Passwater for splotching with spaghetti's red grease his only good suit, Santos' little Lucia laughed with tears and said one's husband was no longer distinguishable from another's, Black Mike and Nazone were chewing the same bundle and kept suck-tugging back and forth until Nazone felt teeth on his nose and let go his end, shirt fronts and shoulders were pasted with sauce spaghetti and wine, and when Amedeo who was properly drunk slipped to the floor and remained on his back Fausta dropped handfuls of spaghetti into his gaping mouth.

Taxed with late hour, hot of stuffing, and smirched in food stains were they all; but at rare espousal one does *not* cry, "Enough!" Giuseppe, Amedeo, Hunt-Hunt, Head-of-Pig and Santos, loaded and reeling, conjourned at the dining-room table for more drinking and exhilarated talk, as the rest pushed the musicians to the front room. Short pock-marked Orangepeel-Face Mike with his bushy black hair, cross-eyes, little sand-colored mustache and large slash of mouth, was drunk to petrifaction. He pushed the paesanos away from the center of the room and remained so that they should behold him. Dressed in shirt, tie, and trousers of black, he stood stuck in pose of imperious ballerino; then, moving about on the same spot woodenly and seeming like statue on edge of toppling he surveyed the ceiling wall-

eyed; from out of his trance he dropped his gaze to
Anzolotti and Ostula, heeled and toed about in circle
wit his arms straight from the side until his eyes found
them again, scissored his arms, slapped his little calloused hands together and away as clash of cymbals and
shouted:

"Tarantella!"

Guitar and accordion began the beating in and out
rhythm under Orangepeel-Face's supreme direction. He
put arms akimbo, circled about swaying his shoulders
and moving with stiff measured grace . . . Tar-an-tell-a
. . . Tar-an-tel-la . . .

After gyrating he remained in the center, spread out
his arms, bent back to the verge of falling, and revolved
with hypnotic movement and roguish stiff grin on his
squat face. As he went about his few short dirty teeth
laughed and the black uncontrolled eyes said: Ahhh . . .
Ahhhh Tar-an-tell! Tarantell! Mouth-open with intoxi-
cation and charming idiocy of expression he approached
Cola and extended rigid hand. She accepted it and part-
nered him. Hands on hips they went about each other
Tarantell—Tarantell! while the paesanos clapped in time
Ta-ra-nn-tell! as dark-haired serious girlish face of Cola
was above the beautiful bouncing breasts la la lala—
Taran-tell!

Fausta 'phoned hands to mouth: "Male and Female—La Tarantella!"

Flushed unsteady men grabbed the women sternly
and in the terrific closeness of the parlor the age-old
rondo held play.

Accordion and guitar lilted with gay stroke and
Fausta raucused directions: "Now forward! And meet—
and about!"

Swing and kick and rub manflesh of Job with soft hip
of Home.

Strum strum strum and swirl.

"Change the woman! Now then . . . Allay!"

Tung-atee-ring-a-tung! and, tambourine held high,
came the Lucy to push Orangepeel-Face from Cola.

More fast is he! Ah, tung-a-tung-tee-ring-tee-ring! Ey!
Tarantell! Whey! Tarantell! Twirl about swinging hips—
twisting swaying torso pushing ahead and circle gay
friendly lusty bump of buttocks away and around to face
and skip forward and circle and now bent frontward and
now fall backward and stamp Tarantell!

Yellow-Fever Giuseppe mapped out lines with wine-
soaked biscuiti upon the tablecloth showing to Amedeo
the fateful battle between Baratire and Menelik.

"Here, here, here, and here were columns of Italia,
my father in the third, then—Zthaaaa! out from the
earth sprang millions and mi-li-ions of hell-toasted
charcoal Ethiops . . . signs of the cross made the sons of
Italia and spine to spine they took to them each a hundred cutlass-in-mouth Nubian fiends . . . Forward,
Baratire! Forward!"

And fighting the battle singlehanded he crushed
biscuiti after biscuiti to crumbs on the table:

"Ztaa Ztaa! Ztaa!ztaa!ztaa! Up, Baratire! Ztaa!ztaa-
ztaa!"

Tarantell!

"It was the Germans who directed the dark assassins
from behind," declared the groggy Santos.

"Nothing like it, sir . . ." drawled Hunt-Hunt, sipping
the last few drops of his wine glass. "Wherever there is
trea-cher-y you will find the whoreface English . . . kerchief in cuff, window stuck in eye, indeterminate between the legs, and mouth convenient—I could do with
a whore right now—properly now!"

"Heads in sinister direction and dexterous direction!
Knobs rolling in the dust! Forward, banner of Italia!
Forward, Baratire!"

La lala lala Tarantell-Tarantell

"Right you are, but I tell you—" insisted Santos in
thick tongue, "the breed Teutonic with their gray
death's-head faces cannot exist without butchery. Who
trusts the Franks trusts the teeth of Carrion—"

"The Albion gend is the Ju—das I tell you. The

water-blooded Englander will sell Christ for pudding with undertaker's smile. How do you like that!"

"One hundred to one—two hundred to one, headless, limbs scattered, half a world separate from his dear mother, drowned in his own regal blood, and yet the heart of Italia fights on ztaa! ztaa! Down, Menelik! Avanti, Baratire!"

Faster, Tarantell, faster, and now leaps Paul gaily and takes mother Annunziata by hand.

Tarantell mother and son Tarantell! And the paesanos dance round with hands on hips. Come Paul! Faster Annunziata!

The floor begins to shake and the walls tremor.

Tarantell! Tarantell!

"Look Conchettina, where Farabutti holds his hand on Regina's backside . . . ! Ey Tarantell!"

Out into the center go the Regina and the Maestro and back go Paul and Annunziata and join hands with Louis and Av-rom—

Good for you Louis, Tarantell!

Jump and joy oh women's lovely heavy breasts!

Kick oh kick stocking-gartered thick matron's legs in Tarantell!

Faster Tambourine! Faster guitar! Faster accordion!

Packed and drunk and raging swifter and swifter go the Tarantellers.

"Mothers' sons flung like grain in the wind here, here, here, and here, but fear not Baratire for I am with you! Fight on! Forward Baratire!" Giuseppe fell face-ward against the wall under the spluttering gaslight and began to retch volcanically.

"I tell you again it was the English!" yelled Hunt-Hunt tiredly. "The Creator made them from a mold of tra-du-cer and filled them with white stink!"

"Yes yes yes," said Santos endlessly, "but I tell you the German will eat his own family and friends in the cold blood, therefore—"

Louder Tarantell! Louder!

Head-of-Pig spilled a glass of cold wine over the

prostrate Amedeo's bald head, and when Amedeo raised
his head he mumbled: "English, German, or Africano—
who pays and pays for the music?—The working asses
who are we . . . !"

Wilder! Tarantella! Madder! Happier! Away! Farther
away! In the parlor's garish whirl all consciousness was
the racing never-ending thundering Tarantella that
shook Tenement and set the sleeping children to sudden
hysterical screaming, and tenants to shouting and cursing, until Tarantella!Tarantella!Tarantella!'s sirening
convulsions hurricaned with crashing end to leave—
"Christians more dead than alive . . ."

In the chill isle of Dawn the paesanos were tangled
one upon and across the other with snoring lips wide in
burned-out exhaustion amongst the children on coats
and hats and piles of clothing throughout the rooms.
Giuseppe was shivering asleep with head hanging over
toilet-bowl completely fouled, and in the kitchen, sitting on the floor clutching a flagon each and with a
rhythm beyond their understanding, the Lucy and the
dame Katarina boned their sore heads together:

"Pa-poo . . . ?"

"Coocoo!"

"Pa-poo . . . ?"

"Coo-coo!"

V

ANNUNZIATA

1

Nineteen Twenty-Nine!

The building boom lay back—and disappeared.

Builders stopped giving out plans to contractors, building owners lost their holdings, building-loan corporations liquidated, the active world of Job shrunk and overnight men were wandering the streets trowel on hip and lunch beneath arm in futile search of wall.

"—Yesterday it was not safe to walk the streets with mortar-whitened shoes, and today, to lay bricks is like winning the lottery!"

"They say the American Bourse has collapsed . . ."

"Proverbially: debacle."

"What dry macaronis is this! We are building workers; and blood of the Virgin what have we to do with the Bourse and the eunuchoids who sport cane, flower in lapel, and carry pot derby on head!"

"And how say the journals? What says the pie-eating coffee-drinking A-merde-can signore the President?"

"—Ahh, that other constipated piece of Christianity—the cocko completely without salt!"

"Moonface jackass proclaimed three months ago that inside thirty days we would all be laying brick."

The paesanos desperately put in a little work on the remaining buildings under construction, and wherever work was obtained they had to "kick back." Their thin savings had given way eagerly before the cataclysm of unemployment, and in their bewildered minds hunger and the fear of hunger set in as quick disease— weakening flesh and pounding sanity.

The sudden and real want that beset the paesanos stupefied them and they had no way to turn. Each day brought more facts of undernourishment, illness, eviction and despair, and now the paesanos rarely laughed or smiled.

Each time the work-whistle blew on the huge Packer building Paul mounted the scaffolds determined to hold his job. No one must outstrip his hands and trowel! But at home the sight of the hungry paesanos depressed him and he worried about his job. One evening he said to Annunziata: "Mama, let's go to the Cripple."

"Haven't I all the time brung you the truth from the spirit woild? . . . Why of course. Now let me see . . . yes, he says to me, he says: 'I ain't never been so happy like now . . .' He holds his hands in prayer and says his prayers has always been listened to by the Lord, and I can see his face is tired-like . . . now don't let that worry you—you know he's been under a super-human strain since the Lord sent for him, and it wasn't exactly easy for him to watch over his dear beloved ones. . . . Yes Missus, like I always told you, he looks at his big boy here and takes him by the hand and shakes it."

Papa. Papa who art in Heaven. Papa . . .

Back and forth rocked the Cripple.

"He says you and your boy has come a long way through the toibulent rivers and thorn-y paths of trials and trib-u-lations and now he looks blessings on youse. Ah, missus, I wisht you could only see him! How lovely he looks! And he says he has somethin' extra special to tell me to tell you from the spirit woild, but now he turns his ear a little to you and says 'What do you want to ask me?' "

"What does he wish to tell us?" asked Paul excitedly.

"He says not to be too impatient and that he'll tell

you after you asked him the questions which he knows is on your mind."

"Ask father ... what our future will be—"

The Cripple caught her thick throat, closed the bulging eyes, and pushed back and forth.

"From the spirit woild he tells me now over my shoulder that anything you have in your minds is something he and God has planted there and 'cause of that it is poifectly safe. He says irregardless what woiks in your mind is gonner woik out right, and everything is bein' done for the best—that's 'cause he and God has figgered it out. Now is there anythin' definite about your ideas? Like—say, money, or goin' someplace?—wait—don't tell me—I got a feeling—See, I knew it was a trip—didn't I feel it and say it! No, the spirit woild has never lied. Now ain't that wonderful, missus, when your boy asked me about the future I got a terrific pull about the waist, like someone wanted to make me go with them someplace—Glory, glory, what a feeling, like I was being taken on a long trip maybe on water—no, it's more like over land on wheels—and yet there's even water to be crossed—" The El trains machined by and she watched them. "My my, I see all of youse riding and goin' through like a country with dairy farms and wheat farms and all of youse wearin' a sunny smile—"

And mother and son living that instant in a dazzling world.

"Your most dearest dreams are gonner come true he says, and you're all gonner experience another and better kind of life! Ah, *now* he says he must tell you that extra special message before he goes."

The Cripple breathed in long rasping breaths.

"My, how lovely, missus, this is the most happiest thing he has ever sent from the spirit woild! He says, he says, 'My dear beloved family has been through enough, they have been through too much, and now the time is over for them to suffer any more. I am goin' to change my family to happiness. The Almighty and I has put ideas (or gonner put) in your minds for good reasons, and when you get to settle in your *new* life—"

She listened with concentrated attention.

"Oh, missus, how wonderful! 'One night when youse are all sitting to the table I'm gonner come. . . .' "

Annunziata and Paul tensed and pushed forward.

"Will we see him? How will we know? How long from now will it be?"

"He says you will know. You will feel it. And you must put a plate on the table and fix a chair for him. He won't eat it though, but it must be there—"

"Oh, tell us what he'll look like!"

"You'll feel a quiet in the house and all of you'll know the time has come and youse must stay still right still in your chairs or if some of you are standing, to just stay like that and look at the doorway and . . . there he'll be, just like when you saw him last, only, dressed in pure white, and with a wonderful smile on his happy face—"

"Geremio . . ."

"—but remember, don't any of youse say anything! I see him just like he's come home from woik . . . yes, he's tired, but he don't mind that—his heart says, 'Nothin' is too good for my family.' . . . Then he puts out his hands to you like the Lord does, and he says, 'You are my own; the time has come for me to show myself like you always asked me in your prayers which I have always heard since I was sent for by my loving Lord by whose right hand I stay.' Then he sees you are all still and reads the love in your eyes and comes into the room without even a sound and comes first to you, missus, and puts his arms around you and kisses you and says, 'This is my wife,' and then he goes to your boy here and puts his arm around him and kisses him, and he even shakes his hand, and says, 'This is my boy Paul, and I thank you for taking my place in the earthly woild, and I am praying that Our Lord will reward you." And then he goes to his dear beloved children one by one and says their name and embraces them with love in his bosom. And then . . . missus, he goes to his

much-deserved happiness with the Angels for then his
woik will be done. . . . See! He stops at the doorway and
turns around with a great smile which means: 'Your life
has changed and now there shan't be any more trouble,
and my children are gonner grow up and marry and
raise'—yes, missus, I see more happy little children—
'beautiful children of their own.' And I see you, missus,
with white-white hair and very old, and your good man
waiting for you in the spirit woild with folded hands and
smiling, and your woik in this earthly woild will be
done. . . . Oh this has been the best message from the
spirit woild. . . . Look at me, I'm flat as a rag—that's
how it's gripped me. . . . Margie! Margie, bring in some
nice tea for the missus and her boy and me! Y'hear me,
Margie?"

2

A mid-July night Paul and Nazone sat on the fire escape.

"Godson, I implore you; you must help me get
work—work that I may go to my wife and children in
Abruzzi. The career of builder in this land is done. This
land has become a soil that has contradicted itself, a
country of Babel where Christians are beginning to
wander about in hungry distress cursing each other in
strange tongues, ripping their hearts, and possessing no
longer even fingernails with which to scratch their des-
peration. Godson, you must find work for me—that I
may return to the beautiful Italia—where I will be content to live and die with a mouthful of bread each day
. . . near my family and that dear earth that gave me
birth."

"Godfather, do not worry—this upset should not last.
Soon, perhaps, there may be more work than we ever
dreamed of. Then, I am sure to be a foreman, and you,

you shall always work for me." Nazone hugged his godson.

"I wish to Dio that will happen. But godson Paul,
what is going on today in this America is not a thing of
temperament, it is something we cannot understand, it
is the beginning, and all shall be shut to the hands that
labor. It is like the war that brings itself and for us only
suffering awaits."

"It shouldn't be like this—there's no sense to it . . ."

"I pray you, godson, speak for me at the job you
work. Be not ashamed to speak for me. . . . I will work
like a fighter! . . . Discovered by an Italian—named
from Italian—But oh, that I may leave this land of dis-
illusion!"

Paul kept after his foreman and pleaded for Nazone
until he got the job for him, and it was understood that
he had to turn back ten dollars a week.

Nazone went each morning to work with him. They
rode together, they sat side by side in the subway train,
they walked to Job together, they went up the scaffolds
together, they troweled and hammered building up together, they lunched together, and together at workday's cease they took sore self home.

On the third morning earth had floated down into
the white hell of day, and as Paul and his godfather
came up from the subway, life stood out in pulsing sunlight photography. Morning-born senses brought vividly
the solarized city into ken. Sharp against sky's light-
light blue concave stood the architectural stance of
buildings—now tall and pointed—now squat and
square—now sandstoney buff in ornate rolls—now with
jail-bar severity—now ugly—and never beautiful.

The few blocks to the job Paul and Nazone stepped
along happy for no apparent reason. They looked at
each other and smiled foolishly. A precious warm breeze
glided down and mingled familiarly with them. Nazone
raised his gentle plump face to it and paused for a moment. After a little way he halted, closed his eyes and

drank in a long breath caressingly. He put his hand to heart and said:

"Ah, summer sweet, how you do perfume these nostrils . . . !"

He gazed up to the sky admiringly, but then caught at his back and cried:

"Ooch, this cocko of a spine seems poinarded! Ah, godson, this skin is too delicate for the wall. Christian man was never meant to blind the light of his short days with bestial toil. This life of mine is inspired now, right now this very moment, to find itself on the rim splay of sea with one naked foot on warm white sand and the other in ocean's wet green. I don't know, but this day is a canzonella of God, a day lucent with colored glass bells. Madonna, with this mood I have a volition for laughing things like this bright circular sun atop our heads, a lust for things natural!"

They were a block from Job when he took Paul by the arm and stopped. "Godson Paul, it is much too beautiful to sweat and stink today! Let us grab two or three paesanos and go with wine flagon and sandwich under arm to some country place or seashore where we may bless the senses with smell of grass and salt of sea. . . . What does one say!"

Nazone's suggestion came on Paul as a sudden good odor, and he hesitated.

"But it will cost us a day's pay . . ."

Nazone waved it away with:

"He who works, eats. He who does not work eats, drinks, and dances. Come, we who work with our hands can live a thousand centuries, and yet will we have to work."

"Is it nice by the seashore? . . . But there, I do not know how to swim."

"Nice? Why, godson, each wave brings in saline bafts

that scour the breathing sacks and impart the appetite of ten Christians, and your skin will consume the touch of sand and sun like a sitting to platter of spaghetti. . . . As for the art of carrying yourself in water, I shall instruct you in the proper European manner—like this—with arms and legs of the frog . . ."

Paul stood consternated and looking to Job near by.

"Godson, come, this day issues as voluptuous woman in heat. It is a rich hour of mammalian desire—a phantasy of Nature—godson, let us disport in dulcent leisure and leave behind Job! Job! Job!"

Two bricklayers went by.

" 'S matter kid, the weather got ya?"

"Godfather, we dare not leave Job."

Nazone shrugged.

"You are just. If we lose our jobs—it is the fish without water."

Job was monstrous-poised on the river front with a wide avenue at its feet, a broad thoroughfare along which were ribboned tracks for railroad trains, and as Paul and Nazone approached it they had their thoughts unconsciously awe-prayered upon it. A white seagull appeared from behind Job. It hovered high above it, winged down, and rested upon the very peak, a concrete column that stuck up from the roof, many floors above the street. It looked about and then flew itself fast away up into nothing. A long train of freight cars was coming slowly along the avenue.

"Come, if we do not hurry it will block our way to the job."

"The good Dio," reflected Nazone, "would have made us with wheels if he had intended for us to hurry so. . . . Aie, but there is at this morning's young hour a surpassing lovely color. . . . There, I must remove me my jacket and open this shirt at neck. Ahh, what a refreshment. . . . Life-life, this plumpiness cares not for Job today—Hmn tee-re-lala, proverbially with tambourine in hand could I do over the sparkling sands of sea!

Godson, godson, again I say let us wrap this tender day
in pocket and steal it to the ocean's side!"

Paul shook his head.

"But godson we sin—beak of gull calls, sands rustle,
ocean's spray waves up, and summer's blue breath above
tries to whisper us there.... Look, my own godson
grins and believe me not.... It really calls to us. Veritably.... Soul of honor—I hear it.... Then we
go ...?"

Paul smiled, shaking his head.

"It was so difficult to get you on. How shall you return to Abruzzi? ... Come, godfather. That train will
hold us back." Nazone, instead, slowed. Nazone, who
walked gracefully in the outward swing of his large feet
and roly-poly buttocks—the chubby chest on paunch—
the open shirt neck revealed red and white of collar-
line—and cushioned in at the sides of the great fine
nose the kind small milk-blue eyes by the flush
cheeks—and the lightness of breath through which he
said:

> "... Also, might the fond hour be
> When I, to lie whole free
> In grass beneath umbrelling tree ...
> To repose in strength
> And dream
> Of this me who bent carnated soul
> On wall of Job's long heat and cold ...?"

"Godfather! Hurry!"

Toil's battle herald had blown, and Paul and Nazone
ran up the twenty flights in a furious effort that left
them aching legs and strained hearts and lungs when
they climbed up over a window sill and out onto the
swinging scaffolds.

The single Job-brain of foreman Jones pressed itself
against two men who had clambered upon scaffold minutes late.

"Hey you Paul take your corner and tell that compara

of yours in Chinese to run up the pier next to the corner! Hey Paul yank up that Goddamn line! The bricklayers are standing-waitin' for it with their pork in their hands—put it up!"

What is he a wise guy? Watch out or I'll fix your wagon! Bastard! See . . . them jump! Jones you've gotta be a reg'lar son-of-a-bitch! I love you Jones. Me. Here. I'm everything! Up! Up! Up!

As the morning hours were muscled and sweated by, Nazone could not focus his being to trowel and mortar, hammer and chisel, line, block, dowel, rule, slicker, brick, scaffold, men, and foreman. An inner rhythm kept radiating his senses farther and farther beyond his immediate physical identification, as though he, a planet of flesh, were sending out the power of his senses over time and space. The concept of his flesh blended with the sun's pure white lust and levitated him past Jones who shouted curses at him to run out the line, past the worried warning face of Paul, past his fellowmen on the scaffold, past the concrete decision of Job Almighty before him, past the overrun street and freighted river, past the steelstone hives, the painful geometry of New Babylon, and out to where warm sands caressed him . . . the cool sea . . . celestial kiss of sky . . . and naked perfect womankind . . . entwined him . . . Yes, that place is . . . But there, where is it?

"Godfather, run out that course, here comes Jones!"

It may be on the shore of Abruzzi near the cove at the bend of the large dune . . . It was there I first saw the little hair 'neath my arms and smelled my flesh . . . perhaps it is there where . . .

He raised his trowel-arm and smelled in the strong sweet wet hair flesh . . .

"Godfather, hurry!"

The sudden message of his flesh told him of earth and sea. He did not hear foreman Jones rushing over the littered scaffold to him.

Jones leaped over a mortar-tub with hand outstretched to snatch Nazone's trowel from him.

"Y'bastard you're's slow's the comin' o' Christ!"

Paul saw Jones's mad foot catch the tub and throw him into his Godfather, pitching Nazone violently from the scaffold trowel in hand. He fell to the sill of a wide window, hit it with his stomach and bounced out into the open. Paul looked over the scaffold rail and through staring mouth and eyes sent out his soul to catch his Godfather who flung out his arms and rested on the speed of space that sucked him down. For an electrical instant their eyes met.

Oh, the surprise . . .

Oh Jesus, the misery he poured up!

Christ-Christ hold him back! Give strength to the air! Christ don't let him drop so fast! Christ have him float gently! Have him land safely! Christ oh Christ he's spinning faster and faster and getting smaller and smaller! Don't! No! Christ! No! Noooooo . . . !

The man Nazone rocketed away from Paul and the scaffold through deathed nothing and smashed to the street bridge twenty floors below. Paul shut his eyes, and when the terrible meaty quash sounded up to him it left him stunned and quaking uncontrollably. As his knees pumped he clung to the scaffold crying hysterically: "Get up, godfather—oh move, godfather—Help! Send for the ambulance! Send for help! Save him oh save him!"

The men climbed off the swinging scaffolds and began running down the stairwells. Foreman Jones lowered his eyes with stupid bitterness. And Paul felt the world going round and round. He moved to get up from the scaffold and gripped the scaffold-cable but his stricken legs refused to move correctly. His heart slammed and fast tears covered his sight. Reuben, a colored hodcarrier, put his arm about Paul's waist and helped him up with foot on terra-cotta and hand at cable onto the next floor.

"Doan' cry, Paulie . . . doan' cry, sonny."

"Oh Reuben, I can't—breathe.... I can't—see ..."

"Jes' take it easy."

"Reuben, my godfather can't be dead ..."

"You sick, Paulie. You better go right straight hoame."

"Reuben, Reuben, the stairs are going all around.... Reuben, the earth is spinning so fast ... so fast! so-so smooth, Reuben!"

"Paulie, sonny, I knows.... Here, lemme carry you.

"Lemme take you hoame, Paulie. Please doan' you go and see."

"I must ..."

"You sick boy. You cain't stand."

"I must go to him. I must talk with him. Talk with him like a few minutes ago."

"Paulie, doan' go. You cain't talk with him ... no more."

"I've got to. To tell him to pull through. To live. That I'll help him—that we'll all help him ..."

He lay forward against the men and said faintedly:

"Let me see my godfather ..."

They made way. He saw. And a ghastly fascination cut across his senses.

Starkly at his feet lay Nazone. A brilliant red wet overalled pulp splotched over broken terra-cotta. Both his feet were snapped off and the flesh-shriven left leg-bone's whittled point had thrust itself into a plank, with the protruding kneebone aiming at the sky. His hips and torso was a distorted sprung hulk. His overflung arms were splintered, and glued in his crushed right hand was his trowel. His head, split wholly through by a jagged terra-cotta fragment, was an exploded human fruit. His skull-top was rolled outward, with the scalp, underlayers, and cartilage leafing from it, and his face halved exactly down the centerline of nose, with the left nostril suspended alone at the lip-end, curled out and facing the right nostril. Only the right half of his face remained attached to his neck. His small right eye was filmed with transparent liquid and fixed at the sun. The crescent of his mouth and teeth was wide askew, and mingled over the sweat of his stubble were the marine contents of his blood and brains that spread as quivering livery vomit, glistening on the bluing flesh a tenuous rainbowed flora of infinite wavering fibrins. . . .

One big green fatbellied fly appeared, and then another and another. They buzzed among his bone and tissue and sucked the anatomy of his soul from the homeless ruddy corpuscles and charged into themselves the dispersed electricity that had powered his light in work, home, and his song and arms to heaven.

Every disfigurement of his godfather echoed in Paul with lightning flashes, shuddering and crushing him. His tongue shrunk.

A laborer laid a tarpaulin over Nazone.

"No lunch for me."

"No more work for me today."

The superintendent pushed back his fedora, put hands on hips, rolled his lips about and said:

"Boys . . . there's a lotta mortar in the mixer and tubs that's gotta be used up. There's a hundred brickies and sixty hodcarriers, and overhead."

He looked at his watch.

"We'll go back after lunch. Men on buildings have to stay on their toes and keep their eyes wide open."

Paul remained by the shattered Nazone. A flame shot through him. "That is your father Geremio!" it cried, "Your father! You!"

Paul bit his hands. He stumbled down into the street. He wandered away, fearing to turn. On the clean sun-bathed sidewalk he saw his bloodied crushed father. He bumped into a woman and looked at her dazedly. He turned and saw Job. It pressed upon him and choked him. He held out his hands and gazed at them. That was he. Those were the limbs that stretched their life force against brick. This was the world, that spun and sickened, making him sit on a doorstep, making him want to clasp the earth and shout for it to stop, the world that would crumple him like his father and

Nazone! Everywhere were their violated selves, helpless, appealing to him in awful dignity. He got to his feet and ran.

This is the street of Tenement, and he arrives weary. Before him on the stoop sits Gloria. Bundle of blonde animal, she sits the July heat in red cotton and bare legs spread.

"Hullo Paul. Gee, it's nice an' hot."

—And her reality's smell.

"I gotta party. Birthday party. Tonight, won'tcha come?"

". . . I have seen a man . . . killed . . ."

"We're gonner have eats and dancin'—what did y'say, huh?"

Annunziata emerged from the dark hallway with Geremino in hand. Behind Gloria she appeared. Ah mother. So heavy worn and early gray.

He walked up past Gloria, and held to the railing.

"Paul my Paul, why are you home shirtless in cemented overall and face shocked? Are you ill of heat?"

He contemplated her burdened face, and said:

"Godfather Vincenz is dead."

Annunziata let go Geremino's hand, and her mouth dried.

". . . Paul . . ."

"Remember, mama, I am talking to you. Remember."

Up Tenement's fetid hallway and into Tenement's Italian smelling kitchen she led him.

Sit oh son while I wet-clothly cool thy hurt self, thy dear dear self oh good beautiful son mine.

The children came, and they wondered.

"Mama," asked Geremino, tugging her apron, "Why is Paul home with overalls, is he sick?"

"Sick, little brother? Geremino, sweat little heart, kiss Paul."

"Paul sick?"

"Play. Find the sun. Play, play, play . . . play."

Annina brought a glass of chill wine to his lips, and as Annunziata applied cool vinegary cloths to his forehead the throb pounded slower and slower in the painful veins of his mind. Tired tears came. And Annunziata wept quietly with him. He closed his lids in the salt of weeping, and began to sink.

"... Mama, did I tell you what happened today? Yes, I do not believe it. But I saw it.... Where is he now? ..."

Annunziata's lachry-rhythm lulled. His head dropped back on the chair-rest and his legs relaxed.

"... Mama, what is today ... ?"

"... Twenty-eighth ... July ..."

"... Good Friday, thirtieth of March ... was papa ..."

Softly-soft. Annunziata helped her Paul to the children's bed. It was dark and still there. She carefully removed his clothes and shoes of Job. Dust, cement, and his Job sweated flesh. She wetted with tongue her finger and signed the cross upon his forehead and pulsing joints. She covered him with a clean white sheet, and kissed the hand that remained without.

Paul mine.

A vibrating gray cloud looms over him and carries him. He knows it is the whistle of Job. He looks above, and Job leans up over him beyond his sight. Job, he sighs, I am so tired. How did you find me out? The soft pad of feet about him. They keep their faces in the shadow and he does not know them but they are living because their breaths are light pink. Why does he not know them? Quick quick up stairwells feet on steps feet on steps and he cannot keep up. But why do they work in the dark; it is so difficult to plumb and level? Next him works a man with a large nose. He will talk in Italian for the man seems a foreigner. Why does the foreman look dangerously at the man? He wants to tell him about the foreman but the man smiles.

When the foreman comes to him the man puts down his arms and surrenders! Do not do it to me, says the man's face. Come, says the foreman's eyes, let's get this over with. The foreman leads the man to the edge of the scaffold. The man looks down and is terribly frightened. The man's large nose quivers excitedly and he cannot keep it still. Stand still, says the foreman, so that I can push you off. The other men stop working and watch, and the man at the edge of the scaffold is ashamed and says, oh please don't push me, I'll do it myself. But he shivers and cannot do it, and he smiles so politely querulous. Now that's right, says the foreman, smile, take it like a good fellow so I can push you off, see, fall down in this direction, do you understand? Yes, says the man with the quivering large nose, but honestly, I am so afraid, I swear I don't want to die, I can't bear it, there is no sense to it, and it will hurt me so. The foreman puts his arm about him and caresses him while tripping him and pushing him off, and says, don't be a child, we don't want to hurt you. He sees that it was his godfather who was sent from the scaffold and he tries to hit the foreman but the foreman picks him up and says, oh so you're on his side, eh? well that's just what I thought, and the foreman pitches him from the scaffold and out into space. He is falling! And he cries, I didn't mean it! I give up! You win! I don't want to play any more! The ground is running up at him faster and faster and he shuts his eyes and makes the sign of the cross. Just as he is about to hit he floats easily and steps to the street bridge.

His godfather is near him with his legs snapped off and kicking the pointy ends about like a woman lying on her back and squirming in desire; he is all twisted, his face chopped in two, and he's trying to keep the lid of his one remaining eye open with his fingers. Godfather, godfather, he cries, keep the light of your eye open until I get help! I'll save you! He wants to pick up his godfather's pieces and put them back on but he is afraid to touch them. I remember, he cries again, I remember who can save you; it is our Lord Christ who will do it; he made us, he loves us and will not deny us; he is our friend and will help us in need! Bear, oh godfather bear until I find Him. His godfather's disrupted being is in parts that yearn away from each other, and his large nose, divided and curled out, quivers like a beating fish. Godson, he says, I can no longer keep the light of this eye. Paul will seek Christ he will seek Christ for that is his mission. He rushes out into the street. Yes, he will run and run until he finds Him. He now will find Him!

On, on, on . . . on—But he has forgotten where to go. Is there no one to tell him? And time will not last.

Hey there, people, he shouts, won't you please tell me which way to go? They do not hear, and he cannot get to them for they are all in passageways as creatures along paddocks. Hey you, hey you and you! But there are no hearings. They stream on. He is lost and knows not the manner of path. Time cannot wait, he will be left behind in a darkness that will not move so that he will not feel himself but will know only that he is waiting and no one will remember to come for him. He must hurry, hurry! And the center of him rushes back suckingly fast. He travels back to the many buildings he helped put up. The men will not speak with him, and when the last brick is laid he wipes his trowel on his overalls and asks, Have you seen Christ? Where may I find him? And they look at the walls. He has built all the jobs and reprinted self on all the brick once before laid. Tired, how tired. He wants to sit, to rest. A slender white Paul-face shakes. It peers from shadow and says, there is no rest, strive and you will find the Job. There is a man approaching. He walks with jaunty and individual grace. He knows it is his father Geremio. Geremio strides along wearing a checkered suit with stiff wing collar, polka-dot bow tie, pork-pie fedora, two-tone buttoned shoes and puffing a Royal Bengal, and his face is a little different, as though he had on heavy makeup. Paul wants to run to him and weep, to embrace his feel and smell, but he does not because his father behaves as an abashed stranger who feigns not to notice him. He wishes so to ask him, Father where have you been this long time? Where have you been living and what have you been doing? What have mother and the children

done that you have run away? Have you forgotten you
are our father? But when his father comes by he does
not ask for he feels that his father is ashamed. He is
hurt to think that his father has betrayed Annunziata.
He loves his father. He will bring him back to
Annunziata and the children without hurting his feel-
ings. He walks with him. He looks up to his face that is
turned slightly to the side, and he says naturally, Hello
papa, I'll walk along with you if you don't mind, I was
going this way. His father nods. He wants to say to his
father, Papa, you are handsome to my eyes with your
white teeth and black wavy hair, and mama always tells
that you are the only man in the world for her. He
knows by the way his father walks that he is going to
Job. He knows the walking-step to Job. He wants to tell
his father with pride that he is a full-fledged journey-
man bricklayer—oh how he will surprise him when they
get to Job.

Job!

It is a maze of caught stone and steel. His heart is
quailed. His father rolls up his coatsleeves and quietly
begins laying bricks. Paul tries to lay bricks with him
but finds his trowel is very heavy, the handle is hardly
big enough to grasp, and the mortar will not stick to the
trowel. He struggles to keep up with his father but the
bricks fall from his fingers and will not lay straight. Fear
swathes him. He looks about Job. He is in a huge choir
loft with scaffolding about the walls. In niches are
Saints. They wear overalls and look like paesanos he
dimly recalls. They step down and carry hods and push
wheelbarrows. But what Saints are they? The little fellow and the curly-headed scaffolder and the mortarman
look like Thomas, Lazarene, and the Snoutnose who
once visited the house. The boss is coming, the boss! A
great big man dressed like a priest punches his father on
the bricklaying muscle of his trowelhand forearm and
shouts, Wop! get it up! That man is Mister Murdin!
Paul points at him and cries, I spy! you are the boss
Murdin! The man turns around like a magician and

each time he revolves and shouts at Geremio and Paul he has on a suit and mask of a general, a mayor, a principal, a policeman, but Paul keeps crying, I spy! I spy!

Mister Murdin sticks his tongue at him and disappears.

Father, Father, calls Paul, why are we here? His father eyes his brickwork and does not listen. Father, I know now that Mister Murdin is our enemy! His father smiles and winks at him. Then Job begins to tumble in gentle silence. Cornices, arches and walls crack apart and roll down. He shouts with all his might to his father to beware, but his father keeps interestedly laying bricks, leaning his head to a side as though listening to flowing music. Huge walls fall out of plumb and cannonade down toward his father and he flies up to meet them holding out his hands to protect his father and the walls break over his arms without hurting him. He hurls himself frantically from scaffold to scaffold to stay the oncoming walls and girders. Father! Men! why don't you try to save yourselves! But they are apathetic and lend themselves dreamily to disaster as fatigued actors. Don't five up! he shouts. Father! Men! Refuse to die! Say no! His father raises a graceful hand, and in defeated chorus they sing, *Good Friday . . . Thirtieth of March . . . Sainted Friday.* The words steal his strength and he cannot keep up with the whelming downthunder of floors and walls, then feels himself giving way and blanketed as sleepy child. He spins through the solids of brick and steel and comes to crucified rest in the concrete forms; concrete pours through him as through soft cotton, and is he Geremio? A slender white Paul-face tells him he is Paul.

A fog carries him to the Cripple, and she awaits him in her rocker. I knowed youse was comin', she says. She clutches her fingers and strains and her neck swells, and from the dark corner of the ceiling behind her whorls out a whiteness that forms into his father. His father is beaten, pale and sublimated. The Cripple writhes and her eyes bulge. Sonny, she says, your father says he's happy in paradise and everything's all right. Let me kiss my father. No, she answers, you can't. But he surges over her shoulder and embraces his father. His father's man-face bristles strongly against his own and his father whispers quickly, I was cheated, my children also will be crushed, cheated. His father begins to absolve and sighs faintly, Ahhh, not even the Death can free us, for we are . . . Christ in concrete . . .

Paul bolted up in darkness, his heart racing and his consciousness groping painfully in resurging maelstrom.

"I am Paul, Paul, Paul, I am Paul."

His blood drained and left him trembling.

"I too, will die . . . and disappear . . ."

And a quiet prisoning terror came into him.

Annunziata weeping with Ci Luigi and the paesanos in the kitchen heard him and hurried into the bedroom. She struck a match and lit the gaslight. His face frightened her. She took the crucifix from the wall and placed it in his hands.

"Paul mine . . . Paul, mother's own . . . what has happened?"

He pushed the crucifix aside and stared into her eyes.

"Mother," he said fearfully, "Papa is not coming back—we shall never meet again."

She was impaled. She shut her eyes and moaned.

He gripped her hands.

"Who nails us to the cross? Mother . . . why are we living!"

She opened her eyes. She remained pierced.

He dropped his head on her shoulder and tearfully whispered:

"Unfair! Unfair! —Our lives—unfair!"

3

"Never back to Job, son my son! We will starve, we will wander the streets and crowd ourselves in holes and corners, we will walk on our hands and knees, we will humble ourselves low, low, rather than you back to Job. Oh hear me son of mine . . ."

To Job he went. He could not talk. He could not say anything.

When Annunziata and the children prepared for mass the Sunday after the funeral, Paul remained in bed thinking.

"Will you not come, Paul? I—will await thee . . ."

As he approached Saint Prisca he felt a dread. In church his head began to ache. He became acutely alive to the strangeness of ceremony, the candles and press of Christian faces, the faces and wings of the statues, the temple architecture, the convolutions of mass, the torment of incantations, the ultimate decision of Father John, and nausea assaulted his bowels, breast and brain.

In the mornings he would eat his breakfast silently and leave; and Annunziata's ". . . Abide thy dear step . . . oh son . . . guard thy every step . . ." came to him tenderer, more beseeching. At evenfall when from the street came distantly his step, at window, her head would bow in thanksgiving. And at kitchen door through eyes her entire love embraced him.

Paul . . . mine. Everything for him. Paul Paul. Quiet the children for Paul. Head-chair of table and richest dish for my Paul. Attention for our Paul! Salt and pepper and clean serviette. Love, love and prayer for him, my Paul.

Silent he returned. Silent he remained. And a trembling came to Annunziata. If only he would speak. But he just looked and listened. For a few Sundays she had waited for him to go to mass. He would turn his head and stay reading the newspapers. And when she wandered off without him she lit candles and prayed, prayed. Would that I could carry for thee thy sentence of Job.

For him she would have borne the world. She wanted to say to him that she had felt ever his crushing duty.

That you are not to mass—Dio—understands—for I know he wants for you to rest on the Sabbath morn—Son son, seek eternally His divine love . . . and sustenance . . . seek Him . . .

She wanted to tell him as mother to child. There was something in his face, and her voice was now powerless. The day he first shaved she wept with admiration, and it added to her fear. As he soaped and shaved at the kitchen mirror it struck her heart. That night she had the cold sensing that told her he no longer said his prayers. The vision of his dark cutting face prided her soul, but where there had been supplication there was intense question; and upon the humbleness had come quiet bitterness. She arose and went to his bed. She knew, she knew he had not prayed. He heard her and remained with closed eyes. Fervently she signed the cross above him and said for him his Our Father and Hail Mary. And he quivered and loved her . . . and hated that which suffered her.

The scaffolds are not safe, for the rich must ever profit more.

The men are driven. And they prefer death or injury to loss of work. Work and die. Today I did not die. I have been let to live today and must be thankful that tomorrow I may return to work—to die.

Somewhere in the countless bendings and twistings he would lose his balance, a derrick would collapse and blot him out, a sledge would hurtle from above and crumple him, a brick would smash through his skull.

Ah no, today's Job had choked him—but let him live. Tomorrow he would die. He will have died without having raised his head and shouted defiance! and would be left with stiff outstretched fingers and gummy stilled mouth—

A severe February morning he was laying up the corner of a parapet fifty floors aloft. Though bundled heavily he was as if naked in the numbing icy wind and blinding dust. He was working on his knees overhand at the very edge of the roof with mortar tubs and bricks behind him and Job-anxious bricklayers swinging their trowels on both sides of him. His sore fingers shot pain each time he picked the frozen brick, the steely furious wind brittled the mortar and blew it into his eyes to stab and bring burning. As he bent over and laid a brick and peered down the endless sharp corner bead a brick-layer in his nervousness jostled him and he pushed forward out over the corner. His foot struck back and caught securely under the mortar tub and held him. He dropped flat on the edge of the roof helplessly and a pressure of fright smothered him.

"It's a long way down, isn't it, kid?" said a foreman's voice behind him. He hit the corner brick weakly with his trowel.

". . . Yes . . ."

O life do not kill me before I have freed my heart—!

At five the foreman came along the parapets with discharge slips in hand. Men shrank and wanted to hide. Their faces went white and they wanted to cry.

"Boys," said the foreman, "that's all there is—there ain't no more!" Today he did not die. Perhaps somewhere tomorrow. And he left Job grimly with level and toolbag.

"Mama! What are you praying for!"

In votive lamp's lume she turned.

". . . Paul . . . ?"

He pointed to the crucifix.

"That's a lie."

His words strangled her.

"—Our Dio?"

"What Dio and Dio!"

She gazed about and falteringly sat back on the bed. She looked to him for minutes. Please, please said her eyes.

You do not understand. He has agonized on the cross for us . . . and complained not. He is the Sun, the Morning, and the Night. He kisses the feet of the little ones, and loves everything, everywhere and always. Yes. Yes, he gave me courage to live for my children, and let me behold child Paul don the long pantaloons. He kept this soul a sheet of white. He made me thankful in sorrow . . . and now . . .

She clasped the scapular of the Sacred Heart to her.

". . . Life, what have you done to the Lord's Paul?"

"Did he ever return papa? Blind, you are blind, mama!"

She wavered dizzily and said with effort: ". . . Jesu . . . has blessed me with thee . . . and to Him praises I sing . . ."

He remained strainedly silent, and then said in lowered voice: "I only know that I am cheated."

". . . But I do not understand . . ."

"Papa's life has been used against me. My toil has been used against me."

". . . What . . . ? I do not know . . . My Paul . . . I am confused . . . so, so tired—"

"We have only one life! One life!"

"On earth, yes—"

"No! It is not like that! Here where we are is our only life!"

Staring to the crucifix, she held her heart.

"We live and suffer not in vain, and our reward awaits . . ."

"I want justice here! I want happiness here! I want life here!"

"In the next world is our salvation—and He is coming—He is coming—"

"Mama, mama, I know so terribly this our only life—"

"He will come—I say he will come—"

"Now! Now! I want salvation now! For I know oh I know we cannot live forever . . ."

She chanted in the eternity of her faith, and that which he could no longer take to him sickened.

"He is coming for us—He will save us—"

"Stop!"

She clutched her breast tighter. The children suddenly awakened, and they lay listening. He reached up
to the crucifix, pulled it from the wall, and Annunziata's
face paled. His eyes sought hers strongly.

"Mama, we must go on to a world of our own. We
need each other more than ever—before we die crushed
like papa!"

She took the crucifix from him and put it to her lips.

"Jesu Jesu Jesu save my Paul save my Paul . . ."

"Mama," he pleaded, "do not kiss the plaster man
and wooden cross!"

"Save save save save . . ."

She proffered the cross in supplicating tears.

"Take the Jesu to your heart—Kiss Jesu—My Paul
my Paul keep forever our Jesu keep Jesu keep Jesu—"

He pulled the crucifix from her and crushed it in his
hands. Annunziata was lightning-struck. Horrified livid
she beheld the pieces fall to the floor. A cloud of mad-
ness swirled and fulminated within her. With closed
eyes, lowered head and chin she threw her mother-
being upon him. She caught him by the throat with a
heart-ripping cry and thrust him to the wall beating his
face hysterically and screaming:

"Out! Out! The Lord's Paul is no more! Out! Ah
Jesu, give me the strength! My sainted son is dead!
Dead! Dead! Ahh dead!" He could not see. He felt his
arms limp. And from his nose and mouth ran blood. Its
wet dropped her hands. And in grace of votive light she
saw his anguished face. He bent his head and turned.
Past the children's dark bedrooms he dazedly swam.
They felt him go by. They lay in torn wonder. Annunziata remained standing, lost. And his blood penetrating
her hands. The kitchen door closed.

Fruit of this belly have I devoured.

Beverage of this womb have I drunk.

Her hands clenched, and quietly-quietly she punched
into her stomach.

Geremio, husband long silent, he of thine and mine

of our cross has borne ... And him have I scourged.
Destroy me!

Hair loosed and hanging chin, she beat her stomach.
Quietly her mother-strength sent shafts against the bag
of life.

... My Paul—forgive me ...

She put swollen hands to mouth and bit until they
bled.

... Lost ...

Annina and the children went to her. She lay in the
grip of awful revolting breaths. As they placed her on
the bed and wept, she gasped:

"—Jesu—remember—the cross of my Paul—was too,
too great ... Christ my Lord—remember—that to me
he came—and prayed me live for the children—To me
he said, 'Mama—do not cry—mama—now I shall be
father—' O Jesu, recall? —Think, my Lord—at tender
twelve—upon Job's scaffold he dared—and yes-yes my
Dio—always loving Thee—I pray Thee as never
before—forgive him—He knows not of what he says or
does—for on the road—'neath burden—and in distort
of pain—of Thee has he lost sight—Jesu Christ, Thou
must hear me—He loves Thee—and vastness of his
love—has overhurt ... Jesu, Jesu, Jesu ... Jesu
Giuseppe e'Mari ...

"Jesu Jesu Jesu

"Jesu Jesu

"Jesu ..."

4

He wandered. Not knowing where. Beyond his stun
noises went off ... and he seemed to hear. Stupid
world. Indifferent. He would have had earth embrace
him. Equality. Justice. That he could sleep silently, sleep
away from all knowing.

At Tenement he found himself. And tiredly up. He

opened the kitchen door weakly, and in Annunziata's rocker sat Annina.

She rose and met him. She spoke as a woman.

"Paul. Paul, mama."

". . . Annina . . ."

"We were awake. And we heard . . ."

". . . How—is Mama . . ." he whispered, "it must never be. Mama . . . forgive . . ."

Annunziata was still.

". . . Mama, you made me, mama . . . I am you . . . in everything."

Without change she remained.

"Mama."

Mama! Let us take the kids and run where none can reach us . . . mama, do you hear? Mama, we'll build a shelter in the forest and dig fruit of wilderness with our hands . . . We'll sing on the hills night and day—Mama, let us find our own world, and never part—Mama, do you hear me . . . ?"

Quiet was Annunziata . . . and staring.

"Mama, this is Paul. . . . Mama . . . ?"

Tarantella . . . Who plays it softly that she dances? And there in the cobbler's shop with shoes slung on shoulder is the boy Geremio smiling to her and telling the cobbler he will marry the little girl with braids who swings sweetly barefoot. She is twelve and as she does Tarantell with the children Geremio's dark eyes travel through the villagers' music to tell her "You shall be mine, Tarantell-Tarantell!" It plays as they are engaged in Aunt Seraphina's big stone room where the giant-muscled Luigi happily follows with Jew's harp in mouth. Tarantell-Tarantell it mischievously calls during wedding's solemn rite in huge chamber of Saint Michael . . . Tarantell-on-Tarantell it waves wildly gay with matrimonial feast under ancient home's thick rafters out into luna-laved vineyards and beneath olive trees and Tarantell! Tarantell! in fierce loveliness on virgin couch! Now it soon sails her to the America where

Geremio's children visit from out of her to become her darling brood. Tarantell—New World—Tarantell her young motherhood in the English-tongued America so hard so ungracious—Tarantell gray striving Tarantell in Tenement America in and about polyglot worker poor as they laugh and scream and moan and weep their cheated fragment selves and she turns twists Tarantell respectfully effortfully from their paths—*Tarantell!*— She Tarantells in sudden airless gloom—Geremio why have you let me go? Where is direction? Oh she must Tarantell and where is he? Geremio, Tarantell? she cries, Geremio Geremio Tarantell! Tarantell Tarantell Geremio . . . ! Child-loaded bosom she staggers in misstep. Dance Annunziata dance yet on and on for Geremio shall return, return—ballet for your children, encore for your little Christians and he shall return! Hey! Whey! Tarantell around and around in neverceasing burdenous strain—

Oh the tune is crushing fast and under she will fall— Jesu Tarantell—Giuseppe Tarantell—Mari! They come not. *Salve! Salve!* And whose small thin hand finds hers to bring her out of the choking shades and witness the little feet of her children in Tarantella whose fervent child hand strengthens her about and about their wisp dancing limbs to lend her sweet of salving dreams and who whispers as warm wind over sea into her soul, Tarantell mother . . . I will not let you fall, Tarantell in lead, mother beautiful . . . ?

Through shadowy religion of night she danced.
"Mama, you must live!"
And call mounted call.
"Mama . . . mama . . . ma . . . ma. . . ."
He reached her from far. His tearful face came nearer and nearer.
Tarantell . . . Tarantell. . . . Tarantell slowly bearing her blood away . . . away . . . away. . . .
Her breath came fast, and she sucked it in from oh-ed mouth. She put her fingers to his lips and sighed:

"... Paul, I tire ... my Paul ... who plays Tarantell?"

"Mama, mama, mama, I thought you would never know me ..."

"... Where oh where have we been in the hour of life ... ?"

"You are here with us, mama, and no one plays Tarantell."

Ey ... ! Tarantell ... away ... away

Memory glowed, and she saw her children.

Wonderful are they ...

"Children mine ..."

They kissed her. And their weeping could not stop.

Warm are they ... dearly warm ...

"Wonderful. ..."

She felt a slow tingling, a heaviness. Paul pressed her closer.

"Mama, you must stay—you have not lived—and soon the kids will be big—mama, please, food or no food—we shall live and laugh—we will be gay and dance differently—we will laugh and laugh and laugh oh how we will laugh ... laugh. ..."

Her limbs were becoming feelingless. She raised her hand. Her fingers were bluing. For a moment she contemplated her hand with gently open mouth, and let it fall upon the sheet. In the light-shaft dark night began to fade. She watched the window, and was becoming cold.

"... Morning shall come ..."

A chillness tremored her. Her pale skin began to shrink and mask. In the silence her features slowly pinched and sharpened. Paul shuddered and tried to swallow his sobs.

"Mama," he whispered, "forgive the hurt I have done thee ... forgive mama dearest ..."

The delicate devotional flame of her being drank fondly from his face, and sang forth quiet tears of love.

She lifted her stiffening fingers to his shoulder and smiled.

Lightly-lightly she caressed his face.

"... son ... everything in my world is for thee. For thee I desire the fullest gifts of Heaven—To thee must the good Dio bestow the world—and lasting health. He must bless thee with the flower of womankind and many-many children as yourself ... and joy and peace without measure—for to me—thou art most precious. ..."

About her they were garlanded, and from the window the dawning gray spoke tonelessly upon their strong faces. She gazed to each of Geremio ... Of mine.

"Mama? ... Are you afraid, mama ...?"

Annunziata faintly shook her head, and murmured:

"... Thy hand ... My Paul.... Paul ....."

And as he cradled her closely close, she receded ... and crooned:

> "Né' ... Né' ... Né' ...
> How beautiful he
> Little Paul my own
> Whose Jesu self
> Glorified our home ...
> Nadi ... Nadi ... Nadi ...
> Gifted to me
> By the Madonna was he
> And of this son
> Shall rise
> A topless lighted Column ...!
> ... Né' .... Né' ..... Né' ..."

With numbing hand she beckoned.

"Children wonderful ... love ... love love ... love ever our Paul.... Follow him."

THE END

WORKS BY
Pietro di Donato

Fiction

Christ in Concrete, 1939 Novel
Three Circles of Light, 1960 Novel
"The House," *Italian American Identity* (February 1977):
23–6.
"The Last Judgement," excerpt from "The American
Gospels," unpub. novel, *Voices in Italian Americana*,
2.2 (Fall 1991): 23–43.

Non-Fiction

Immigrant Saint: The Life of Mother Cabrini, Biography,
1960, New York: St. Martin's Press, 1991.
The Penitent, Biography, New York: Prentice Hall, 1962.
"A Rinasciamento on Long Island," *New York Times*,
Sec. 1A (November 14, 1971): 1+.
"The Laborer," *Fra Noi* (September 1986): 1+.

Anthology

Naked Author (selected writings), New York: Phaedra,
1970.

READ THE TOP 25 SIGNET CLASSICS

❏ ANIMAL FARM BY GEORGE ORWELL   0-451-52634-1 $5.95

❏ 1984 BY GEORGE ORWELL   0-451-52493-4 $5.95

❏ LES MISERABLES BY VICTOR HUGO   0-451-52526-4 $7.95

❏ THE ODYSSEY (W.H.D. ROUSE, TRANSLATOR)   0-451-52736-4 $5.95

❏ GREAT EXPECTATIONS BY CHARLES DICKENS   0-451-52671-6 $4.95

❏ NARRATIVE OF THE LIFE OF FREDERICK DOUGLASS
   BY FREDERICK DOUGLASS   0-451-52673-2 $4.95

❏ ADVENTURES OF HUCKLEBERRY FINN BY MARK TWAIN   0-451-52650-3 $4.95

❏ THE COUNT OF MONTE CRISTO BY ALEXANDER DUMAS   0-451-52195-1 $6.95

❏ JANE EYRE BY CHARLOTTE BRONTE   0-451-52655-4 $4.95

❏ HAMLET BY WILLIAM SHAKESPEARE   0-451-52692-9 $3.95

❏ HEART OF DARKNESS & THE SECRET SHARER
   BY JOSEPH CONRAD   0-451-52657-0 $4.95

❏ THE JUNGLE BY UPTON SINCLAIR   0-451-52420-9 $5.95

❏ A TALE OF TWO CITIES BY CHARLES DICKENS   0-451-52656-2 $4.95

❏ THE SCARLET LETTER BY NATHANIEL HAWTHORNE   0-451-52608-2 $3.95

❏ CRIME AND PUNISHMENT BY FYODOR DOSTOYEVSKY   0-451-52723-2 $7.95

❏ FRANKENSTEIN BY MARY SHELLEY   0-451-52771-2 $3.95

❏ BEOWULF (B. RAFFEL, TRANSLATOR)   0-451-52740-2 $4.95

❏ UNCLE TOM'S CABIN BY HARRIET BEECHER STOWE   0-451-52670-8 $5.95

❏ A MIDSUMMER NIGHT'S DREAM BY W. SHAKESPEARE   0-451-52696-1 $3.95

❏ WAR AND PEACE BY LEO TOLSTOY   0-451-52326-1 $8.95

❏ ONE DAY IN THE LIFE OF IVAN DENISOVICH
   BY ALEXANDER SOLZHENITSYN   0-451-52709-7 $4.95

❏ PRIDE AND PREJUDICE BY JANE AUSTEN   0-451-52588-4 $4.95

❏ ROMEO AND JULIET BY WILLIAM SHAKESPEARE   0-451-52686-4 $3.95

❏ MACBETH BY WILLIAM SHAKESPEARE   0-451-52677-5 $3.95

❏ ETHAN FROME BY EDITH WHARTON   0-451-52766-6 $4.95

TO ORDER CALL: 1-800-788-6262